MW00448361

A novel by
Joe C. Ellis

Outer Banks Murder Series

Upper Ohio Valley Books
Joe C. Ellis
71299 Skyview Drive
Martins Ferry, Ohio 43935
Email: **JoeCEllisNovels@comcast.net**
www.joecellis.com

PUBLISHER'S NOTE

Although this novel, The Treasure of Portsmouth Island, is set in actual places, the Outer Banks of North Carolina, various locations in North Carolina, and Virginia, it is a work of fiction. The characters, names, and plot are the products of the author's imagination. Any resemblance of these characters to real people is entirely coincidental. Many of the places mentioned in the novel—Buxton Village Books; Manteo, NC; Buxton, NC; Hatteras, NC; Wheeling, WV, Morgantown, WV, etc., are real locations. However, their involvement in the plot of the story is purely fictional. It is the author's hope that this novel generates great interest in these wonderful regions of the U.S.A., and, as a result, many people will plan a vacation at these locations and experience the beauty of these settings firsthand.

CATALOGING INFORMATION
Ellis, Joe C., 1956-
The Treasure of Portsmouth Island by Joe C. Ellis
ISBN 978-0-9796655-8-5
1.Outer Banks—Fiction. 2. Portsmouth, NC—Fiction
3. Mystery—Fiction 4. Suspense—Fiction
5. Ocracoke, NC—Fiction 6. , Hatteras, NC--Fiction
7. Buxton, NC—Fiction 8. Wheeling, WV—Fiction

©2019 by Joe C. Ellis

OUTER BANKS MURDER SERIES
By Joe C. Ellis

The Healing Place--
Prequel to Murder at Whalehead

Murder at Whalehead

Murder at Hatteras

Murder on the Outer Banks

Murder at Ocracoke

All books available in hardcopy and ebook formats.

Before you begin ... I wanted to let you know that a gift awaits you at the end of the novel. I am hopeful that this gift will complete your experience and enjoyment of this book.
Good reading,   Joe C. Ellis

Chapter 1

In the dim light of predawn, I stand barefoot in the sand, waiting. The Atlantic Ocean, blue-gray and bleak, waits with me. The sun is about to blaze the horizon. Its bright yellow rim breaks the surface. Orange flares out along the edge of the sea as the fireball rises, brightening the blue sky above. Watching the sunrise at the beach never gets old. It brings me to life. I need to come back to life. Finishing up the semester zapped me—too many all-nighters cramming for exams. The chains of responsibility and duty have fallen away. On this narrow strip of island I feel alive again. I'm free.

When I was a freshman in high school, I'd hike up to the limestone quarry on Sunday afternoons to get away from everything and everybody. The workers had Sundays off. Huge excavators with their toothed shovels rested in the gorges like sleeping dinosaurs. The stripped landscape was desolate but peaceful. I needed a break from my arguing parents and my yelling and screaming sisters. I'd stand at the top of a huge mound of limestone under a big azure sky, raise my hands, and let the breeze blow my hair. Freedom!

My hair was longer back then. When I went off to college three years ago I got it cut shorter to look more mature. I tried growing a beard, but it was scraggly, so I shaved it off. I still look like a high school kid.

College women seem to be going for guys with beards nowadays. Just my luck. Obviously, I've never been a Casanova. Don't get me wrong. I like girls, but I'm not obsessed with sex like half the guys in my dorm. The girls from WVU staying next to us are incredibly good looking, though. I wonder if they're cheerleaders. I hope not. A cheerleader has never given me the time of day. My buddies want to invite them over for a cookout, but Don and Johnny are more awkward than I am when it comes to women. Computer science majors aren't known for their romantic prowess. I'm an art major. The only time I get to see a naked lady is during my life drawing classes.

But this vacation isn't about chasing women. It's about rebirth and freedom. I need to clear my mind. No term papers to complete. No drawings to finish. No designs to turn in. No work-study chores in that damn cafeteria. The weight of the world has been lifted, if only for a week. I don't want to think about school or even what's happening in the world. If Kim Jung Ill and President Stamp get into a fist fight at their next summit meeting, I don't want to know about it.

Maybe that's why I love walking along the beach so much. It's just me and the sand and the waves. My buddies think I'm crazy for getting up at five-thirty in the morning to look for seashells, but that was one of the main reasons I came to Portsmouth Island. It certainly wasn't for the nightlife or comforts or attractions. To say this island is primitive is an understatement. No restaurants. No grocery stores. No swimming pools. No hot tubs. No conveniences. That's the way I like it. They call it the Ghost Island.

A huge wave rolls a large, white object up the slope of sand just ahead. Wait a minute. Are you kidding me? That's a . . . that's a humongous shell, a lightning whelk. I've never seen one that big. I've got to get it before another wave sucks it back into the ocean.

I tromp through the foamy backwash. The water is wonderfully warm this morning. I reach for the shell. Got it! It's amazing. I turn it over. No cracks. It's huge and perfect. An amber swirl runs along its surface like beautiful brushwork. I open my collection bag and peek inside. I've already found about ten excellent shells. This is the Holy Grail.

"Find a good one?" A girl's voice says.

Crimenetly! 'Bout crapped myself. I wasn't expecting to run into anyone out here this early. She's tall and skinny, wearing an oversized white sun hat. Looks like a junior high kid. Her loose white top whipping in the wind makes her appear wraithlike.

I hold up the shell. "Yeah. Best lightning whelk I've ever found."

"Can I see it?" Her voice is melodious.

"Sure." I hand her the shell. The youngster is a cutie, a pixie face with huge dark eyes and long eyelashes. Her short black hair contrasts with her light complexion. She reminds me of that actress from Hollywood's heyday. What was her name?

She edges to the water and washes the shell off in the shallows. "It's magnificent! I've found a few good ones today but nothing like this. Can I have it?"

"Are you kidding me? I've been shelling most of my life. That's the best I've ever found. This one'll go in the place of honor on my dorm room bookshelf."

She shrugs and smiles. "Doesn't hurt to ask."

"What's your name?"

"Give me the shell, and I'll tell you."

"Yeah, right."

"You'll find out soon enough anyway."

What does she mean by that? "Okay. Whatever."

"If I guess your name, will you give me the shell?"

Man, this girl doesn't give up. No way could she ever guess my name. "Okay, what's my name?"

She touches her finger to the tip of her petite nose and stares at me, eyes narrowing. "It's either Joe or Tom."

A chill jolts down through me. "Nice try. My name's Joel Thomas."

She clasps the shell to her chest. "Close enough to give me the shell?"

"Close but no shell. Give it back."

"Wait a minute. Do you want to see what I found?"

What's she up to? "Sure, but give me my shell back first."

She shakes her head, slowly reaches inside the cavity of the shell, and pulls out a golden coin. It glistens in the sunlight.

My eyes widen. "Let me see that." She hands me the coin. It's about the size of a fifty-cent piece and very worn. I can make out a large cross with rudimentary lion symbols and crowns decorating the four spaces between the bars.

She holds out her palm. "Finders keepers. Give it back."

I clutch the coin in my hand. "I don't think so. Possession is nine tenths of the law. Besides, you found the coin inside of my shell. I would have found it when I cleaned it."

She screws up her face and closes one eye. "I'll tell you what. I'll trade you the coin for the shell."

"Please." I reach out my hand. "Just give me the shell."

She tucks the shell into the crook of her arm. "Possession is nine tenths of the law."

"Hmmph." This gal is pretty sharp for a junior high kid. "How old are you?"

"I'll be thirteen next month on the Fourth of July."

"Really? You were born on Independence Day?"

She nods.

I look at the coin. "Are you sure you want to trade a coin for a shell? This might be a gold doubloon. Could be worth hundreds of dollars. Maybe more."

"Sure I'm sure. With this shell I can take the ocean with me." She places the cavity of the shell against her ear. "What's a few hundred dollars compared to the ocean?"

"You are a strange girl."

"Elsa!" A harsh voice yells.

I look up and see a tall, thin, old man with a salt-and-pepper beard. He's holding a long walking stick and wearing a baggy white shirt that ripples in the wind. The guy looks like John Carradine from the old monster movies.

"Coming, Grandfather!" She glances back and says, "See ya around, Joel Thomas. Thanks for the shell."

"Goodbye . . . Elsa." Elsa. So that's her name. I shake my head. She said I'd find out soon enough. Crimenetly! She's different, that's for sure.

Chapter 2

The coin glows in my hand. How old is it? What's it worth? It better be worth something. I gave away the Holy Grail to get this thing.

"You son of a bitch!" a man yells.

What in the world? I glance up. About a hundred yards ahead a man yanks on a fishing pole, the thick rod bending like a sapling in a thunderstorm. A red ATV sits higher on the bank. I slip the coin into my shorts pocket and pick up my pace. He's hooked a big fish. Look at that! The man leans back against the strain of the line. Out in the shallows about forty yards a fin cuts through the surface, and a tail slings a sheet of water into the air. A shark! He's caught a big shark, maybe seven feet long. I trot toward him.

The man is wearing a denim shirt with cut-off sleeves and a cowboy hat. He's about six feet tall and muscular. Can you believe that? He's got a prosthetic leg, one of those blades—the kind the Paralympic athletes wear. Crimenetly! He looks like a wrestler. He pulls back on the rod again, and his hat falls off, one of those oilskin cowboy hats with white jagged objects around the band. Are they teeth? He has a shaved head and goatee.

I slow to a stop and pick up his hat. "You've hooked a monster." The white things on the hat band *are* teeth. Large shark's teeth!

"You showed up just in time." His voice is gravelly.

"Can I help?"

"Yeah. Drop the hat. I want you to take the rod."

"What!"

"You take the rod and reel!"

I'm no weakling, but physical strength is not one of my greatest assets. I drop the hat and my shell bag onto the sand. "You want me to pull the fish in?"

Below thick eyebrows, his eyes widen. "No! Just hang on to the rod and reel!"

"Okay." He hands me the fishing tackle, and I almost lose my balance, tugged forward by the shark.

"Hang in there, buddy. This'll only take a minute or two."

What in the hell is he going to do? I hold the rod closer to my body and dig my feet into the sand. The pole is bending almost to the ground. He's marching into the water. You've got to be kidding. He's going out toward the shark.

Can he keep his balance in the waves with that blade-leg? The shark suddenly eases its struggle. I can see the fin about twenty-five yards out. Does it sense that someone is in the water nearby? A wave slaps against the man, but it doesn't faze him. He plows on toward the shark. Now he's within five yards. He turns and yells, "Pull hard on the line! Walk backwards if you can!"

With all my might I yank the rod back. This brings the shark back to life. I manage a step or two backwards. The man is circling behind the shark, waist-high in the water. I take another step back, leaning against the strain of the line. Will it break?

Now the guy is directly behind the shark. He reaches and grabs its tail. "Keep the line tight! I'm dragging the bastard in!" Step by step he progresses to the shoreline. Another wave smacks him, but he shakes it off. I do my best to keep tension on the line so the beast doesn't whip around on the guy. He trudges onto the bank, yanking the tail. The shark, a dark gray, blunt-nosed brute with a white belly, flops violently but can't escape the man's grip. I reel in the slackening line. He pulls the fish farther up the bank and lets go. It flaps its tail a few times but then settles. I can tell by its widening gills that it's struggling for oxygen.

The man slaps his hands together several times and walks in my direction. "Thanks, buddy. Couldn't have done it without you."

I hand him the fishing tackle. "I've never seen anything like that before."

"I do it all the time." He waves his hand toward his red ATV. "As you can see, I've got quite a collection."

Mounted on the front of the ATV are large shark jaws, maybe two feet wide. Several smaller sets are attached at various places on the vehicle—handle bars, front fenders, the back of the seat. Crimenetly! This guy's a shark serial killer.

The man inserts the rod handle into a white tube that's been embedded into the sand. He picks up his hat, positions it on his head, faces me, and holds out his hand. "Quentin Porter's my name."

I shake his hand. "Joel Thomas. Nice to meet you." His hand is rough like a scouring pad. "You come here to fish often?"

"Oh yeah. Been coming to Portsmouth Island for years. Good place to catch sharks." He glances over his shoulder. "That's a female bull shark, probably about 250 pounds."

"How can you tell it's a female?"

"No claspers."

"Claspers?"

Porter laughs and grabs his crotch. "Claspers."

"I get it. Will you release it since it's a female?"

"Hell no. They're a menace. I'll make sure she doesn't get back in the water."

"You're not too fond of sharks, are you?"

"No." He looks down and scrapes the blade of his prosthetic leg across the sand several times as if erasing someone's etched profanity. "Don't like them at all." He points at the ground beyond me. "Are you a beachcomber?"

I glance over my shoulder and spy my bag full of shells. "Yeah. That's mine."

"The tide's rising. Better get it before the ocean does."

I snatch it up just as a wave swoops up the bank and around my feet. "That was close."

"Is that why you came to Portsmouth Island? For the shelling?"

"Partly." I take a deep breath of fresh sea air. "It's my first time here. I love it. My family has vacationed on the Outer Banks all my life—Corolla, Duck, Rodanthe, Hatteras. I've been beachcombing since I was a kid. Then I heard about this island just south of Ocracoke. Best shelling anywhere they say. My family wasn't crazy about the idea of staying in a tent or cabin, so I convinced my roommates to spend a week here with me. They were up for it. Besides, the price is right for poor college kids."

Porter glances up and down the shoreline. His face muscles tense up. "About fifteen years ago me and my buddies came here for the first time to drink beer, fish, and surf."

"So you've been coming back here for fifteen years?"

He nods slowly and then motions toward my shell bag. "Can I see what you found this morning?"

"Sure." I open the bag.

He steps closer and peeks in. "You've got some good ones in there."

"Yeah. Unfortunately, I gave away the best of the bunch a few minutes ago to some junior high kid."

"Why'd you do that?"

I reach into my pocket and pull out the coin. "Traded for this."

"Whoa! Is that gold?"

I shrug. "Looks like gold to me."

Porter takes the coin. "I'll be damned. That is gold. You made a helluva deal."

"Thanks. Wish I knew how much it was worth."

He hands back the coin. "You should show that to One-Eyed Jack. He'd know."

"Who?"

"A friend of mine. Jack Graham. He's renting one of the cabins this week." He points inland. You'll find him up over the dunes not far from here with his metal detector. He's a treasure hunter."

"Metal detector? I thought they were illegal on these federally protected islands."

"They are. That's why he stays out of sight. Guess you could say he's a part-time pirate."

A flapping sound startles me—the shark's tale swishing across the sand, its body writhing, mouth opening and closing.

I point to the shark. "She must be suffering awful."

Porter nods. "Time to put her out of her misery."

"How'll you kill it?"

He paces over to his ATV and pulls a good sized machete out of a sheath attached to the back side. An odd smile forms on his face as he raises the blade. "You wanna watch?"

I feel queasy inside. "No thanks. I think I'll go find your buddy, One-Eyed Jack."

"Suit yourself."

I turn and stride toward the dunes. Behind me I hear the whumps of a machete slashing shark flesh and a few final swishes of its tail through the sand.

Chapter 3

I check my watch—a little past six. It's been an eventful morning. The sun feels warm on my back. This long sleeve, black t-shirt doesn't help. I peel off the shirt and tie it around my waist as I climb the first dune. I stare down at my bare chest. I'm thin but not scrawny. I should do more pushups. Women go for broader chests and six-packs. Very few art majors have six-packs. I'll have to work on that.

The dunes aren't as steep on this island compared to Hatteras Island and the ones farther north. At the top, scrub brush and live oaks pepper the land that stretches several hundred yards toward Core Sound. Marshy grasses flourish here and there. I don't want to step in a bog. I swat away some mosquitoes. The diminished winds on this side of the dunes don't keep them off of me as well. Fortunately, I sprayed half a can of mosquito repellent all over my body before I left the cabin this morning.

Quentin Porter said that One-Eyed Jack would be somewhere out there with his metal detector. Hope I don't spook him. He sounds like a real character. So's Porter for that matter. Strange man. Wonder why he's so obsessed with killing sharks? This island would be a great setting for a horror movie. I can picture Quentin Porter going crazy with that machete, roaming from cabin to cabin chopping people up. Better not let my imagination get carried away. Actually, he seems like a fairly normal guy except for all the muscles, the blade leg, the sandpaper hands, the shark grabbing, and machete chopping. Crimenetly!

About a hundred yards away I see some odd colors moving through the scrub brush. I stop and focus. I can make out a figure. Must be One-Eyed Jack. I assess the possible pathways to get from here to there. If I go to the right toward that live oak and then turn left, I can avoid a marsh. A sudden fluttering explodes to my right. Some kind of white heron or egret takes flight. I can feel my heart thumping. I take in a deep breath and blow it out to calm myself. That was a damn big bird!

When I'm within fifty yards of the guy, I shout, "Hey! Are you One-Eyed Jack?" He straightens and stares at me. I see why they call him One-Eyed Jack. He's wearing an eye patch.

"Who the hell are you?" Sporting a faded Hawaiian shirt and cut-off blue jeans, he looks like a beach bum. Streaks of gray stream through his long, brown hair and beard.

"I just met Quentin Porter. He told me I could find you out here. Don't worry. I'm not a ranger." I can tell he's trying to hide the metal detector behind him.

"What do you want?"

"I've got a question about a gold coin."

"A gold coin? Did you find it on this island?"

"Yeah."

"Okay. Come on over, matey. I'll take a look at it."

The tension had gone out of his voice, and he actually sounded like a pirate. That's a good thing. I don't like to make people nervous. He looks to be about forty-five years old, has a substantial paunch, and is very tan. He reminds me of my Uncle Jim, who dresses up like a pirate to do commercials for local businesses back home.

need repairs. He made the decision to preserve the four chests of gold from the *El Salvador* by burying them on one of the barrier islands off the North Carolina coast. He safely anchored the Nuestra Señora de Guadalupe fifteen miles south of Ocracoke Inlet. Four chests along with a smaller chest were placed onto a dinghy and rowed to the beach at Core Banks, the very island on which we stand. If you factor in today's prices, the gold coins from the four chests would be worth millions of dollars. The fifth chest, a smaller one, was rumored to contain an ancient relic, but no one knows for sure what it may be. "

"Wow. I could be holding a rare doubloon from the *Lost Treasure of El Salvador*."

Graham brushes his knuckles against his beard. "Believe me. It's possible."

Chapter 4

The coin feels alive in my hand. I rub it gently as I walk toward the cabins. One-Eyed Jack must be right: Elsa planted the coin in the shell. Does she know something about the *Treasure of El Salvador*? Why would she trade an important clue for a shell? It doesn't make sense. If she found the coin somewhere on the island by dumb luck, could the treasure chests be buried nearby? That's a possibility. Several coins could have been dropped when the chests were being buried. Maybe she'll tell me where she *really* found it.

I look up and see the row of cabins. There are ten of them right along the beachfront. The first four are shaped like octagons. The next six are more traditional, rectangular buildings. All of them are duplexes and mounted five feet above the ground on posts to keep them safe from high water when bad weather hits. These are the only lodgings that can be rented on Portsmouth Island. No million dollar beach homes. No hotels. No stores. No mini golf courses. If you're a minimalist, it's an ideal vacation spot. And cheap! Where else can you stay in a beachfront bungalow for less than $700 a week?

Someone is standing near the first cabin, a red-headed guy. What's he doing? Some church group is staying in the first two cabins. I think they're having some kind of religious retreat. It looks like he's trying to hear what's going on inside. Is he spying? He glances up and sees me. Now he's walking away, kind of sheepishly, heading in my direction. Interesting. He's about six feet tall and lean, maybe thirty-five or forty years old. I recognize him. He and his family are renting one of the cabins.

I nod and say, "Good morning."

"Morning," he mumbles as he walks by me.

Hmmmm. Wonder what's going on in that cabin? I decide to drift in that direction. There's a side by side recreational vehicle, the kind with the two front seats, parked next to the building. As I near I can hear a deep voice speaking with a rhythmic delivery. Must be the pastor preaching a sermon. Now I can make out his words.

"What kind of country are we living in at this time in history? I'll tell you what—a country where men act more like women, and women act more like men. There's been a mix up in the natural order of things."

A spattering of amens erupts.

"A country where good is labeled evil, and evil is labeled good. A country where if you stand up for what you believe, you could go to jail because you're treading on someone's so called rights. Be careful if you believe it's not right for two men to sleep together. Be careful if you say a women's place is in the home. You'll be put on a black list, maybe arrested. Yet millions of babies are slaughtered in the name of human rights. What about the rights of the unborn?"

More amens.

"Our politicians are all liars, both republicans and democrats. You can't trust the government. It's a big deception. They all get elected by lying their way into office. Our president is a womanizer, a braggart, a scammer, and a fool. He has the diplomacy skills of a five-year-old child. He deals with our enemies like a kid on the playground, calling names and making threats. I'm telling you, we are living in an unstable world. I have seen a vision of our future. The apocalypse is on the horizon. This time the good ol' USA will not be spared war's destruction and devastation. We need to be prepared. That's why God called us to gather on this island—to prepare us for what's to come. We have an opportunity to build a new kind of kingdom from the rubble of destruction."

Crimenetly! This guy's on a roll. That's not the kind of preaching I'm used to hearing. Much different from the sermons I've heard all my life at Vance Memorial Church back in good ol' Wheeling, West Virginia. I guess Presbyterians aren't so extreme when it comes to end-time theology. I glance over to the far side of the porch and see smoke drifting upwards like a spirit rising. What in the world? I meander in that direction.

Sitting on the porch steps, a woman, probably in her mid-thirties, smokes a cigarette. She has wiry brown hair. Her eyes are dark brown with the deep etching of crow's feet extending from the corners. She has that worn-around–the-edges look like a favorite pair of jeans.

She blows out a stream of smoke. "Good morning."

I wave and nod toward the cabin door. "That's some preaching."

She chuckles. "They're preparing for the end of the world in there. I'm not quite up to it yet. Reverend Swagger says I still got this tobacco demon in me. My name's Mary. What's yours?"

"Joel."

"Nice to meet you, Joel." She eyes my sack of shells. "Find anything interesting on the beach?"

I step closer and open the bag.

She opens it wider with her forefinger and peers in. "Not bad. You've found some beauties."

For some reason I feel a strong urge to show her the coin. "That's not all. Take a look at this." I unfold my hand.

She lifts it with her finger and thumb and examines it. "Wow. Impressive. That is a really old coin." She waggles it. "Shines like gold."

The door opens, and a tall, broad man with black hair combed straight back strides onto the porch. He has Elvis sideburns and a prominent chin. He peers down at the coin and then shifts his gaze toward me. "May I take a look at it?"

"Sure."

He takes the coin from Mary's hand and raises it chest high, tilting it so that the morning sun flashes on its surface.

"This is definitely gold. Where did you find it?"

"On the island."

"I don't believe anything happens by chance. God meant for you to find this coin." He extends his hand. "I'm Reverend Noah Swagger, head pastor of the New Kingdom Church."

I shake his hand. "Nice to meet you. I'm Joel Thomas."

"Now whereabouts on the island did you find this?"

"To tell the truth, I actually traded for it. Some young girl found it. She wanted to trade for one of my shells."

"I see. What was her name?"

"Elsa." I feel a sudden pang of regret for saying her name. Why is this guy giving me the third degree anyway? I glance at Mary as she smashes out her cigarette on the porch step.

"Again, I don't believe anything happens by random accident. You were meant to trade that shell for this coin." He motions toward the door. "I just finished my morning teaching when I heard you two talking out here." He pats his chest. "The Spirit spoke to me and moved me to step out onto the porch to meet you."

Now this is getting creepy. Presbyterians believe in predestination, but I'm not so sure I'm buying what this guy is selling. "Well, the Spirit is sorta like the wind. That's what I've always heard, anyway." I didn't know what else to say.

"You're right. You seem to be a young man who is sensitive to the moving of the Spirit. Do you believe God has a purpose and plan for your life?"

Oh no. Now we're moving out of my religious comfort zone. "I guess so."

"I know so. You and I have met for a reason. Let me ask you an important question. Is it possible, with the world in its current circumstances that world war could break out tomorrow or any time in the near future?"

"Sure."

"In all probability, what kind of war would it be, conventional or nuclear?"

"Probably nuclear."

"You're right. Only a fool would deny that possibility, and you're no fool. My church is preparing for that outcome in the most practical ways. We believe we can survive the apocalypse and begin again. But we need funds. I want to give you the opportunity to join us and help us. By helping us you will be advancing God's New Kingdom in this world. Would you be willing to join us and donate this coin to our ministry?"

I shake my head. "Sorry. I belong to the Presbyterian Church."

"The Frozen Chosen."

"What? Oh, yeah." Very funny but sometimes true. "We are a little more formal than most."

"Your Presbyterianism doesn't prevent you from supporting this ministry. Will you donate the coin?"

Man, this guy doesn't quit. "No, I think I'll hold on to it for now." I reach and tug the coin out of his hand. "Nice meeting you both."

I nod at Mary, and she smiles. Gotta get out of here. I turn and head toward my cabin.

Chapter 5

The variety of people renting the cabins this week is fascinating. A Dodge Ram pickup is parked next to the third cabin. Several ATVs with fishing equipment mounted on them surround the pickup. I figure it's a buddy trip—a bunch of guys in their late twenties and early thirties with beards and beer guts. They spend their days fishing and drinking. Wonder if Reverend Swagger invited them to join the New Kingdom Church.

The cabins are all duplexes with just the basics on each side—six bunks, a propane stove, cabinets, a kitchen table, and a small bathroom. We have to keep our food and drinks cold in coolers packed with ice. Fortunately, we can buy ice at the nearby Long Point Cabin Camp Office. We brought our food and drinks with us on the small ferry that transported us here from Ocracoke. You need a four-wheel-drive vehicle to get around on this island. No paved roads. None of us own a 4 x 4, so we decided to rent ATVs for the week. When we crossed the Pamlico Sound on the ferry with our ATVs, suitcases, and boxes of food, it felt like we were setting off on a great adventure. I've been vacationing on the Outer Banks with my family as long as I can remember, but this place is nothing like the beach communities north of here with their beautiful rental homes. To me it's more thrilling, rugged, and untamed.

Not sure if my two college buddies agree with me. Don and Johnny are a little soft and nerdy. Hopefully, as the week goes on, they'll adjust. We've introduced ourselves to the WVU girls staying on the other side of our cabin, but that's about all. We'd like to invite them to a cookout. That'll probably be up to me or Don. I can't imagine Johnny getting up the nerve.

I think the redheaded guy and his family are renting one side of the fifth cabin. He's got a good-looking wife and a couple kids. Another couple, probably in their fifties or early sixties, is staying on the other side of that cabin. They might be related to the young family. I've seen all six of them walking on the beach together.

One-Eyed Jack and Quentin Porter must be renting cabins too. I'm not sure which ones are theirs. I'd say all in all there're about forty people staying in the cabins this week. Another twenty or thirty are camping in tents. You can set up a campsite wherever you want on the island. Most people erect their tents on the ocean side of the dunes to avoid the mosquitoes. It's definitely not overcrowded on Portsmouth Island. Thirteen miles of pristine beaches for seventy people? Crimenetly! It's kinda like paradise.

We're in the last cabin. The WVU girls parked their lime green Jeep Wrangler on the left side of the duplex. We've got our three ATVs parked on the right. I wonder if anyone's up yet. I doubt it. When on vacation, most college kids stay up late and sleep in 'til noon. I ought to wake up the boys and show them my coin. I fill my lungs with the fresh ocean air and gaze down the shoreline. It's good to be here.

What's that? There's a pile of stuff about a hundred yards up the beach. Did something unusual wash up? I'll go check it out. I pick up my pace to a jog. It looks like clothing. As I near I can make out a colorful beach towel, a yellow t-shirt, a white, fluffy robe, and . . . . . panties!

What in the world? The yellow t-shirt has a WVU logo on it.

I peer out to sea and notice a girl's head bobbing above the surface. I yell, "Good morning!" It's one of the WVU girls, the blond with the athletic body. I think she said her name was Holly. She has that Mariel Hemmingway look.

As the water dips, she crosses her arms in front of her breasts. "Good morning."

"Are you skinny dipping?"

"Yes. I always wanted to swim naked in the ocean. I didn't think anybody would be up at this time of the morning. It was a . . . a spur of the moment thing."

"You're . . . adventurous." I wonder if she'll ask me to join her. Crimenetly! I've never skinny dipped. I don't know if I could get up the nerve. "How's the water?"

"It's fine. Warmer than I figured. Why are you up so early?"

I lift up my shell bag. "I like to beachcomb in the mornings."

"Sounds like fun. Did you see anyone else out on the beach?"

"Yeah. Several people."

"Really?"

"'Bout a half mile south of here a guy caught a big shark. I helped him pull it in."

Her eyes widen. "Are you kidding?"

"No. A bull shark about seven feet long."

She swivels her head and scans the surface of the water. Her eyes tense, lines forming on her forehead. "I'm coming back in."

I reach down and pick up her towel. "Do you want me to throw you this?"

"No! Just drop it on the beach and face the other direction."

I can't help smiling as I drop the towel and turn slowly. Is this really happening? It feels like a dream. I can hear her feet splashing through the surf.

"Don't turn around!"

I feel a wet hand on my shoulder.

"Did you hear me?"

"Yes, but I've seen naked women before. I'm an art major. It won't shock me."

She removes her hand. "You haven't seen this naked girl. Keep looking at the dunes. This'll only take a second.

The temptation to take a peek is overwhelming, but somehow I maintain control of myself.

Thirty seconds later she says, "Okay. I'm dressed."

I turn around. "That was fast."

She dries her hair with the towel, her robe cinched tightly around her. "I can move fast when I need to." She drapes the towel around her shoulders.

"Guess you can check that one off your bucket list."

"Yeah." She makes an imaginary checkmark in the air. "Skinny dipping in the ocean—done."

She has that clean, no-makeup look. Her dark eyebrows and light blonde hair remind me of the appearance of Nordic women. My mind scrambles to think of something else to say. "The morning is too beautiful to waste snoozing in the cabins. My buddies are snoring away."

She smiles. Perfect teeth. "I agree. I'd rather be out here with the dolphins." She nods toward the ocean. "They're singing. Can you hear them?"

I focus on the surface of the sea and catch the arced backs of dolphins gracefully gliding through the water about two hundred yards out. "I can see them, but I can't hear them."

"It's a beautiful song."

"You've got good ears."

She raises those sensuous, dark eyebrows. "I do have exceptional hearing. As soon as I stepped out on the beach this morning I heard them. Sounded like the song of mermaids. That's when I took my clothes off and jumped in."

"You are quite . . . serendipitous." As soon as I said the word, I knew it sounded corny.

She smiled oddly up at me. "Well . . . I am a marine biology major." She spread her hands. "This is the perfect setting for what rocks my socks."

"Were you going to swim all the way out to the dolphins?"

"I was thinking about it until you came along. Your shark story changed my mind. Did you really help catch a seven foot bull shark?"

I raise my hand. "God's honest truth. I may have saved your life. You never know, her brother may be prowling these waters."

She shakes her head and touches my shoulder. "Thanks, Joel. I certainly didn't want to end my vacation feeding a shark."

Cool. She remembered my name. "So that's why you came to Portsmouth Island? You like marine biology."

"Yeah. I convinced Lisa and Stephanie to come along. They're nursing majors, but they got excited when I told them about this place. We're not your normal college girls. We don't mind roughing it. Why'd you and your buddies come here?"

"To do something different. I love the ocean, but I'm tired of the same old beach vacation. Don and Johnny were up for trying something new." I lift up my shell bag. "Besides that, I'm obsessed with shelling."

"Can I see what you found?"

"Sure." I hand her the bag.

She opens it. "Nice. Some knobbed whelks. A couple shark eyes. You even found a Scotch bonnet and a nutmeg."

Wow. She knows her stuff. "The shelling's incredible here."

She hands my bag back. "Very productive morning."

I've got to show her the coin. "Those were nothing compared to the huge lightning whelk I found."

"Where is it?"

"I traded it for this." I extract the coin from my pants pocket and hold it up.

She takes it. "Someone traded you a seashell for this?"

I nod.

"That must have been an amazing shell."

I laugh. "Yeah, the Holy Grail of a shell. Some junior high kid wanted it. She reached inside the shell and pulled out the coin, almost like a magic trick. Then she traded me."

"Was she tall and thin with short, black hair?"

"Yeah. Do you know her?"

"I've seen her walking along the beach. She was singing a song about angels. She's an unusual girl."

"Her name's Elsa. She's definitely different."

"I'd like to meet her."

"I'm sure you'll cross paths sometime this week."

"Hey, what are you and your friends doing this afternoon?"

"Don't think there's anything planned. Why? What's up?"

"My gals and I would like to go to the north end of the island and check out the abandoned village."

"That would be fun. We've got three ATVs if you'd like to ride with us."

"Awesome. That would be more exciting than going up in our Jeep."

"Great." I raise my hand for a high five. "The journey to the abandoned village."

She slaps my hand. "What time do you want to go? About noon?"

"Sounds good. The boys should be bright-eyed and fresh-faced by then."

She laughs.

As we walk back toward the cabins, I feel like I'm in a dream. Can this really be happening? Don and Johnny won't believe it. They'll think I'm trying to punk them. Can't wait to see their faces when the girls show up.

Chapter 6

Don and Johnny aren't bad looking for nerds. Most girls would find them somewhat attractive. They don't have great bodies, that's for sure. Neither do I for that matter. I'm about six feet tall and weigh 150 pounds. Most chicks think I'm too skinny. Don is an inch or two shorter, and Johnny is two inches taller. They both weigh fifteen or twenty pounds more than me, but they're not slobs. We just don't have bulging muscles. If these girls go for gym rats, then we're out of luck. Don has dark brown hair and a three-day beard that's looking pretty good. Johnny has a baby face, worse than mine, but he's got the long blond locks that some girls go crazy over. Unfortunately, his black-rimmed glasses give him that computer geek look.

"I'm nervous," Johnny says.

"Why?" I ask. "You wanted to get together with these girls."

"I know." He rakes his fingers through his long hair. "I just am. Maybe they're too good looking, you know, out of our league."

"Whaddaya mean out of our league?" Don says. "They're not world class models. They're just college babes. Good ol' West Virginia girls."

"What if they're wearing bikinis?" Johnny asks. "How can I concentrate on driving that ATV with a half-naked girl hanging on to me?"

Don snorts. "That's the difference between you and me. Your fears are my fantasies. If they show up wearing bikinis, I just may propose marriage."

"Yeah, right," Johnny says. "I'm sure we'll end up marrying these girls."

"Just relax and have fun," I say. "We're not looking for any long term relationships here. If we hit it off, fine. If we don't, fine. "

"Right," Johnny says. "If they don't like us, it's not the end of the world."

"That's right," Don tilts his straw cowboy hat back on his head. "You never know, though. We might get lucky."

"You think so?" Johnny's eyes widen slightly.

Don slaps Johnny's back. "Sure. You might just land your space probe on Venus this week."

Johnny shakes his head. "Yeah. With my luck, the world would end right before my rocket launches."

I glance out the screen door. "Let's go. They're waiting for us out by the ATVs."

"Crap," Johnny whispers. "I hope they didn't hear us shooting our mouths off in here."

Don slips on his Oakley sunglasses and peers out the screen door. "I've got good news and bad news, Johnny."

"Yeah. What's that?"

"They're not wearing bikinis. That's good news for you and bad news for me."

Although the temperature has climbed up into the eighties, the girls are all wearing long-sleeved, light-colored t-shirts and loose-fitting white pants. No doubt, they're prepared for the mosquito onslaught coming our way once we turn off the beach and head toward the village. Holly is looking sharp with wire-rimmed shades and a straw sunhat tied under her chin. I hope she wants to ride with me.

Stephanie, a pony-tailed brunette, has a great body, not quite a Salma Hayek but close. She's shorter than Holly, maybe five feet six inches. I could see how she could make a guy jumpy pressed up against him on an ATV. If she rides with Johnny, he may end up driving right into the ocean.

Lisa is almost six feet tall with sandy blonde hair. She has that model look about her. She'd be the better match for Johnny height-wise. We'll see what happens. I guess we'll just climb onto our ATVs and let them choose their partners.

I step onto the porch and wave. "Hi ladies. Beautiful afternoon for a ride along the beach."

"Couldn't ask for a more splendiferous day," the tall one, Lisa, says. She's wearing a red ball cap turned backwards on her head and white-framed sunglasses.

I turn and motion to my buddies. "You remember Don and Johnny?"

"How could we forget?" Stephanie says. She's got her eyes fixed on Johnny.

Oh no. If she gets on the ATV with him, he's going to lose it. Must be his long blond locks. I glance at Don, and he's staring at Lisa. Figures he'd go for the world-class-model type. She's got to be two inches taller than he is.

"You're Lisa, right?" Don says.

"You got it."

Don points to the blue ATV. "You wanna ride with me?"

"Sure. I'll take my chances."

Don's boldness surprises me. He may be a computer science major, but he's growing some giggleberries.

I glance at Holly, and she smiles and says, "I'll ride with you, Joel."

Excellent! I want to give a big fist pump. Cool it, Romeo. Don't act too excited.

Lisa walks over to Johnny and puts her hand on his shoulder. "Looks like we're partners, big guy."

Johnny takes a deep breath and blows it out. "L-L-Looks we are." His face is almost white. How about that Fickle Finger of Fate! That boy may not survive this trip with Selma Hayek riding on the back of his ATV.

Leading the way, flying north along the beach with a pretty girl hanging on to me, I feel free. I don't think I've ever felt this alive in my life. Everything is beautiful. The sky. The ocean. The sand. The dunes. The seagulls. Is this what heaven is like?

It's funny how things work out. If we were vacationing at Myrtle Beach, these girls wouldn't give us a second look. Too much competition there. Here we're the cream of the crop. I wonder if the scarcity of people on this island impacts how we interact socially. There's less pressure to try to impress the crowd. These girls don't feel the need to go after the stereotypical stud. They can sample a more exotic flavor of male, one that doesn't meet their sorority's checklist. I love it. Freedom!

Holly squeezes me tighter. "Joel, look up ahead. There's a nice shell bank. Can we stop?"

"We sure can. We've got the whole afternoon. No schedules to follow. No deadlines to meet."

"Don't you just love it? This place is paradise."

"Hell yeah." Love and paradise—those two words go together.

I slow the ATV and skid to a stop at the top of a slope where a ton of shells have collected. Don and Lisa pull up beside us. "What's up?" Don says.

Johnny and Stephanie arrive. Johnny 's smile is wider than a king bed in a swanky hotel room. He looks like a Golden Retriever waiting for a dog biscuit. I cut off the engine and motion for them to follow suit.

I wave toward the shells. "We're in no hurry. Let's beachcomb for a few minutes."

Stephanie steps off the ATV and extends her hand. "Come on, big guy, let's see what we can find." She pulls Johnny off the ATV and leads him down the beach. That girl is definitely not shy.

We climb off the ATV. Holly nods in their direction and says, "They seem to be hitting it off."

That's an understatement. Johnny looks like the guy who found the winning Powerball ticket in a 7-Eleven trashcan.

"Let's check out the shells," Holly says.

"Maybe we'll get lucky, like Joel," Don says.

Lisa leans on Don's back as she stands and draws one of her long legs over the seat. "Why is Joel so lucky?"

"He found a golden coin inside a seashell this morning." Don springs off the seat and they amble toward us.

"That's splendiferous. I've heard of finding pearls in clams," Lisa says, "but a coin inside of a seashell?"

Crimenetly. Everything's splendiferous with this girl. I don't even know what that means. "Well, to be exact, I didn't find it in the shell. Some kid did. But it was my shell."

"Still," Lisa says, "that's an unlikely happenstance. Maybe it's a harbinger."

Happenstance? "Whadaya mean, harbinger?"

Lisa rotates her ball cap around and lowers the brim to shade her face. "A portent. An augury. A sign that something's about to happen."

"Oh." Learn something new every day. "Hopefully, it's a good sign."

"Yeah, like finding a sand dollar," Holly says. "Whenever I find a sand dollar, something good happens. Let's see if we can find one."

"I'm in," Don says. "What do they look like?"

Lisa lowers her shades and peers at Don. "You are not a regular beach-goer, are you?"

"Naaah." He holds up two fingers. "This is my second trip to the ocean."

She puts her arm around his shoulders. "Come with me, neophyte. I'll educate you."

Neophyte? Crimenetly! As they head down the beach, Don turns and smiles at me. We're definitely having fun.

Once Don and Lisa are out of earshot, I say, "Do your friends have steady boyfriends?"

"Stephanie's been dating the same guy for about three months. I don't like him. He's a linebacker for the Mountaineers, a senior. I don't think she's in love with him, although she does 'stay over' sometimes, if you know what I mean."

I nod. "So meeting Johnny may be a nice diversion for her?"

"Sure. You never know. I can tell she's really attracted to him."

"How about Lisa?"

"She goes out every once in a while. Nobody steady. Believe it not, she's a bookworm."

"She knows some big words." I chuckle. "As you can clearly see, none of us are lady killers. We're just glad that you gals are willing to hang out with us for a while."

Holly stops and faces me. She reaches and locks onto my chin with her thumb and forefinger. "I think you're kinda cute, Joel Thomas. I like hanging out with you."

I smile. She's incredible. I want to ask her if she's dating someone seriously. I want to tell her how beautiful she is. Get a hold of yourself, Romeo. Don't act like some lovesick schoolboy. Be a man. I straighten up and point to the shell bank. "Let's see what we can find."

I can't believe it. Two steps in front of me is a large, white sand dollar. I reach down and pick it up. "Whadaya think? Is something good about to happen?"

She takes the sand dollar. "I believe something good is already happening."

She hands it back to me, but I raise my hand. "It's all yours."

"Thanks, Joel." She leans and kisses my cheek.

"You're welcome." I want to hug her, but she's already looking for more shells. Instead, I take a deep breath and savor the moment. That spot on my cheek where she kissed me is still wet.

After about twenty minutes of beachcombing, we gather at the ATVs. Stephanie can't keep her hands off Johnny. At least some color has come back into his face. That boy is definitely under her spell.

Lisa smiles and holds up a long brownish-beige chain-like object. "Look what Don gave me, a mermaid's necklace."

Don holds up his hands, palms out. "I spare no expense when it comes to good-looking women."

Lisa laughs and elbows his ribs.

Holly says, "You know those necklaces play an important part in the life cycle of the knobbed whelk."

"Oh yeah," Don says, "what part?"

"Reproduction. That chain is filled with miniature whelk shells."

Don gulps. "A necklace for making babies?"

Lisa wags her finger. "Don't get any ideas."

Laughter erupts. I can tell this week is going to be a blast, one of those rare weeks you don't want to end.

Don and Lisa seem to be flirting and joking a lot. They both have a good sense of humor. Who knows? Maybe this is more like Cupid Island than Ghost Island. We climb onto the ATVs and head north along the shoreline.

It's about a ten mile ride from the cabins to the village. I'm guessing the island itself is about thirteen miles long. Up ahead I see a sign that points toward a trail that goes over the dunes. That's gotta be the one we need to take. Yep. The sign, crudely painted with white letters, says, "Portsmouth Village." I turn left and take the trail. The landscape is incredible. The sand cuts a path through tall sea grasses that wave in the wind, almost like a rolling wheat field. Occasionally, a small bush or tree pops up, a tiny green island in a yellow sea.

Holly squeezes my arm. "Look over there." She points over my shoulder to the northeast. "It's the Ocracoke Lighthouse."

Even though it's one of the smaller lighthouses on the Outer Banks, I can see it clearly. The islands are only about a mile apart, across the Ocracoke Inlet from each other.

Up ahead I can see a small sign. I slow the ATV and come to a stop. It's another hand-painted sign: "Welcome to Portsmouth Village. Established in 1753. Population in 1860 – 685. Today – 0." The others stop directly behind us.

"Look at that," Don says. "Today -0. Kinda spooky, isn't it?"

"Sure," Lisa says. "That's why they call this the Ghost Island."

"I ain't afraid of no ghosts," Stephanie says.

"Me neither," Johnny shouts over the motors.

I chuckle to myself. We've got a couple of Ghostbusters with us. "Okay then. Let' see if we can conjure up a couple dearly departeds." I crank the throttle and spin out onto the path toward the village.

Above a thick patch of bushes I can see a two-story building with a small lookout room protruding from its roof. It's covered with gray wooden shingles and outlined with red trim around its edges and windows. It almost looks like an A-frame because of the tall second story but it's not. A covered porch wraps around the front half of the building supported by red posts. It's a neat looking structure.

"That's the United States Life Saving Station," Holly says.

We stop at an informational sign that displays a picture of the building and a large rowboat resting on a ramp.

I point to the sign. "There's quite a few of these old lifesaving stations along the Outer Banks. There's one in Kitty Hawk they turned into a restaurant."

"Right," Holly says. "The Black Pelican. I've eaten there several times. Good food."

The others pull up beside us.

"Can we go inside?" Don says.

"A lot of these buildings are open to the public," Lisa says. "Maybe the doors are unlocked."

We park the ATVs in the grass near the porch. There's a bench and an old picnic table sitting on the deck. On the side of the building I can see a huge white cylinder. Must have been used for water storage. As I pan my surroundings, I can see Ocracoke Island across the inlet. What an amazing view!

"Look there." Lisa points across the yard to a smaller gray building. "That's the stable."

"Why'd they need a stable?" Don asks.

"These lifesaving stations were the predecessors to the Coast Guard. Members of the crew would ride horses up and down the beach looking for ships in distress. It was their responsibility to rescue people from any boat that had foundered on the shoals."

Don takes off his Oakleys and blinks. "How do you know all this?"

"I read, my boy, I read."

"Hey! Check this out." Johnny has drifted across the yard to the corner of the building. "One of the garage doors on this side is open."

Stephanie, standing next to him, says, "We can get in this way."

We walk around the corner and see two ramps leading to two barn-type doors. The one on the right is swung wide open.

"That's not a car garage," Lisa says. "That's where they kept the surfboats. I betcha there's one inside. Let's check it out."

We walk up the ramp and enter the boat room. The wall to the right is lined with informational posters. The right side of the large space is empty except for a few displays and a couple support posts. On the other side of the room a large white rowboat rests on a transport cart with wagon wheels. Lisa makes a beeline to the informational posters, and Don follows her like an obedient Irish setter. Man, we nerds can be pathetic. Holly walks over to a display box featuring a small cannon. Lisa and Johnny cut through the displays to the big rowboat.

"Look at that," I say, peering over Holly's shoulder, "a Lilliputian cannon."

She points to a poster on the right. "It's called a Lyle Gun. They used it to shoot a line out to a vessel hung up on the shoals. Then they rigged up a rope and pulley system to rescue the people stranded on the boat."

I inspect the poster and notice how they used a wooden support to raise the rope on shore. With the pulley system they transported the victims from the boat using what looked like a life saver with a seat in it. Just above the display hangs an example of the life saver, strung from the ceiling.

"That is so cool," Holly says. "Can you imagine saving someone's life like that? Living on an island like this and saving lives—what a dream life."

There's a wonderment in the tone of her voice. She really does marvel at the way life was lived here. She's definitely different from any girl I've ever met. "It would be a unique experience—living in this village and helping to save lives."

"Yeah. Unique and fulfilling." She takes my hand. "Let's take a look at the surfboat."

We cut around a white support post and stride over to the big rowboat. Stephanie and Johnny are standing there, Stephanie leaning her head on his shoulder. I can't quite hear what she's saying to him. The boat has been painted white with black trim around the edges. U.S. LIFE-SAVING SERVICE has been lettered in black on the bow. A bunch of oars and floaters are scattered inside.

Lisa and Don sidle up to us.

"Learning anything new?" Lisa asks.

"This place is amazing," Holly says.

Don reaches and grips the top edge of the boat. "It's definitely different from my world. I sit in front of a computer screen all day, writing code, playing games, checking my phone, and posting on Instagram. This place is . . . this place is real. It has a feel to it." He pivots and looks out the open door. "It has a smell."

I pat Don on the back. "I promised you wouldn't regret coming here. It'll be one of those weeks you won't forget."

"It's been great so far," Holly says.

"Very interesting," Lisa says. "Whenever there was a shipwreck, they must have pushed the cart out the doors and hooked it up to the horses. Then down the beach they would scramble."

Holly nods. "When they got to the scene, they'd use that Lyle Gun to shoot a line out to the ship and then set up the rescue pulley system. I would have loved to see them in action."

Don swivels his head. "Talk about action, what happened to Johnny and Stephanie?"

I quickly inspect the large room. They've disappeared.

"Listen," Holly says. "Do you hear those footsteps?"

I don't hear a thing.

She looks up. "Right above us."

A wide smile breaks across Don's face. "They're heading up to the lookout room."

"Well." Lisa claps her hands together. "Shall we go rescue Johnny from the clutches of our libidinous roommate?"

"Libidinous?" Don snorts. "Does that mean horny?"

Lisa raises one eyebrow. "Someone is in peril on the high seas of lust. C'mon lifesaving crew." She points to a door that's ajar on the opposite wall. "They went thata way."

Chapter 7

Lisa leads the way through the door into the living quarters. The walls are a dull white with peach-painted wainscot trim and doors. A small table surrounded by four wooden chairs occupies one corner of the room. A couple of bookshelves loaded with shells and duck decoys sit against the walls. More informational posters hang here and there. These old boys definitely lived a rustic life.

Lisa turns and presses her index finger to her lips. "Shhhhhhh." She points to a doorway and heads in that direction.

We follow as quietly as we can and enter a short hallway. At the end of the hallway, some gray steps lead up to a landing. She heads up the steps, using the railing to help keep her footfalls as light as possible. I want to laugh out loud, thinking about catching Johnny and Stephanie in some kind of amorous embrace or even worse.

At the landing, an open door to the left reveals the bunk room. Eight or so beds are stationed between closet doors. A wooden storage chest, the size of a small casket, sits at the foot of each bed. A large chimney cuts through the middle of the room with a wood stove piped into it. I can feel Holly's hand on my back as she leans against me to get a look inside the room. Man, does she smell good. I feel like I'm going to catch on fire inside.

Lisa turns right on the landing and ascends another set of stairs. Those must be the ones going up to the lookout room. We stop halfway up and listen.

"We've got a great view from up here," Johnny says.

"A car just parked next to the ATVs," Stephanie says.

"Yeah, that's a Land Rover. Those vehicles can go anywhere."

"Ahhh. It's a family. A couple kids, a mom and dad, and grandparents. Would you like to have a family one day, Johnny?"

"Sure. That'd be great."

"Me too."

Things get quiet. What are they doing now?

"Johnny . . . . . You're different than most guys I date."

"Is that a good different or a bad different?"

"Definitely a good different."

"May I . . . may I . . ."

"Do you want to kiss me?"

"Yes."

I glance at Holly, and a big smile breaks across her face. Johnny has got to be shaking in his shoes. Should we go charging up the stairs and interrupt their first kiss? That would be nasty. Oh no. There goes Lisa on cue, flying up the steps. We tromp after her.

Johnny and Stephanie separate and glare at us with wide eyes.

"We caughcha!" Lisa shouts.

We file into the small room. It's only about a seven by seven foot space with two small windows on each side.

"What's the matter, Johnny boy?" Don Says. "You look like the kid who just missed the ice cream truck."

Johnny's face glows bright red. "We were just checking out the lookout room."

Lisa laughs. "That's not all you were checking out."

Stephanie crosses her arms "Lisa, you can sure be a pain in the ass."

"Uh, uh, uh!" Lisa raises her finger. "I'm just trying to protect an innocent."

"Well . . ." Stephanie puts her hands on her hips. " . . . I don't need protecting."

"I'm not talking about you. I'm trying to protect old Johnny here." Lisa slaps Johnny's shoulder.

"Hey, be quiet." Holly is staring out the window.

Everyone looks in her direction.

"That's the family staying a couple cabins down from us."

I step to the window, look down, and see the redheaded guy with his wife and kids. An older guy is standing next to them. His wife, pointing here and there, seems to be giving some kind of speech. Everyone crowds around the window.

"Can you hear her?" I ask.

"Yeah," Holly says. "She's talking about the history of the village."

"You've got Super Girl ears," Lisa says. "I'd really like to know why Portsmouth was abandoned. Let's go down and listen to what she has to say."

"Good idea," Holly says. "I'd like to know too."

"Follow me, gang." Lisa turns from the window and scrambles down the steps. We hustle through the hallway, into the living quarters and out through the surfboat garage. As we descend the ramp, the family turns in our direction.

Lisa waves. "Hi. Do you mind if we listen in? We're interested in hearing about the village's history."

The lady, wearing wire-rimmed glasses, has light-streaked, sandy brown hair gathered into a ponytail. She's thin but fit, probably about sixty years old. Like the WVU girls, she has on a long sleeved t-shirt and light colored pants. The man standing next to her is tall, muscular, and imposing. His close-cropped, almost white hair and granite-carved face gives him the appearance of an old drill sergeant.

The woman spreads her hands. "You're certainly welcome. I didn't know I'd be speaking to an audience this morning. Aren't you the young people staying in the last cabin?"

"Yes." Holly points at me. "The boys are staying on one side. That's Joel, Don, and Johnny." She motions toward her buddies. "Lisa, Stephanie, and I are renting the other side."

"Nice to meet all of you. I'm Mee Mee." She tilts her head toward the tall guy. "This is my good friend, Russell Goodwin." She gestures toward the family. "These are the Waltons, Dugan, Marla, and their two kids, Gabriel and Azalea. We call her Azy for short."

The dark-haired boy looks to be about ten years old. He's the splitting image of his mother, who, by the way, is incredibly attractive. She has long sable-colored hair and full red lips which contrasts with her light complexion. You can tell she works out. The little girl, about two years old, looks more like her dad with that bright red hair. He looks in shape, too. This crew must be fitness fanatics.

"We all attend college in West Virginia," Holly says. "We girls go to WVU, and the guys attend West Liberty University."

"Really." Mee Mee's eyebrows raise high above her wire-rimmed glasses. "I graduated from WVU. What a coincidence. It's good to meet some fellow Mountaineers. What brings you to Portsmouth Island? Don't kids your age prefer Daytona Beach?"

"We girls are all into biological science," Holly says. "I'm going into marine biology, and my friends are nursing majors. A place like this is much more interesting than Daytona Beach."

Don raises his hand. "I'm here because Joel made me come, and the price was right."

Everybody laughs.

Dugan Walton says, "For sure it's an economical vacation and a very unique place." His black ball cap has a Dare County Sheriff patch on it with the Hatteras Lighthouse symbol.

I point to his hat. "Are you in law enforcement?"

He nods. "I'm the sheriff of Dare County just north of here. My wife is a deputy."

"We've always wanted to vacation on Portsmouth Island," his wife says. "Just get away from all the hassles of police work. It's a beautiful place. So much history."

"Yeah," Lisa says. "We want to know more about its history. Why in the world was it abandoned? Most of these other barrier islands are thriving."

"Well," Mee Mee says, "this island did thrive at one time. The town was established in 1753 by the North Carolina Colonial Assembly." She turns and waves toward the village.

I swat away a horde of mosquitos and peer in that direction. There are about a dozen buildings spread out across a flat, grassy stretch of land with a few live oaks scattered here and there. The farthest building is a small church with its tall steeple, maybe 250 yards away.

"As you can see," she says, "the village has been well preserved by the National Park Service. Portsmouth became an important lightering port. Because the sound was so shallow, ships had to transfer their cargo onto flatter-bottomed boats that could take the goods across the Pamlico and Core Sounds to the mainland. By 1860 the population had grown to 680. Little ol' Portsmouth became one of the most important ports-of-entry along the Atlantic coast after the Revolutionary War."

"That's amazing," Lisa says. "How did it go from prominence to pot?"

From prominence to pot? Crimenetly, the girl comes up with the words.

Mee Mee shakes her head. "Unfortunately, decline began when two strong hurricanes cut the Oregon Inlet and deepened the Hatteras Inlet to the north. Those inlets became more favored by shipping companies. The Civil War struck another blow when Union soldiers occupied the Outer Banks, causing many people to flee to the mainland. After the Lifesaving Station was decommissioned in 1939 and the Post Office closed in 1959, the population dwindled down to a handful of tenacious inhabitants. Two elderly ladies were the last to leave the island in 1971." She spreads her hands. "That's when the island became officially uninhabited. As the years went by, the island became a vacation destination for campers who didn't mind roughing it. Now the village's only occupants are ghosts."

Holly points toward the trail we arrived on. "Talk about ghosts!"

Everyone turns and looks. A tall, thin man with a salt-and-pepper beard and long walking stick stands there. The wind whips his loose fitting, white, long-sleeved shirt and gray baggy pants. He raises his hand and shades his brow, staring at us. His image wavers in the rising heat.

"Holy Moses," Stephanie says. "That *is* a ghost."

"He's coming this way," Holly says.

I squint against the bright sunshine to clear my vision. I know that guy. "That's Elsa's grandfather."

"Who's Elsa?" Russell Goodwin asks.

"A kid I met this morning."

He picks up his pace and draws near. His face is pale and eyes tense. Wrinkles score his cheeks and forehead. "My name's Jonah Newland. My granddaughter is missing. I've covered the length of the island. I can't find her. Have you seen a tall, thin, black-haired girl?"

Chapter 8

I shake my head. "We rode up along the beach. No sign of her."

Dugan Walton steps forward. "When was the last time you saw her?"

"About three hours ago. She took off on her ATV to go shelling. She would have stayed along the shoreline. I should have run into her by now. This is the end of the island."

Mee Mee turns and waves across the open expanse. "She may have crossed over to the sound side. Maybe she decided to go exploring."

"It's possible," the old man says. "But I told her to stay along the shore. I didn't want her to get that ATV hung up in a bog. There're lots of marshy land between the beach and the sound."

Marla Walton reaches and grasps her son's shoulder. "Kids don't always listen."

"That's true." Jonah Newland rubs his beard. "Elsa does have a mind of her own."

"We'll help you hunt for her," Stephanie says.

"Sure." Johnny points to the lifesaving station. "Our ATVs are right over there. We can head back along the sound side."

Dugan Walton and Mee Mee's friend, Russell Goodwin, look at each other as if an alarm went off in their minds. They drift away from the group toward the Land Rover.

"Can I help hunt for the girl, too?" the dark-haired boy says.

"Of course, Gabriel," Marla Walton says. "We'll all help."

Holly stares at the two men. I glance at them and notice they're engaged in a private conversation but can't make out their words. Can she hear what they're saying? I wouldn't be surprised.

Holly tugs on my arm and whispers, "The sheriff is worried about the girl."

I keep my voice low. "What did he say?"

"He told Mr. Goodwin that there're a couple of ex-cons on the island. They're staying with the church group. He considers them dangerous. He said something about drug deals and extortion."

My heart ramps up. They sound like mob thugs. Elsa's pixie-like face appears in my mind. The thought of a cute kid like that in the hands of a couple of creeps jolts me.

Jonah Newland says, "I'd appreciate any help you could give me. Elsa's all I got. Her mother died a few years ago in a car accident. Her father's a no-account-good-for-nothin'. She'd rather live with her old granddad than him."

Sheriff Walton and Mr. Goodwin walk toward us. They look as if they had just seen a pack of wolves.

"Mr. Newland, I'm Sheriff Dugan Walton. This is my friend, Russell Goodwin. He also has a background in law enforcement. Have you or your granddaughter encountered anyone on the island that has made you feel uneasy or uncomfortable?"

Jonah Newland twists the bottom of his beard and stares at the ground. "Well . . . Now that you mention it, a couple of men and a woman stopped by our camp and invited us to one of their church meetings. They were going on about the end of the world coming soon. I'm a Methodist. I believe in all that, but these people seemed a little wild-eyed to me. I told them thanks but no thanks. Elsa kept asking questions about the end times. She reads the Bible a lot. They finally left."

"Do you think she may have gone to one of their meetings?" Russell Goodwin asks.

Newland shakes his head. "No. She told me she had a bad feeling about them. That girl's got good instincts when it comes to people."

"Still," Sheriff Walton says, "if we don't find her in the next half hour, Russell and I will go talk to that church group to see if they've had contact with her. Then we'll question the other campers. In the meantime, let's comb the island from here back to the cabins."

"I truly appreciate your help," Newland says.

Russell Goodwin motions toward the sound side of the island. "You college kids can take your ATVs along the sound. Be careful. It can get swampy over that way. There may even be some soft spots similar to quicksand. Don't take any chances. If the ground looks questionable, go around."

"My Land Rover can handle the terrain on the other side of the dunes," Sheriff Walton says. "We can get a good view of the area between the dunes and the sound."

"My old pickup is parked on the beach," Newland says. "I'll head back down along the shore to the south end of the island."

"Sounds good," Goodwin says. "If your granddaughter cut up over the dunes for a few minutes, you may have missed her on the way up."

Jonah Newland nods. "I pray that's what happened."

Marla Walton picks up her daughter. "Let's go Azy. Gabriel, get back into the car."

The boy stamps his foot. "Aw, Mom, can't me and Dad walk back? We can search better that way."

Sheriff Walton tousles his hair. "No, Gabe. We'll cover more ground faster in the car."

Russell Goodwin reaches for Mee Mee's hand. "Let's get going."

"Wait a minute," Holly says. "Can't anyone hear that?"

Everyone stops in their tracks and stares at her.

I tilt my head and cup my ear in the direction she's looking but don't hear anything unusual.

"What do you hear?" Marla Walton asks.

"It's very melodic like a Gregorian chant, but it's definitely a girl's voice."

"That's got to be her," says Jonah Newland. "Where's the song coming from?"

Holly points across the clearing. "It's coming from over there."

"That's the Methodist church," Mee Mee says.

The church is only a couple hundred yards away. I take off running in that direction, and Holly keeps right up with me. In less than two minutes the whole crew reaches the building, even old Jonah Newland. The building looks like one of those little old country churches you see in paintings. It's white with a three-story-high steeple. Red-brick supports raise the structure about two feet off the ground. The few windows are frosted glass and come to a point on top.

Now even I can hear the song. The voice is somewhat otherworldly, and the words hard to understand.

Although Jonah Newland is heaving for air, he rushes up the few steps and opens the door to the entry foyer. We all try to peer in at once. The center aisle splits two rows of wooden pews. A thin girl with short black hair is kneeling at the altar rail. I can't see her face, but she has to be Elsa. She's holding something in front of her face. A seashell? Her strange song is distorted by the shell. Wait a minute. That's the whelk shell I traded her for the gold coin.

"Elsa!" her grandfather yells. "I've been looking for you for almost two hours."

She snaps out of her chant, turns, and faces us. "Grandfather, it's here. I've had a vision. I've seen where it is. There's a tree and a big white bird. I know we can find it."

Chapter 9

There's nothing like sitting on the porch steps and watching the sunrise over the ocean. I check my watch: 5:50, right on schedule. The sun looks like a ball of fire on the horizon, turning the sea a light blue-green and the breaking waves into tumbling shadows. The sky above spreads out all orange and pink, and the backlit clouds hover in holy silence. It's a spiritual experience to me—the new day's light breaking through earth's darkness once again.

I take a deep breath. I want to hold on to this feeling of freedom and life. I let the air out slowly. I'll turn twenty-two this fall. The world and all of its responsibilities await somewhere out there. Sooner or later I'll have to grow up, get a job, get married, and raise a family. I look forward to those days, but for now I want to enjoy this feeling of being one with the universe. These are rare minutes in life. Don't think. Just enjoy.

But I can't help thinking about Holly. She's incredible. I need to put the brakes on. I don't want to end up heartbroken over a girl who's out of my reach under normal circumstances. She wouldn't give me a second look if I walked by her on WVU's campus. Here, though, she noticed me. She even likes me. I wonder how much she likes me. I can't let myself get carried away. In this environment the romance juices flow, but once we head back to normal life, she won't have the time to think about me. I'll be a fading memory. I need to establish a firm stance on the reality of this relationship. Accept this week for what it is—a week in paradise with a beautiful girl. Enjoy it, but don't expect much once it's over.

I hear a door open on the other side of the cabin. That's got to be Holly. She said her friends like to sleep in. I glance over my shoulder and see her walking my way dressed in pink and white striped pajamas. She's barefoot and carrying a cup of coffee.

"Hey, Joel. Up early again, huh?"

"Yeah. I don't like to miss the sunrise."

She sits down next to me. "It's beautiful."

I smile at her. "Sleep well?" Even without makeup she looks great, her light blonde hair gathered into a ponytail with one of those pink scrunchies and her dark eyebrows above those China blue eyes.

She wavers her hand. "I woke up in the middle of the night and couldn't fall back to sleep for a couple of hours. Kept thinking about finding Elsa in that church and what she said."

"You mean about the vision?"

"Yeah." She takes a sip of coffee.

"I know what you mean. The girl is . . . uhhh . . . otherworldly."

"What kind of vision do you think she had?"

"Hard to say. Some kind of object, maybe a relic or something like that. Whatever it is, she said she thinks she can find it on this island. "

"Did you find it weird that she was singing into that seashell?"

I feel an odd sensation scurry up my spine. "When I found that shell, I knew it was something special. She definitely wanted it. Can you imagine trading a golden coin for a seashell?"

"I think she has a gift."

"Whaddaya mean, a gift?"

Her eyes narrow. "Some people have a super sensitivity when it comes to processing what happens around them in the world."

"Like you with your hearing?"

"Yeah. When I was a kid I was diagnosed with golden ears."

I chuckle and lightly brush her earlobe with the tip of my forefinger. "They seem normal to me."

She shakes her head. "They're not. I can hear very soft sounds like whispering and high frequency sounds that most people don't hear. Loud noises used to scare me out of my rompers, but I've learned how to manage my fright response."

"You definitely have super hearing. So you think Elsa is some kind of savant?"

She shrugs. "More like a visionary. She reminds me of Joan of Arc."

"I've heard of Joan of Arc but don't know much about her. She was a Catholic saint, right?"

Holly nods. "I'm Catholic. Went to Catholic schools all my life, so I've heard all about her. She was a French peasant girl during the Hundred Years' War. She claimed to have received a vision from the Archangel Michael instructing her to support France's effort to gain independence from England. Many people believed she was the one who would fulfill an ancient prophecy claiming that a young virgin would save France. The French King was impressed by her spirituality. He gave her permission to put on armor and lead the French army into battle. She became an inspiration, and the tide of the war turned. Some people thought she was a sorceress but others a saint. Unfortunately, the English captured her and burned her at the stake."

"Not a great way to go."

"Not at all. Anyway, that's who Elsa reminds me of. She has this aura about her."

I stretch my arms behind me, plant my hands on the deck, and arch my back. "I'm just glad we found her. The possibility of Elsa falling into the hands of a couple of creeps freaked me out."

"Me too. As soon as I heard Sheriff Walton mention those ex-cons I felt jittery."

"Who knows? They may not be a threat anymore. They're with that church group. Maybe they've been converted."

"Yeah." Holly takes another sip of coffee. "God only knows."

"Anyway, let's forget about it, relax, and enjoy the day."

"That reminds me. We gals have a great idea for later on."

"What's on your mind?"

"We'd like to have a storytelling evening with a big bonfire. Roast marshmallows and hotdogs, that sort of thing."

"Sounds great. Who's invited?"

"The whole neighborhood. We'll go from cabin to cabin and any campsites nearby and tell people to bring their own hotdogs, marshmallows, and a good story to tell."

"Are you going to invite the ex-cons?"

"Well . . . maybe we'll skip the two church cabins. They probably have their own agenda anyway."

"That's probably wise. What do you want me and the boys to do?"

She wiggles her fingers in front of my face. "You guys are in charge of the fire."

***

I'm definitely no boy scout. Fortunately, Don takes charge of the fire. An Eagle Scout with all the merit badges, he relishes the opportunity. Within ten minutes he has flames leaping into the sky from a neatly stacked circle of wood. With the sun setting over the Core Sound, the fading light offers the ideal backdrop to the dancing blaze.

"Hey, what's going on here," a woman's voice calls out.

I turn to see Mary, the thirty-something gal from the church group I met yesterday. She drops her cigarette, stamps it out, and blows a jet of smoke.

"We're having a campfire story night. You're welcome to join us."

"Don't mind if I do." She tilts her head toward the church cabins. "I need a break from all that end-times indoctrination."

Holly strolls over toward us. "Hi. I'm Holly." She extends her hand. "I'm a friend of Joel's."

"Nice to meet ya." Mary shakes her hand. "I'm Mary." She thumbs over her shoulder. "I'm with the New Kingdom Church group, but don't worry, I didn't come to thump you with my Bible. In fact, I don't even have it with me."

Holly shrugs. "We figured your group had meetings scheduled this evening. We should have offered an invitation."

Mary holds up her hands. "No, no, no. Too many wet blankets amongst that crowd. You were smart not to invite them. Reverend Swagger would have showed up and preached a sermon."

Holly laughs. "Well, we hope you stick around. There's plenty of marshmallows and hotdogs. If you have any good stories to tell, we'll be happy to listen."

"Thanks, Sweetie. I think I will hang out for a while." She takes a deep breath. "I need some fresh air and free rein."

Within ten minutes about twenty people show up, the Waltons, Mee Mee and Russell Goodwin, Elsa and her grandfather, Quentin Porter, Jack Graham, and several other campers. I sit down on a nice size log next to Holly and spear a couple of hotdogs on one of those long cooking forks. Laughter and conversations jangle around the campfire. Holly and I lean on each other now and again. She feels so warm when her body presses against me. Stephanie and Johnny sit next to us on another log, Stephanie's head planted on Johnny's shoulder. Lisa and Don are sitting next to each other on beach chairs. The Walton kids, Azy and Gabe, are giggling because their mom's marshmallow just caught fire and fell off the stick. Mary found a spot between Jack Graham and Quentin Porter. Hmmmmm. This is going to be an interesting evening.

After about ten minutes Lisa clears her throat. "Can I have everybody's attention?"

The laughter and conversations dwindle down to silence except for the crackling of the fire.

She spreads her hands. "We'd like to thank you all for coming to our little community bonfire party tonight. We hope you brought some stories to tell. I'm going to break the ice with a true story of a mysterious event that occurred very near here back in the 1920s. I've been doing a lot of reading lately about local history, and this account truly captured my attention."

Lisa clasps her hands on her lap and pans the circle of faces. "There was a ship, a five-masted schooner called the Carroll A. Deering. She was making a return trip to Hampton Roads, Virginia from Barbados in late January of 1921. Not long after sailing through the Bermuda Triangle, strange things began to happen. The schooner passed the Cape Lookout Lightship, a vessel fitted with a strong warning light to help other ships navigate away from the shoals. The lightship keeper reported that the crew was wandering about the top deck in an odd fashion. One of the crewmen yelled out that they had lost their anchors.

"The next day the Deering passed the S.S. Lake Elon southwest of the Diamond Shoals. A crew member of the Lake Elon reported that the ship seemed to be steering an odd course as if they did not know where they were going. On January 31 the lookout man of the Cape Hatteras Lifesaving Station spotted the schooner in the morning light run aground on the Diamond Shoals not far from Portsmouth Island.

"Because of the rough seas, a rescue attempt couldn't be made until four days later on February 4th. When rescuers boarded the ship, they discovered the crew had vanished. Oddly, food was laid out below deck in the dining room as if dinner was about to be served. None of the crew was ever seen again. No bodies washed to shore. Despite an exhaustive government investigation, no clues were ever found and no clear explanation given. Were these crew members in possession of some forbidden treasure or cursed idol? Perhaps they slipped into some kind of time portal. If so, it's possible they could reappear here tonight."

Lisa waves toward the ocean. "Sometime this evening if you wander along the beach, don't be surprised if you cross paths with the lost souls of the Carroll A. Deering."

Jack Graham stands up and adjusts his eye patch. Flickering light from the fire dances over his blue-and-white-striped shirt and red bandana. His black baggy pants and leather boots add a swashbuckling flavor to his appearance. "I believe what you say to be true, young maiden. In fact, I arrived on this island via a time portal."

Everyone laughs at his pirate's inflection. What in the world? I can't believe it. Sometime during the evening he slipped on a fake hook hand. I shake my head and whisper to Holly, "This guy is quite the thespian."

"Aye, don't laugh. It be true. I was once a crew member of the Queen Anne's Revenge, the very ship commanded by the infamous Blackbeard." He went on to tell a story about a fierce battle between Blackbeard's crew and Lieutenant Robert Maynard's naval force. He held up his hook. "It was in a sword fight with Lieutenant Maynard himself that I lost me hand. He was about to plunge the sword into me heart when I slipped through a time portal and I ended up in Jamaica three years into the future. Luckily for me I found a good surgeon who fixed me up with this hook."

Quentin Porter, the shark fisherman, asks, "How'd you lose your eye?"

"Shiver me timbers. That's another story. In Jamaica I joined another band of pirates under Calico Jack. One day as we were sailing on the open sea and drinking too much rum, I heard a screech, looked up, and saw a seagull. The damn bird shat right in my eye."

Giggling jingles around the fire.

Lisa asks, "How did bird crap put your eye out?"

"Well, my pretty young maiden, I wasn't quite used to me hook." With an explosion of laughter, Jack Graham bows and takes his seat.

Chapter 10

Everyone glances around the circle waiting for the next story to begin. It becomes awkwardly quiet. Hoping to get the ball rolling again, I say, "Mr. Porter, how about you? With all the sharks you've caught, certainly you can drum up a good fish tale."

All eyes focus on Porter. He's wearing a faded-gray tank top, and the fire's light deepens the shadows carved out by his muscular arms and shoulders. His shaved head gives him that Yul Brynner look. He scans the listeners, nodding. "Okay. I'll tell a story." He stretches out his good leg and crosses his prosthetic leg over the other. The fire glints off the bowed metal of the foot. "It's not as mysterious as the young lady's or as funny as One-Eyed Jack's pirate tale, but I promise you it is a true story.

"Fifteen years ago when I was a young man, about the age of you college kids, me and a couple buddies came to Portsmouth Island to party and surf. We loved the idea of roughing it on an island where you didn't have to fight through the crowd to get to the ocean." He stares at the fire as if he's looking into another dimension. "Have you ever had friends that were kindred spirits? All for one and one for all? Sometimes we'd say the same thing at the same time. That's how close we were.

"About the middle of the week there was a storm at sea, which stirred up some incredible waves. These bad boys were ten to twelve feet high. We paddled way out to where the big ones were breaking. I was the first one to catch the curl perfectly. I rode it all the way in to shore.

"Once I finally tumbled into the surf and got back to my feet, I heard screaming. My buddies were about a hundred yards out, but I could see a violent struggle, arms flailing and legs kicking. Then I saw the whipping tale and fin of a large shark. I threw my board onto the sand and dove through a crashing wave. I swam as hard as I could to get to them. It seemed like it took forever. When I finally got out there, I saw Billy floating on the water, head back, kinda bobbing up and down. The water was red with blood. When I reached and grabbed his arm to pull him to me, he felt so light. Then I saw what had happened. The shark, a big bull shark, had bitten him almost in half.

"I didn't have time to process it because I heard Franky shrieking. I glanced up in time to see him ripped under the surface. Then up he came again, screaming and thrashing. The shark kept pulling him under, but he managed to keep shaking loose. By the time I got to him he was in shock. I could see he was losing a lot of blood. The shark had disappeared. I clasped Franky around the neck and began one-armed swimming back to the shore."

Porter pauses and gazes into the smoke rising into the night sky. He takes a deep breath and blows it out. "I was about thirty yards from shore when I felt something dig into my calf just below my knee. It hurt like hell, but I didn't let go of Franky. I managed to turn slightly and kick the son of a bitch on his blunt nose with my left foot. It wouldn't let go. It kept on twisting back and forth, its teeth digging deeper until my leg came off. A big wave carried us the rest of the way onto the beach.

"It was too late for Franky. He was pale gray, not breathing. I had my own troubles. I knew I'd bleed out unless I could tie a tourniquet just above my knee. I crawled over to my surfboard and grabbed the leash. Some people call it a leg rope. I was getting dizzier than hell but somehow managed to tie a knot tight enough to slow down the bleeding. I jammed the end of the stump into the sand, thinking maybe the grains would help to clog the blood. Then I passed out.

"I woke up a few hours later in the Engelhard Medical Center about twenty miles across the Pamlico Sound. I lost three precious things that day: my two best friends and the lower half of my right leg." Porter lifts his prosthetic leg into the air. "Most of you were probably wondering how I got this technological marvel. Now you know."

Dead silence descends on the circle of listeners except for the crackling of the fire. I stare at the ground and swallow, feeling like someone just punched me in the gut. I'm definitely inept when it comes to handling awkward moments in life. What in the hell do you say when someone tells a story like that? I want to get the party back on track, but the words that form in my mind seem foolish and inadequate.

Finally, Holly speaks up. "Well, Mr. Porter, that was quite a traumatic experience. We're sorry for all you've suffered because of that day. Your love for your friends and your courage is something I'll always admire and take to heart."

Porter nods.

Crimenetly, Holly's good at smoothing things out.

Holly glances around the circle of faces. "Does anyone have something else they would like to share? How about you, Mee Mee? Could you acquaint us with some local history?"

"Certainly." Mee Mee stands up. She is a thin but strong looking woman with a face that registers a high degree of intelligence. The flames flash off her wire-rimmed glasses as she clasps her hands in front of her like an enthusiastic teacher getting ready present a lesson. "Believe it or not, there was a two-story hospital on this island built back in 1845. I'll tell you a little bit about its history. It had twelve rooms and its own dock for unloading supplies and patients. However, when the Civil War broke out, the hospital was shut down so that it could house Confederate troops. In 1861 soldiers from Greenville, North Carolina known as the Tar River Boys were stationed at the hospital.

"At that time the Confederates had constructed forts on Hatteras Island, Fort Clark and Fort Hatteras. You see, the barrier islands of the North Carolina coast were the gateway to the rest of the state. Whoever controlled these barrier islands could control North Carolina. Of course, the Union Army knew this and made it a priority to attack the forts and take Hatteras Inlet. They started with Fort Clark.

"The great Union ships were equipped with long cannons that could batter the forts from a great distance. The firepower of the Confederate artillery could not reach the ships. Eventually the Rebel soldiers fled Fort Clark and took refuge at Fort Hatteras. That's when the Union Navy turned their guns on Fort Hatteras. After hours of suffering intense shelling, the Confederate commander surrendered the fort.

"With the loss of these two forts, the people and Confederate troops on Portsmouth Island fled. The Union took over the hospital and used it to treat their wounded and sick soldiers. After the war the building was occupied by the Army Signal Corps for a short while. Then it was abandoned in 1883. In the late 1890's the building caught fire and burnt to the . . ."

Mee Mee shifts her gaze to the darkness beyond the fire. The sound of swishing footsteps through sea grass and sand distracts my attention from the halted history lesson. I stare in the direction of the sound.

"War and destruction," a deep voice intones.

Three tall, dark figures stand against the violet star-studded sky. They move toward the firelight, and the faces of Reverend Noah Swagger and two of his disciples, rough-looking, dark-haired men, reflect the red-amber glow.

Chapter 11

"Things haven't changed much, have they? This world is full of war and destruction," Swagger says. "My name is Reverend Noah Swagger." He gestures to his right. "This is Disciple Clint," then to his left, "and this is Disciple Tanner."

Disciple Clint, tall and thin with a patchy beard and shaggy brown hair, raises his chin and squints around the circle. Tanner, an ugly man with crooked teeth and a large nose, is a few inches shorter but muscular with receding dark hair and a thick mustache. He raises his hand and lowers it.

Swagger motions toward the woman. "I see you've already met Disciple Mary. We missed you at the prayer meeting tonight, Mary."

The woman finishes a drag on her cigarette and blows out a stream of smoke. "Sorry, Reverend Swagger. These good people invited me to join them around the campfire. I didn't want to decline such a friendly gesture."

"I see. Most of the disciples are back at the cabin praying for our ministry goals. Perhaps you should go back and join them."

"No thanks. I'm enjoying myself too much. It's been a nice change of pace getting to know these people and hearing their stories. I do believe I'll hang out for a while longer."

The preacher frowns but nods. "Please don't let us interrupt the storytelling. If you don't mind, we'll just take a seat and listen a while."

Holly says, "You're welcome to join us."

Swagger and his two followers sit down on the ground next to One-Eyed Jack.

I glance around the campfire and notice Sheriff Walton's stare is transfixed on Swagger and his companions. Goodwin, sitting next to Walton, also eyes the newcomers.

"I'd like to tell the next story," Sheriff Walton says. "A lot of people wonder why I went into law enforcement. Currently, I'm the sheriff of Dare County just north of here." His focus shifts back in the direction of Swagger.

"When I was a boy, about ten years old, my Uncle Elijah and Aunt Annie took me on vacation with them to the Outer Banks. We stayed up in Corolla just above Duck. One day I went out riding my bike on some paths in the woods north of the old Whalehead Club. I hit a fallen branch and tumbled over my handlebars. The first thing I noticed when I got my bearings was a terrible odor. I'll never forget that smell. When I looked up I saw a girl, about nineteen years old. Her skin was pale gray, and a horde of flies was buzzing around her."

Lisa and Stephanie gasp.

"Her eyes were blank but they seemed to be staring at me. I hightailed it out of there and back to the beach house. I was known for being the boy who cried wolf. I admit I had an active imagination. None of the adults believed my story. They said it was probably just a dead animal.

"The next day, I convinced a friend of my uncle to go back to the crime scene with me. When we got there, we found a dead deer. I couldn't believe my eyes. How could I mistake a deer for a young woman? Then I noticed something. Someone had swept away all my footprints and tire marks. The killer had come back to the scene of the crime and noticed a kid had been there on a bike. So he did what he could to eliminate the evidence. When another girl disappeared, people began to listen to me. The sheriff brought in a cadaver dog, and the body was located in a shallow grave not far from where I found the girl.

"When the killer was arrested, I felt a great sense of purpose, knowing justice had been served. After high school I earned a law enforcement degree. Then I moved to the Outer Banks and got a job as a deputy. Ten years later the good people of Dare County elected me as their sheriff.

"My experience as a young crime solver taught me something about the criminal psyche I'll never forget." Walton paused and glanced around the faces, stopping again at Swagger and his cronies. "First, the sociopath's mind lacks conscience and compassion. To the hardened criminal, people are objects to be used or abused for their own aims. Second, they believe they can get away with their crimes, but they always make a mistake."

Reverend Swagger nods. "It's good to know we have a man on the island committed to the protection and safety of our citizens. I appreciate your service and dedication to the good people of your community. I haven't been here for the entire storytelling session, but clearly a common theme has been established: The nature of fallen man— war, destruction, murder, violence and evil. Most human beings have a penchant for violence and power and greed. None of us are exempt from the touch of evil. It's this fallen nature that will bring about mankind's destruction."

Swagger motions toward the flames. "The Bible talks about the world meeting its end by fire. I truly believe we are in the last days of this earth. Drugs, crime, and sexual immorality are rampant. We are living in a time when anything goes."

Stephanie and Johnny straighten up as if Swagger's words jolted them. They each scoot to the end of their side of the log, creating a space between them.

Swagger lowers his thick eyebrows. "The Apostle Peter says the very elements of the air will be incinerated. Of course, Jesus himself said in the last days stars will fall from the sky like missiles, there will be wars and rumors of wars, and the earth will see destruction that it has never experienced before in its history."

Jonah Newland interrupts, "That's a pretty dim outlook, Reverend. Isn't mankind capable of great good also? Don't we have the choice between good or evil? Certainly, there's hope of working out our problems and disagreements peacefully?"

Swagger shakes his head. "I wouldn't count on that. Just look at the world situation: the nuclear threat from North Korea, China, and Russia is growing. Our self-absorbed president lacks basic diplomacy skills. They are all itching to be the first to press the so-called red button on their desks. I tell you the current world situation is a recipe for annihilation—the beginning of the end." Swagger raises his hand, index finger pointing upward. "God has raised me up as a prophet to warn those who will listen. Destruction is coming upon us soon.

"I don't mean to frighten you. In fact, I want to offer all of you an opportunity. We are determined to survive the coming Apocalypse and begin a new community of faith on earth. This is the vision God has given me. This is my divine mission. That's why we're here on this island. We're preparing for the end. We're growing together spiritually and making plans for what's to come. We have purchased a large underground shelter that will withstand a nuclear war. It was built during the Cold War in the 1950s. We hope to raise enough money to not only pay off the shelter but also stock food and water to insure our survival underground for more than a year. Soon there will be a worldwide nuclear war. Civilization as we know it will end. However, the New Kingdom Church will survive. We will emerge and begin the rebuilding process. Just as the Israelites returned from Babylon and rebuilt Jerusalem, God has called us to build a new kingdom. I'm offering all of you an opportunity to join us and help us."

Elsa Newland stands up. Her tall, thin figure seems ablaze in the firelight's glow, her large dark eyes reflecting the flames. "I've received a vision from God, too. But it's much different than yours."

Chapter 12

Reverend Swagger sits back, somewhat startled. "Well, go ahead young lady. Tell us about your vision from God."

Elsa takes a deep breath and glances skyward for a few seconds. Then she stares at the fire. "When Grandfather and I arrived on the island a few days ago, I found a golden coin along the shore. Grandfather said it was a good omen. He's convinced the *Lost Treasure of El Salvador* is buried on this island—four chests of gold. There's also a legend that another chest, smaller than the others, is buried with them. It contains something very powerful.

"When I was praying at the church in the village yesterday, God gave me a vision of where the chests are buried. I could see a large white bird near an old tree. The Spirit revealed to me that the contents of the smaller chest are incredibly important. World leaders will even take notice. Somehow this ancient object will open their eyes to a new way of thinking. God has called me to find this chest. The world doesn't have to go up in flames. This object, whatever it is, will bring these leaders to a new level of understanding of the importance of human life. It will raise them up to a place where they can see more clearly, like when you stand on top of a mountain and see the whole valley below."

Swagger laughs and shakes his head. "That's not going

to happen. That's just a young girl's idealistic dream. I have seen the destruction that is coming upon this world. Nothing can stop it. Evil has possessed the hearts of humanity like a virus. It grows and spreads. Our leaders have been infected. The sooner all of you understand the fate of this world, the better. Come to your senses and join us. We hold the hope for the New Kingdom. We have a solid plan to insure our future and yours."

Russell Goodwin stands up. "Who says your sect or cult or whatever it is offers us the best hope for the future?"

"I do," Swagger says.

"That's right. You do. Who are you? You're just a person like me or anyone else around this campfire." He motions toward Elsa. "Who says this young girl's vision is just a fantasy? Same answer. You do. What credentials do you have to be the judge? How about your two sidekicks there? What credentials do they have?"

Swagger springs to his feet and places his hands on his hips. "Who are you to question our credentials?"

Sheriff Walton stands up. "Let's just say that we know your background. In my eyes this young girl here has ten times more credibility than you."

"Is that right?" Swagger motions toward Elsa. "So, young lady, you've received this wonderful vision of an amazing treasure that's going to save the world? This island is thirteen miles long. Did God show you exactly where to dig?"

"Not exactly, but I've seen the scene in my mind. It's just a matter of locating it."

Jonah Newland struggles to his feet and says, "I'm afraid it's getting late. Elsa and I must be leaving."

"No!" Swagger growls. "We're all very interested in these chests of gold and this incredible object. Apparently, it has the power to cast evil out of the hearts of men." He motions toward Sheriff Walton and Russell

Goodwin. "These two gentlemen have become true believers. Tell us more. Convince me, and I'll rally my church to help you dig. We don't have shovels, but we'll use our bare hands to uncover this amazing treasure."

"Listen to me you bogus, Bible thumper." Jonah Newland raises the little finger on his right hand. "My granddaughter has more spiritual perception in the end of her little finger than you could ever muster with a whole stack of bibles and a boatload of half-baked disciples." Jonah takes his granddaughter by her hand. "Come on, Elsa. We're getting out of here." They hurry away from the fire and disappear into the darkness.

Swagger turns and faces Sheriff Walton and Russell Goodwin. "Maybe your young friend will find the gold and the magic box. Maybe she will save the world. I wouldn't count on it if I were you. To me, she's just a kid with a vivid imagination. But what's happening in this world is real. Watch the news. Read your daily paper. You'll see. Destruction is coming our way. Unfortunately, most of you will remain blind. The elephant is standing in the room, but you ignore it." He scans the other faces around the campfire. "If you do come to your senses, please come and talk to me. You're welcome to join us. Don't wait until it's too late. Once the door closes, it stays closed."

Disciple Clint and Disciple Tanner stand up and dust off their pants.

Swagger says, "It seems like we have worn out our welcome here tonight." He gazes across the circle of people. "Mary, come along. It's time to go back to the family of faith."

"I'm not going back," Mary says.

Swagger lowers his head, those thick eyebrows hooding his eyes. "I said it's time to go back." He nudges Disciple Clint at his side. "Help her up and bring her along,"

The two disciples step toward the woman.

One-Eyed Jack and Quentin Porter jump to their feet and stand in front of her. The two goons stop abruptly and take a step back.

"This is a free country," Quentin Porter says. "I believe the lady has a right to decide for herself whether or not she wants to go back to your cult."

"We're not a cult. We believe what the Bible says like most other churches." Swagger raises his hands pleadingly. "Disciple Mary has no place else to stay. I'm concerned for her safety."

Mee Mee rises to her feet and says, "She can stay in our cabin. We have plenty of room."

Swagger glares at the woman. "Mary, is this what you really want? To turn your back on your church family? We have become brothers and sisters in the Lord."

She takes a deep breath. "Yeah. That's what I want. I'm tired of all your fire and brimstone, end of the world fear mongering. I'm leaving the family."

Swagger nods slowly. "You've just made a big mistake."

Chapter 13

This morning's sunrise seems even more fantastic because Holly is with me. Hand in hand we walk barefoot along the gentle slope of sand, the warm sea water rushing up, dousing our feet with every wave. We turn and face the flaming ball hovering above the horizon. Seven pelicans glide by just over the water's surface, effortlessly, freely. She squeezes my hand, and a surge of joy flows through me.

Holly says, "There's nothing like a good walk along the beach in the morning."

"No doubt about it. When that sun comes up, I feel reborn."

"Yeah. Everything seems new again."

"This world can be dark and disturbing, but there's always a new day."

"Some of those stories last night were somewhat disturbing," Holly says.

Crimenetly! She's got that right. "Quentin Porter's shark tale was brutal."

Holly releases my hand and slips her arm around my waist. "It almost made me cry. I had to gather myself just to try to keep the evening from becoming a downer."

I place my arm around her shoulders and pull her tightly against me. "You were amazing. I'm not good in those kinds of situations, but you said all the right things."

"Well . . . Mee Mee helped with her talk about the hospital and Civil War battles. She's really knowledgeable about this place."

"Yeah. She reminds me of my favorite high school teacher, Ms. Tencate. She was a petite lady, but when she talked, you listened. She commanded your attention because she always had something interesting to say."

"Mee Mee definitely had my attention until Swagger and his two henchmen showed up."

"Henchmen?"

"That's what they reminded me of."

"Yeah, they did look like a couple of thugs."

"Swagger is a man who doesn't like to be crossed, but Elsa stood right up to him."

I picture the tall, thin girl in the glow of the firelight and remember her words about her hope for world peace. "I don't know what to think. She truly believes in her vision of finding that treasure. Swagger's end-of-days rant didn't dampen her enthusiasm about the contents of the mysterious chest."

Holly leans her head on my shoulder. "I wonder what's inside of it."

"You're assuming that it exists."

"Joel! I didn't know you were such a skeptic."

"I'm just being realistic. Elsa is a junior high kid. At that age there's a fine line between fantasy and reality."

Holly drops her arm from my waist and pulls away from me. "I believe her."

"Okay." Man, can a girl get touchy in a flash.

"She's different. There's a Joan-of-Arc quality about her. Sheriff Walton and Mr. Goodwin sure stood up for her."

"Well . . ." I pause to figure out the right words to say. I don't want to put a kink in the outset of a promising day. ". . . Sheriff Walton and Mr. Goodwin weren't going to let

Swagger bully a kid just because she had a different perspective than his."

"It's more than that, Joel. The girl has a calling. Sheriff Walton and Mr. Goodwin could sense it. I got the feeling that even Swagger noticed it."

I nod. "You might be right. She is different."

"The thing is . . ." Holly eases closer and leans her head on my shoulder again. ". . . the things that Swagger said are true. This world is on the brink of destruction. Our future is under the constant threat of nuclear war."

"Right. No one can deny that."

"When we got back to the cabin last night, Stephanie wasn't her usual self. Did you notice that she and Johnny cooled their romance jets after hearing Swagger's spiel?"

"Yeah. I thought that was odd. They went from frisky sweethearts to straight-laced listeners in an instant."

"Swagger's words were like a cold shower. Back at the cabin Stephanie said she had some thinking to do. The rest of the evening she kept to herself."

"Now that you mention it, Johnny didn't say much once everyone left. Lately, he hasn't been able to keep his mouth shut about how wonderful Stephanie is. I guess I figured he was tired. It's been a busy week so far. We're all tired. I'm amazed that you and I got up so early this morning."

Holly glances northward down the beach. "We're not the only ones up at sunrise."

I see three people huddled together on the shore about two hundred yards away. "I can't make out who they are, but it looks like a man and two women."

"Let's go see."

We clasp hands and walk toward them. As we near I can identify them. My ears can't compete with Holly's, but my vision is pretty sharp. "That's Mee Mee, Mary, and Russell Goodwin. They're looking at something Mee Mee is holding in her hand."

"Come on." Holly tugs my arm and starts jogging. "I want to see what they found."

We run along the firm sand, occasionally splashing through seawater that rushes up the slope and then drifts back. As we near them we slow to a stop. They are focusing on Mee Mee's cell phone.

"Good morning," Holly says.

They glance up, concern etching their faces.

"G'morning," Mee Mee says.

"What's going on?" I ask.

Mee Mee turns her phone in our direction. "North Korea just captured one of our ships in international waters."

"Oh no" Holly says.

"What kind of ship?" I ask, wondering how they could capture a huge ship.

Goodwin says, "It was the U.S.S. Shawnee, a Banner-class research ship. I'm guessing it was on a spy mission."

"But it was in international waters," Holly says.

"That's right," Goodwin says. "They were several miles from North Korea's maritime border. Kim Jung Ill claims they had crossed over earlier in the day, which gave him justification for capturing the ship. The U.S. denies his claim."

That sounds odd to me. "But why didn't they just take off and get away?"

Mee Mee glances at her phone. "According to the report, a heavily-armed North Korean subchaser arrived. The Shawnee stood her ground and claimed they had every right to sail in international waters. Before they knew it, four small torpedo boats showed up and began circling the ship. When the captain of the Shawnee refused to follow the subchaser into port, several salvos were fired, and a couple of crew members were injured. That's when the captain of the Shawnee relented."

"I feel terrible for the crew members," Goodwin says. "There's no doubt the North Koreans will find evidence that they were on an espionage mission. The ship will be loaded with high tech recording devices and other top secret information. In all probability, Kim Jung Ill will have the crew members tortured to get confessions."

Mee Mee shakes her head as she focuses on her phone. "President Stamp is considering retaliatory military actions. He may even declare war." She glances up at us. "This doesn't look good at all."

Goodwin shakes his head. "I'm afraid this will be a battle of egos. Who's the toughest kid on the playground? Who has the biggest bomb? If it comes down to trading blows, I don't think it will be a conventional war."

Holly's eyes widen. "What do you mean? Do you think this will turn into a nuclear war?"

Goodwin nods. "It's very possible. What's worse, it may turn global. Who knows what Russia and China will do? They may just side with North Korea. If that happens, this world may not survive the destruction that would be unleashed."

My throat feels dry, and I try to swallow. "B-but that would be crazy. No one wins in that kind of war."

"You're right," Goodwin says, "but these world leaders aren't known for their diplomacy or wisdom. Pride and power can blind them to the ultimate consequences of their actions."

Mary takes a quivering breath. "Reverend Swagger must be reveling in this latest news. His plans seem to be falling into place. He and his followers will head to their underground shelter and wait for the bombs to drop."

Holly reaches and touches Mary's shoulder. "Do you regret leaving the church?"

Mary shrugs. "Not really. I don't trust Swagger. He's as crazy as Stamp and Kim Jung Ill. But facing the possibility of nuclear war is scary."

Goodwin shakes his head. "You've got good instincts as far as Swagger is concerned. He has a shady background. He was arrested for internet fraud about five years ago and served some time in a minimum security facility. Before that he was accused of embezzlement where he served as a county commissioner in western North Carolina, but they couldn't make that charge stick. He's a slippery snake. The two goons with him served time for extortion. One of them, Harry Clint, was suspected of murder for hire but beat that charge for lack of evidence."

Mary nods. "I figured as much. Of course, they all claim to be born again. Swagger says all the right words to draw you into his web. He knows the Bible backwards and forwards. Most of us followers were lost souls looking for love and acceptance. When I first joined the church, it felt like a big family, I guess I needed to fit in somewhere. They welcomed me with open arms."

Goodwin says, "Did they try to force you to do things you didn't want to do?"

"Do you mean sexually?" Mary asks.

Goodwin nods.

"Not really. According to his teachings, women were to be submissive to men, but no one made any moves on me. I'm sure some hanky-panky went on among some of the members, but he frowned upon that sort of thing. With Swagger, it's all about recognizing his authority. "

"What about Clint and Tanner?" Goodwin asks. "Did they push people around?"

"They were the enforcers. If you got out of line, they definitely let you know it. They could be intimidating. Don't get me wrong. I never saw anyone physically abused. It was more verbal and psychological. If you were a part of the family, you needed to abide by the rules and yield to what Swagger called 'Biblical authority.' Whenever I disagreed with one of Swagger's decisions, I was accused of being rebellious and grieving the Spirit. Members were conditioned to go along by being shamed and embarrassed. During the last few days I've realized what was going on. Swagger claims God's authority in order to control what you think and do."

Goodwin nods. "It's typical cult M.O. There's always an opposition to critical thinking, isolation of members, obsession with particular doctrines, unquestioned loyalty to the leader, and separation from family or the traditional church. You were wise to leave."

"Yeah . . . but . . . but . . . now I feel alone. At least as a member I belonged somewhere. Now I am on my own again."

Mee Mee steps toward Mary and clutches her arm. "You are not alone. You've made some new friends."

"You've been good to me, but soon we'll go our separate ways. I'll head back to my apartment in Raleigh and the drudgery of cleaning houses." She holds out her hands, palms up. "Look how cracked, dry, and calloused these hands are. That's what my life feels like back in Raleigh—dry, cracked, and calloused." She shakes her head.

"Listen," Mee Mee says. "I'm looking for a new employee to help run my bookstore in Buxton. Would you consider moving to the Outer Banks? You could stay with me until you got on your feet."

Mary's head lifted and her eyes widened. "Are you serious?"

"You bet I'm serious. Buxton would be the perfect place for you. It's a great community with compassionate people. There's a lot of activity. If you're interested in joining a local congregation, there are several good churches you could visit. Besides that, the ocean is less than a quarter mile away from where I live. There's nothing like a morning walk along the beach to get you into a positive mental state."

Mary smiles and glances out to sea. "I can't argue that point." She turns and hugs Mee Mee. "I'll seriously consider your offer." She releases her, steps back, and takes a deep breath. "I thank God that I met all of you. I feel like I've been given a new start."

"I know what you mean." Holly reaches and grasps Mary's hand. "New friends and new starts can make a big difference in life."

I pat Mary on the shoulder. "Let's just hope that Reverend Swagger isn't a true prophet. These world leaders need to put aside their egos and work out their disagreements."

Mary smiles. "Amen to that."

"We better head to the cabin," Goodwin glances at his watch. "Marla promised us a big breakfast at 6 a.m. That gives us about fifteen minutes to get back."

Mee Mee smiles. "You kids keep your chins up. Don't get too upset about this incident. It might blow over in day or two."

"Let's hope so," Holly says. "We'll talk to you later."

Mee Mee waves and then turns to join Goodwin and Mary as they head in the direction of the cabins.

Holly takes my hand, and we walk a few hundred yards farther along the beach in silence. The waves and cries of seagulls offer a soothing background to help assimilate this latest news. We stop and face each other, and she grasps my other hand.

"Joel, are you afraid to die?"

"I guess so. I know I don't want to die."

"Me either."

"I feel like I haven't lived life yet."

"Exactly." She steps closer. "We're just getting started. I want to know what it means to love someone for years and years, to go to work every day at a job I enjoy, and hopefully, have a family."

I release her hands and place my hands on her shoulders. "I want the same things."

She slides her hands around my waist and clasps them behind me. I pull her closer, and she nestles her head just under my chin. She takes a deep breath, her body pressed against mine.

"I guess all we can count on is the now," she says.

"Right now the now is pretty good."

She lifts her head and gazes at me, those China blue eyes glistening. "Kiss me."

The wind presses wisps of blonde hair across her cheek. Can she feel my heart pounding? I turn my head slightly and press my lips to hers. The connection is warm and wet and wonderful.

She suddenly pulls away. "Did you hear that?"

Are you kidding? I was lost in ecstasy. "Not really, just the waves. Did you hear something?"

She nods and points beyond my shoulder. "Over the dunes in that direction."

"What was it?"

"It sounded like metal clanking against something. Let's check it out."

She takes my hand and leads me across the warm stretch of sand to the dunes. We struggle up the slope, the sand spilling away as our feet slide and shift.

"Over that way." Holly points to the right where another dune rises up, tufts of sea grass wavering across its crown.

We shuffle down the shifting surface and plod to the top of the next one.

"There!" Holly motions toward a stand of live oaks about a hundred yards away.

I can see two people, a tall thin girl and an old man digging with shovels.

Chapter 14

Elsa and her grandfather stand next to a large hole, shading their eyes from the rising sun and peering up at us. An old Ford 4 x 4 pickup truck is parked nearby under the gnarled boughs of a live oak. In the shadow of the hole I can make out the corner of some kind of box. We scurry down the side of the dune. Jonah is breathing hard, sweat pouring from the old man's forehead.

"Do you need some help?" I ask.

Jonah smiles and wipes his face with a soiled handkerchief. "We found it! *The Lost Treasure of El Salvador*. I knew it was buried somewhere on this island."

I more closely inspect the hole and can see they've uncovered half of a chest, about two feet wide and three feet long.

"How did you know to dig here?" Holly says.

Jonah points to Elsa. "She knew."

Elsa waves her hands and twirls, a three-hundred-and-sixty-degree pirouette. "This is the exact place I saw in my vision. We got up early this morning and drove on the backside of the dunes until I saw a white egret. It flew over our heads and landed by that that old tree." She points toward the live oak by the truck. "I knew this was the place."

"That's incredible," Holly says.

Elsa motions toward Jonah. "Grandfather is exhausted. The humidity is smothering us. Will you help us dig?"

"Sure. We'll help." I step toward Jonah and reach to take his shovel. "We can take turns."

He pulls the shovel away. "I don't mind the help, but just remember, we're the ones who found the treasure."

I raise my hands. "Of course. We're just here to give you a hand, right Holly?"

"Yes. That's what friends are for, Mr. Newland. We don't want any of your treasure."

"Well," Jonah leans the shovel toward me, "I just wanted to make things clear."

Holly reaches for Elsa's shovel. "You take a break. We'll get this chest uncovered in no time. "

Holly and I go at it, working around the edges of the chest, deepening the hole. Sweat runs into my eyes. I blink and wipe it away with my forearm. I glance up at Holly and notice the definition of her arm muscles as she digs. Crimenetly! She's a strong girl. After about ten minutes we have cleared away the sand from the bottom edge of the container. It's made of old cedar wood but has tarnished copper bracing riveted around all the edges and corners with large metal hinges. An old tarnished lock fastens the copper hasp.

"That should be good enough," Jonah says. "Let's each get on a side and see if we can pull it out of the hole."

We lay down the shovels and position ourselves on our knees around the chest, Jonah and I on the ends and the two girls on the front and back. There are handles on each end. Jonah and I reach and grab the handles, and the girls get a grip on the lid.

Jonah raises his head. "Ready?"

We nod.

"One, two, three, lift!"

The box is heavy but we manage to extract it from the hole and shove it onto the level sand in front of Jonah.

Jonah staggers to his feet and rubs his hands together, eyes wide. "Let's see what we got!"

We get to our feet and brush the sand off our knees.

Jonah picks up a shovel. "Shouldn't be too hard to bust that old lock." He raises the handle and clangs the shovel blade against the lock. No luck. He grits his teeth, face muscles scoring deep wrinkles across his cheeks, raises the shovel again, and jams the blade against the lock. This time it breaks.

"Ha! I did it!" Jonah takes a deep breath and blows it out slowly. He snaps his fingers and smiles at each of us. "It's time for the grand opening." With his fingertips he grips the bottom edge of the lid and lifts.

I blink and refocus on the contents. I can't believe it— the chest is filled with golden coins glowing in the sunshine. They look similar to the coin Elsa gave me except less worn.

"Hallelujah!" Jonah jumps into the air with fists raised. He steps sideways and then backwards as if dancing to fiddle music. "Yiiiiipeeee!" He circles around us and the treasure chest, continuing his awkward dance, skipping, jumping and shaking his body to music only he can hear.

I step backwards out of his way. With his long beard and white hair, he reminds me of a half-crazy prospector in one of those black and white westerns.

Elsa reaches and grasps his arm. "Grandfather, stop! You're acting like a drunk."

Jonah steadies himself. "I am drunk! Drunk with happiness! We're rich, Elsa! We're rich!"

"No." Elsa shakes her head. "It's not happiness. It's greed."

"Don't be foolish, girl." Jonah spreads his hands above the coins. "Can't you see what we've found? Our future is secure. I can buy a new truck. Hell, I can buy a new house. This will pay for your college tuition. Shoot! You don't even have to go to college. We'll be independently wealthy."

"This isn't what I've come to find. There's another chest here somewhere with something very important in it."

"You're right!" Jonah says. "According to the legend there're three more chests of gold. Let's keep digging."

Elsa puts her hands on her hips. "I'm not talking about gold."

"Get that shovel, Joel," the old man says. "We've got work to do."

As I glance around for the shovel, I catch sight of a face just above the dune. The person immediately ducks out of sight. Was I seeing things? I squint to clear my vision and wait to see if someone reappears.—nothing but sea grass on top of the mound.

"Did you see something, boy?" Jonah asks.

"I . . . I thought I saw somebody watching us."

Jonah stares at the dune. "Are you sure?"

I shake my head. "Maybe it was my imagination."

Jonah funnels his beard through his hand, staring at the gold. "Joel, help me get this chest onto the back of my truck. Let's see if we can find the other three chests before someone else shows up."

We each grab a handle and lift. The thing must weigh nearly a hundred pounds. Holly rushes to brace the bottom as we edge toward the truck. That helps. Fortunately, the tailgate is already down, and we heave the chest onto the truck bed.

Jonah struggles to catch his breath as he turns and faces the hole. "Listen. They probably laid the four chests out in a nice square pattern maybe six or eight feet apart parallel to the sea." He strides to the hole, pivots to get the correct angle, and takes three steps. "Here. This would be my best guess. Give me that shovel, Elsa."

Elsa grimaces but picks up the shovel and hands it to her grandfather.

I pick up the other shovel and begin digging. The mix of sand and dirt isn't hard to remove, but the heat definitely amps up the stress of the task. I take a break to wipe the sweat from my brow.

Jonah hands Holly the shovel and retreats to the shade of the tree. "You young people dig for a while. Don't worry. I'll pay you well."

Holly drives the shovel into the sand. "You don't have to pay us, Mr. Newland. Like I said, we're here to help."

Elsa walks over to the truck. "Are you okay, Grandfather?"

"I'm fine. Get me some water out of the cooler."

She opens the passenger door and reaches inside. When she turns toward us, I notice she has a jug of water in one hand and large seashell in the other—the lightning whelk I traded her for the coin.

"Here." She hands her grandfather the jug of water.

Jonah points at the shell. "What are you going to do with that?"

"That's my business."

The man shakes his head, pops the cap off the jug, takes a long drink, then recaps the jug. "You kids want some water."

"I'm fine." I'd rather not drink from that same jug. We dig for about five more minutes, and my shovel clanks into a hard object. "I hit something."

Jonah bolts from under the tree like a hyperactive kid. "Keep going! Keep digging!"

It's definitely another chest. Holly and I work around the edges, clearing the sand from the top of the box. Within minutes we have the chest halfway uncovered.

Jonah's hands shake as they hover over the top of the lid. "It's just like the other one. Holy macaroni. We've hit the mother lode." He straightens and raises his hands to the sky. "I can see my new oceanfront beach house now with a big new Ford F150 in the driveway. Hallelujah!"

I meet Holly's gaze, and she shakes her head. I glance to my right and see Elsa holding the seashell in front of her, eyes closed as if she's trying to channel some kind of spirit. She turns slowly, takes several steps and places the shell on the ground. That was strange.

"Here, give me that shovel. Elsa! Give Holly a break!" Jonah commands.

I hand him the shovel and swipe the sweat off my brow.

Elsa marches over and takes the shovel from Holly. "Grandfather, you're ordering people around like you're the big boss. I want to look for the other chest, the smaller one."

Jonah stamps his foot and frowns. "Be patient, young lady. There'll be time to look for the others. A chest uncovered is worth two buried, and this one's right in front of our eyes. Let's get the dirt cleared away and the chest on the truck before we dig more holes—one step at a time, one chest at a time."

Elsa fights back tears and jams the shovel into the sand. She lifts out a heap of dirt, throws it to the side, and with fury in her eyes, repeats the motion.

"That's the way to do it, young lady." Her grandfather bangs the end of his shovel on the ground. "We'll have this thing out of that pit in no time if you dig like that."

A shadow of a person stretches across the ground in front of Jonah, then two more. I glance up to see three tall figures standing on top of the dune and several more rising up behind them. Elsa and Jonah stop their digging, straighten, and peer up at them.

"I can see the young girl is truly a prophet," Reverend Noah Swagger says. "You've found the treasure that she saw in her vision."

Jonah shades his eyes with his hand. "That's right. We found it. What of it?"

"We've come to help you dig just like I promised last night. If you don't have extra shovels, we'll use our hands."

"We don't need your help," Jonah growls.

"Don't be foolish, old man. God has sent us here to help you." Swagger sidesteps down the slope and his disciples follow.

I take a quick count—twelve including Swagger.

Disciple Clint and Disciple Tanner step toward Jonah and Elsa. "We'll handle this," Clint says. "Give us the shovels."

Jonah raises his shovel. "Stay back. We don't need your help. Get the hell outta here before I crown you with this damn thing."

Clint whirls, grabs the handle, and jerks the shovel out of Jonah's hands.

"Take it easy, old man," Swagger says. "I told you, we're here to help you."

"Give me the shovel, kid," Tanner says.

Elsa tosses it to the ground, and Tanner picks it up.

Swagger edges to the hole. "Okay, boys, start digging."

Clint and Tanner begin clearing out the sand around the second chest.

I glance at Elsa. She backs away and stands in front of the seashell.

Swagger looks up at the other disciples and points just beyond the two holes. "Begin digging in this general area. We're out of shovels. You'll have to use your hands. The girl said there are four, maybe five chests."

The other disciples circle around us, fall to their knees, and claw at the sand. They remind me of zombies, mindlessly swiping the dirt away as if driven by some involuntary urge.

Clint and Tanner make fast work of clearing the sand around the second chest. They drop to their knees, grab the handles, and lift the chest out of the hole.

Swagger picks up a shovel. "Stand back." He thrusts the blade at the lock and breaks it with a loud clank.

Disciple Clint opens the lid, and the gold coins sparkle in the sun.

Swagger puts down the shovel and spreads his hands. "All praise to God Almighty!"

"We've found another chest!" a disciple calls out. He's a middle-aged man with a receding hairline. His face is sweaty and hands filthy. "Here's the top corner."

"Excellent!" Swagger motions toward his grubbing disciples. "Disciple Clint and Disciple Tanner, use the shovels to dig up the chest they just found. Everyone else, move over and keep digging. The Lord has answered our prayers. God has poured out his blessings upon us."

Jonah steps in front of Swagger. "Are you crazy? We found this gold, not you."

Swagger places his hands on his hips. "I want everyone to listen carefully to me. God sent my church to this island to prepare for the end. Today we received news that North Korea has captured one of our ships in international waters. They've taken the crew hostage. Our president will declare war soon. I have no doubt that nuclear war will follow after this declaration. But through us God is going to build the New Kingdom. There is a reason God sent us here." He spreads his hands above the golden coins. "Now I know. The Lord has appointed us to find these chests of gold and use this mammon for the advancement of Gods Kingdom on earth." He lifts his hand toward Elsa. "This young girl was the prophet who opened all of our eyes to this discovery. I praise God that she has led us to this place."

Jonah's face turns blood red. "You are full of unholy bullshit! I found this gold. It's mine."

Swagger waves his hand in front of Jonah's face. "You've been blinded by greed. Your eyes cannot see what I see."

"I see a thief and a conman," Jonah says.

Clint drops his shovel, wheels, and smacks Jonah in the mouth with an open hand. The old man falls backward into the sand, blood spurting from his lower lip.

Swagger raises his hand. "Please, Disciple Clint! You're too impulsive, just like the Apostle Peter. There's no need for violence!"

Elsa drops to her grandfather's side. "Give me your handkerchief."

He withdraws the cloth from his shirt pocket, and she takes it and presses it to his lip.

Swagger leans on his knees and stares at Jonah. "The New Kingdom is a kingdom of peace. You must understand, old man, that we will obey what God says and not what you say."

"Here's the fourth chest!" shouts the middle-aged guy with the receding hairline.

The disciples claw at the ground, uncovering the cedar box one handful of dirt at a time. Clint and Tanner finish digging around the third chest, lift it out of the hole, and set it next to the second chest. With all the cult members clawing away, it doesn't take them long to uncover the fourth chest.

"Hallelujah!" Swagger shouts. He can't keep his hands from trembling. "God's abundance flows forth upon us. Church members, please help me carry these chests back to our cabin. The Lord has provided this earthly mammon for spiritual purposes. We'll be able to pay off the underground shelter and buy the supplies we need to survive the coming Apocalypse. But then we will rise from the depths of the earth to live again. We are the chosen ones of God. Like the children of Israel who rebuilt Jerusalem, we will build the New Kingdom."

A gravely voice shouts from above, "I wouldn't count on that!" Two figures stand at the top of the dune, the sun burning through their silhouettes. One of them raises a machete and says, "You may not survive beyond the next five minutes."

Chapter 15

Quentin Porter and Jack Graham scurry down the dune. Porter has no trouble maintaining his balance as his prosthetic blade slices through the sand. Porter's cut-off denim shirt reveals ripped shoulder and arm muscles, his right hand firmly gripping the handle of the long machete. Wearing a black bandana cap and eye patch, Graham looks like he just stepped off the Queen Anne's Revenge.

Porter points his machete at Swagger. "Back away from the chests. They don't belong to you."

Swagger shakes his head. "Don't listen to him." He faces Porter. "The chests belong to us. We dug them up."

"They're lying," Jonah struggles to his feet. "They showed up after we found the treasure and tried to take over. "

I can't keep my mouth shut. "That's true. Holly and I got here before Reverend Swagger and his disciples. Jonah and Elsa had already found the gold."

Swagger puts his hands on his hips. "Show me your ownership papers."

"What are you talking about?" Jonah says.

"You don't have any ownership papers? Could it be because these chests have been buried here for hundreds of years?" He digs his hand into the mass of coins and pulls out one coin. "Tell me, whose image is on this coin."

"The King of Spain," Jonah says.

"Right. Then we should we send this gold back to the King of Spain."

"He's long dead."

"Right again. Therefore, whoever claims ownership becomes the possessor. We dug up the chests. We claim ownership."

"Your claim won't stand up in court," Jack Graham says. "We saw your spy skulk on back to your cabin. I was metal detecting up on the dunes, and Quentin was fishing along the shore. We figured something was up. Then you and your gang came marching up the beach. After you passed by, Quentin and I decided to mosey on over to the other side of the dunes and listen. We heard everything. "

Swagger's bushy eyebrows lower, hooding his dark eyes. "I'm telling you we claim ownership over these chests and their contents. A judge or jury won't dispute my claim. We dug it up, and we're taking it."

"I'm telling *you*," Graham says, "that the law will be on the side of Mr. Newland and his granddaughter. Believe it or not, in the real world I'm a lawyer. I am well versed in right of ownership when it comes to found treasure. I treasure hunt in my spare time. It's clear that your gang moved in and appropriated what did not belong to them. I will represent Jonah in court pro bono. I guarantee you with the evidence and witnesses aligned against you, you have no chance."

Swagger laughs. "Funny thing about lawyers, they only lie . . . when their lips move. Ownership is a matter of possession, and we have taken possession." He motions toward Clint and Tanner. "Pick up that chest."

The two disciples step forward, close the lid, grasp the handles, and lift the chest.

Porter extends his prosthetic blade toward the two men and whips his machete through the air like a sword.

They flinch, jerking backwards, but manage to maintain their balance while steadying the swaying burden.

Porter raises the machete above his right shoulder. "Drop the chest!"

"Make me," Disciple Clint says.

"On the count of three I'm going to swing this machete at your wrist. If you don't drop the chest, you will lose your hand. One . . . Two . . . Three." Porter slashes the machete, but Disciple Clint releases the handle and whips his hand away just in time. Clint's side of the chest clunks to the ground, but Disciple Tanner manages to hold on to his side.

"S-s-sonovabitch!" Clint stammers. "You almost cut my hand off!"

"You're sharper than a Ginsu knife." Porter turns to Tanner and raises his machete. "One . . . Two . . ."

Tanner lets go, and his end thuds to the ground.

With the machete still raised, Porter points in the direction of the cabins. "Now get the hell out of here."

Swagger says, "You're going to take on all of us?"

"In the last ten years I've whacked hundreds of sharks. I'm ready to whack a few more. If you want to tangle, let's go at it."

Swagger glances around his group of disciples and shakes his head. "We seek a kingdom of peace, not violence."

"Bullshit," Jonah thrusts his chin forward and protrudes his bottom bloody lip.

Swagger turns and faces his disciples. "Let's head back to the cabin. We're done here for now."

The disciples slowly get to their feet, faces sweaty and smeared with dirt, hands filthy. With heads lowered, they trudge toward the dune and follow Swagger up the slope. When they get to the top, Swagger turns and raises his hands. "Revenge is mine sayeth the Lord. Mark my words. The wrath of God is going to come down upon you."

Chapter 16

Jonah Newland shakes his head. "Can you believe that guy and his crew of bozos? He thought he could march in here and steal my gold." He faces Porter and Graham. "And he would have if it weren't for you two. I owe you big time, boys. I promise you, I don't forget my friends. I plan on giving both of you a generous reward once I get this treasure home and secured."

Quentin Porter slides his machete back into his belt. "I didn't defend you because I wanted money. I just can't stomach greedy preachers."

Graham adjusts his eye patch. "I don't want any kind of reward either, matey. I'll find me own treasure. Besides, I enjoy the pursuit more than the catch." He pats Jonah on the shoulder. "Seriously, though, I stood up for you because it was the right thing to do. I meant it when I said I'd represent you in court free of charge."

Elsa steps up to Porter and hugs him. He blinks, raises his eyebrows, and pats her on the back. She turns to Graham, gives him a quick hug and a kiss on the cheek. "God sent us a couple of guardian angels."

When she steps back, Graham raises his finger. "A kiss from a beautiful young maiden is reward enough for me."

Everyone laughs.

Porter motions toward the chests at their feet. "I wouldn't store the treasure in your tent. That preacher and his apostles have made an underground deal with the devil. They'll come for it again."

Jonah shrugs. "We plan on heading home tomorrow morning. Where should I hide it till then?"

An idea pops into my mind. "How about keeping the chests at Sheriff Walton's cabin? He knows all about Swagger and his ex-cons. I'm guessing the sheriff and his friend, Mr. Goodwin, have firearms. Certainly, Swagger wouldn't take the chance of breaking into a lawman's cabin."

"Good idea," Graham says.

Jonah slaps me on the back. "That sounds like a fine plan."

Porter says, "We'll help you load it onto your truck. We'll even ride on the back to make sure you get to the sheriff's cabin without being molested again by that crazy cult."

Holly, Elsa, and I clear the sand from around the bottom of the fourth chest. Porter and Graham heave the other two onto the back of the truck next to the first one. With help from Jonah, we lift the fourth chest out of the hole and slide it onto level ground.

Jonah taps the top of the cedar box. His bottom lip is swollen and bright red in the middle where Disciple Clint's slap split it. "This is my lucky day." He smiles but winces with pain, gently touching his lip. "Those sons of bitches." He shakes his head and peers up at Porter and Graham. "Elsa's right. You two were heaven sent. I'll do you both right."

"Don't worry about us," Porter says. "You've got enough to worry about."

"That's right." Graham eyes the chest and then glances at the back of the truck. "You may have ten million dollars in gold coins here. Your worries have just begun. You need to figure out how you're going to get it safely back home. It might be wise to get professional help."

The old man rakes his beard. "What are you talking about?"

"You might want to contact Brink's Armored Transportation and have them move the treasure to a secure location."

"Well . . ." Jonah nods. "That's something to consider. For now, though, lets haul it on over to Sheriff Walton's cabin. Maybe he has some ideas on the best way to handle it."

"Sure," Graham says. "Let's climb aboard ye old Ford and set sail."

Porter and Graham load the fourth chest onto the truck and then clamber onto the bed. They each take a seat on one of the chests. Jonah yanks open the driver's side door and climbs into the cab. As if in a trance, Elsa drifts over between the holes and piles of sand and stares at the lightning whelk shell sitting on the ground about ten yards away.

Jonah juts his head out the window. "Elsa! Get in the truck. We've got to go."

"But Grandfather, I want to look for . . ."

"Not now. We need to go talk to Sheriff Walton and secure this gold. There's no time for that now."

Elsa glances at Joel and then back at the seashell.

"Elsa, c'mon! I'm not leaving you here after what just happened. We'll come back later."

Elsa blinks, fighting back tears. She turns, walks to the pickup, climbs into the front seat, and slams the door. They drive away, cutting between two dunes in the direction of the beach.

Holly's eyes grow wide. "She wanted to stay and look for the smaller chest, the one she said could save the world."

"I know. She thinks it's buried somewhere close by." I walk over to the seashell. "I wonder if . . ."

"If what?"

"This is the shell I traded for the gold coin. I wonder if she placed it here for a reason."

Holly hurries over and kneels by the shell. "It's beautiful."

"I know. It's perfect. Not a chip or imperfection on it."

Holly gently touches the shell. "She held this as if it were sacred."

"Right. Like some kind of spiritual communication device."

"Do you think the smaller chest could be buried right here?"

I shrug. "Why not? She knew where to find the four bigger chests. It wouldn't hurt to dig down a few feet and find out."

Holly springs to her feet and scans the ground beyond the holes. "Look! They left a shovel behind."

I spot the wooden handle almost hidden in a patch of sea grass. "I'll do the digging. You keep your eye out for Swagger's spies."

"Okay." Holly pans the tops of the dunes.

I start by edging a four feet circle around the shell. "Go ahead and pick the shell up."

Holly picks it up and holds the cavity to her ear. "Wow. I can hear the ocean loud and clear."

"Yeah. Elsa claimed she could take the ocean with her with that shell."

After about fifteen minutes, I have dug down about three feet, slightly deeper than the depths of the other chests. "I don't think it's here."

Holly closes her eyes. Her hands, clasping the shell, tremble slightly. "Keep digging. It's gotta be there."

I take a deep breath and jam the shovel into the dirt. Clank. "Bingo! I hit something." I scrape the shovel several times horizontally and uncover copper metal bracing on the corner of a wooden box. "We've found it!"

Holly inspects the tops of the dunes. "Hurry. We need to get it up and out of here."

I dig furiously around the edges. My arms are tired, but adrenalin has recharged me. The chest is definitely smaller than the other ones but has the same style of metal bracing and rivets. Within five minutes I have the thing unearthed and ready to lift out.

Holly falls to her knees and gently places the whelk shell off to the side. "There's a handle on this end."

"There's one on my end too." I swipe the sweat from my forehead and lower myself to the ground. "Hopefully, it won't be too heavy."

We each grab a handle and lift. It feels like a feather compared to the other chests, maybe twenty-five pounds. We set it next to the seashell. The box is about eighteen inches long and twelve inches wide. It has a tarnished padlock similar to the other chests.

"That was easy enough," Holly says. "What're we gonna do with it now?"

I check the surroundings to make sure no one is watching. The coast is clear. "Let's haul it back to my cabin. Then I guess we'll open it and see what's inside."

"Shouldn't we talk to Elsa before we open it?"

I shrug. "I don't know. Maybe." Don't I get any credit for digging this thing up? I found it. Isn't possession nine-tenths of the law? Why should Elsa have any say? I glance at Holly and notice that look of disappointment on her face, those China blue eyes narrowing. Can she read my mind?

"Joel, Elsa is the one who knew this chest was here."

I stare at the lock. I'm not Elsa's errand boy. She didn't give me the order to dig this thing up. I made that decision myself. I have a right to find out what's inside. I take a deep breath and blow it out. Whatever is in there could secure my future. I need some time to clear my mind.

"We better head back," Holly says.

"I agree with you there. Pick up Elsa's seashell and the shovel. I'll carry the chest. We need to keep on this side of the dunes. Walking back along the beach is too risky."

On the way back to the cabin we don't say much. Holly keeps scanning the top of the dunes to make sure Swagger's lurkers aren't keeping tabs on us. I can't help wondering if I just dug up the key to my financial independence.

Ours is the first in a line of ten cabins heading southward. That's a good thing. We don't have to pass the other nine to get to the door. We hurry across the top of a dune and race walk to the steps and onto the porch. Holly opens the screen, and I rush in and plunk the chest onto the kitchen table. We stand in silence, just listening.

"Where are Don and Johnny?" Holly asks.

"I don't know." A piece of paper to the left of the chest catches my eye. "Wait. Here's a note." I pick it up. "*We went to explore the north side of the island with the girls. Be back in a couple of hours.*" I glance up. "I guess they took the ATVs out again."

"Good. It's better that you and I are the only ones that know about this fifth chest for now. Less chance of word spreading."

I reach for the padlock and shake it.

"Don't get any ideas, Joel."

"But what if there're more gold coins inside? I found it. We're talking hundreds of thousands of dollars here. Maybe a million."

She points to me and then back to her, swishing her finger back and forth. "Didn't we find it? Didn't I tell you to dig where Elsa placed the shell?"

Ah c'mon. I don't remember her saying those exact words. I close my eyes. Okay. Maybe she's right. We both found it. "Listen, there may be enough wealth here to provide a good life for both of us. We'll split it evenly."

"What about Elsa?"

"What about her?"

Holly touches the tip of her forefinger to the other. "First, she knew where to find the treasure." She raises a second finger and touches it. "Second, she had a vision of this smaller chest. Third, she claims it could save the world. Fourth, she placed the shell exactly where we found it. Fifth, the only reason she didn't dig it up is because her grandfather made her get in the truck . . ."

"Okay, okay, I get your point." Crimenetly. Am I losing my sense of integrity over what's inside this box? No. I'm just curious. I need to know in order to decide what to do. "What if it's worthless? Maybe it's just another Maltese Falcon."

"What's that?"

"Haven't you ever seen the movie?"

"No."

"It was a statue of bird that was supposed to be worth millions, but it was a fake—a lead figurine painted over with black enamel. Humphrey Bogart called it the stuff dreams are made of."

"Maybe it is worthless. That's more reason not to open the box. Why beg the question when Elsa's privilege to open it is at stake? We know it's not filled with gold coins. It would weigh twice as much."

"That's true." Her words hit me like a splash of cold seawater. I shake it off, pondering other possibilities. "Then again, maybe there's something inside worth more than gold coins. I'm sorry, but there's only one way to find out what we're dealing with here."

"Don't do it, Joel."

I pick the chest up and place it on the floor. "Hand me the shovel."

Holly shakes her head.

I reach for the shovel. "If there's something inside that could save the world, we'll give it to Elsa."

"Elsa should be the one to decide when to open the chest."

I pull the shovel out of her hand. "This was a team effort. I have the right to open it."

"Joel, don't. Please."

I focus on the lock and raise the shovel. Something doesn't feel right. I glance at Holly and notice her eyes are wide and watering. Is she going to cry? I try to shake off the feeling and grip the handle tighter. C'mon, man. Don't let a pretty girl control your every decision. Break the lock. I take a step back and focus again. The feeling comes back even stronger. Is it guilt or my own lack of backbone?

Pounding rattles the screen door. I lower the shovel, slide the chest under the kitchen table, and throw a beach towel on top of it.

Chapter 17

Holly strides to the door and pushes open the screen. It's Elsa.

She enters the cabin and faces me. Her large dark eyes are slightly red around the rims. "Grandfather is down a few cabins talking to Sheriff Walton."

I glance under the table at the beach towel covering the chest and then back up at Elsa. "What's the verdict? Will the sheriff guard the gold?"

"Yeah. Sheriff Walton isn't afraid of Swagger and his bullies. He wants Grandfather to press charges and have Disciple Clint arrested." She frowns. "I don't think he'll press charges, though. He just wants to get the treasure home and stashed away in some vault."

My throat feels like a tightening knot, so I cough to try to relieve it before speaking. "You should be set for life. All that gold must be worth millions of dollars."

"I don't care about that gold. There're more important things to consider." Elsa lifts the seashell from the table. "I see you found my shell."

Holly glares at me. "Yes, we did. It was on the ground, not far from all the digging."

"That's right," I say, ignoring Holly's dirty look. "I'm curious. Why'd you bring it with you on the treasure hunt?"

Elsa holds the shell with both hands in front of her as if she is presenting an offering. "Man didn't create this, God did. It's beautiful and perfect. I feel a strong connection to the Spirit when I hold it. When I was at the church yesterday, I held the shell in front of me and drifted into another world. That's when God gave me the vision of the white egret and the tree. "

"I see." I glance at the beach towel again and try to swallow away the weird feeling in my throat. "Is that why you left it at the site?"

Elsa nods. "I placed it exactly where I sensed the smaller chest would be buried. I wish you wouldn't have moved it."

I glance at Holly, and her eyes burn through me.

Elsa looks from Holly to me. "Joel, is there something you're not telling me?"

I bow my head, stare at the towel, and wring my hands. "Okay. I'm not sure about what to do here. Things are a little murky."

"You found the chest, didn't you?" Now Elsa's eyes are on fire.

I nod. "Yes. I found it." Bending over, I whip the towel away and pull the chest out from under the table.

Elsa falls to her knees and places the shell on top of the chest. "This is it."

I clear my throat again. "This is what? We have no idea what this is."

Elsa peers up at me. "I'm not sure what's inside, but I know the contents of this box have the power to bring peace to this world, maybe even prevent a nuclear war."

I cross my arms. "That's a tall order for an inanimate object. I'm not so sure. Besides, I'm the one who dug it up. I'm the one who found it."

"Wait a minute," Holly says. "We found it, not you. And the only reason we found it is because we knew where to dig."

I hold my hands up. "I'm just saying, things aren't black and white here. Let's open the box and then decide."

"No!" Elsa springs to her feet. "We can't open the box."

"Hear me out. If there's something inside the chest that can save the world, fine. It's all yours, but if it's jewels or silver chains or gold coins, then we should split the profits equally. What's inside this chest could make a big difference in our lives."

"Joel Thomas! You're starting to sound just like my grandfather. Your vision has become clouded by dollar signs."

I reach for the shovel. "That's easy for you to say. You're already a millionaire. Holly and I are college kids with huge school loans."

"Don't include me in your selfish rationale," Holly says. "I'm with Elsa. If God gave her a vision, I believe her. We shouldn't open the chest unless she's proven wrong. So far she's been on the money."

"On the money. Yeah, that's a good way to put it. I work in that damn cafeteria all semester just to make enough to pay for my books. All I'm asking is what's fair. Let's open it up and see what's inside. We won't know whether it can save the world or not unless we see what it is."

"No!" Elsa shouts and jerks the shovel out of my hand. "It's not meant to be opened here."

Crimenetly! I can't believe a junior high kid just overpowered me. "Fine. That's great. You and your grandfather can go off and buy a mansion by the sea. I'll go back to the school cafeteria and load the dishwasher so I can scrape by on a measly work study check."

Holly reaches and touches my shoulder. "Joel, don't be such a Silas Marner."

I raise my hands. "I'm just being practical."

"Listen," Elsa says, "I'll make a deal with you."

"A deal? Okay. Let me think . . . I'll give you this smaller chest for one of the bigger chests. If what's inside this can save the world, that's quite a deal."

She shakes her head. "Those belong to my grandfather." She raises the shell. "I'll give you this."

"Very funny."

"I'm serious. This shell means a lot to me. It will represent a covenant between you and me. I promise you that when the box is opened, whatever is inside is all yours if it doesn't have the power to save the world. At that time you can trade the shell back to me for the contents of the box."

I stare at the chest. That sounds fair enough. "A covenant, huh?"

Elsa nods.

"What about Holly?"

"I haven't made any demands," Holly says. "Besides, I don't believe we'll have to cross that bridge."

"I just have one question then. When will you open it?"

Elsa leans the shovel against the table. "As soon as I can get President Stamp and Kim Jung Ill together for a peace summit."

I try to muzzle a surge of laughter, but it bursts out. "How in the world will you do that?"

Elsa smiles. "With your help."

"Yeah, sure, I have a direct line to the Oval Office."

"Don't be so obtuse." Elsa slips her cell phone out of her pants pocket, taps the screen a couple of times, and raises the phone so I can see. "I made this video to prove ownership."

It's a video of her standing in front of the four chests. She lifts the lid on each one, giving the viewer a close-up of the golden coins and says, "This is the *Lost Treasure of El Salvador*. My grandfather and I found it on Portsmouth Island. I'm documenting the find because there is a religious group camping on the island that tried to steal it from us. Their leader, Reverend Noah Swagger, claims that God wants them to have the treasure. Two men, Quentin Porter and Jack Graham, came to our rescue and prevented them from taking the chests. Sheriff Dugan Walton is helping us by guarding the treasure. He will verify my story."

The camera is focused on Walton. He's wearing a black ball cap with a logo of the Cape Hatteras Lighthouse. "My name is Dugan Walton. I'm the Sheriff of Dare County, North Carolina. I confirm that what this young lady said is true. She and her grandfather, Jonah Newland, found the treasure. We are storing it in my cabin on Portsmouth Island until we can make arrangements to transport it safely to the mainland. The proper steps will then be taken to establish the rights and ownership claim of Jonah and Elsa Newland as the finders of the treasure."

Elsa lowers her phone. "This video proves that Grandfather and I found the treasure."

"Okay." I must admit her documentation of the treasure find was a good idea. "Now what? How in the world will you get President Stamp and Kim Jung Ill together for peace talks?"

"I intend to make another video that I hope will go viral."

I take a deep breath and blow it out. I'm beginning to see the direction she's heading. I dip my hand toward the smaller treasure box. "And that video will focus on the contents of this chest."

She nods. "That's right. It's well known that Kim Jung Ill's son is battling leukemia. Kim Jung Ill is also fascinated by ancient relics. The contents of this chest is rumored to have spiritual powers—powers to heal relationships and bodies."

Holly drops to her knees and touches the chest. "Wow. Do you think what's inside this box could heal his son?"

Elsa crouches and touches the chest. "Things don't heal. Faith heals. What's inside this box may inspire the faith needed to heal his son."

"I get it." I shrug. "Who knows? It might just work. If the video goes viral, certainly President Stamp and Kim Jung Ill will hear about it. When are you going to make the video?"

Elsa rises to her feet. "We could do it right now." She slips her cell phone out of her back pocket and extends it to me.

"You want me to make the video? I'm the one losing millions of dollars in this deal."

Holly rises. "I'll do it if he refuses."

"Thanks, but I'd like Joel to do it. He's the one who found the shell. We made a connection. I believe things happen for a reason. Joel, this is your opportunity to put greed aside for the sake of peace. It's up to you."

Now I feel guilty, Mr. Greedy Gut standing in the way of world peace. "Okay, okay. Give me the phone."

Elsa hands me the phone. "You won't regret this."

I take a couple steps back and focus on her. She stands behind the chest, the immaculate whelk shell still positioned on top of the center of the lid.

"Elsa!" Jonah Newland shouts from just outside the cabin.

Chapter 18

"Grandfather's here," Elsa whispers. "We'll have to make the video tomorrow morning when I come to pick up the chest."

"What do you mean when you come to pick up the chest?" I ask.

"I can't take it with me. Grandfather will insist on opening it. Can you hide it somewhere here in your cabin?"

My mind whirls with possible hiding place options. "Well . . . I guess I can hide it under my bunk. Just don't tell anyone it's here."

"I won't tell anyone. Make sure you two don't say a word to anyone."

"No one will say a word," Holly says.

"Elsa!" Jonah Newland shouts from just outside the cabin.

"I've gotta go." Elsa turns and hugs Holly with her free arm. Then she pivots, lifts the shell from the chest and faces me. "You are now officially a peacemaker." She hands me the shell.

"Wonderful. It doesn't pay much, but the benefits are good—the survival of humankind."

"Elsa! Come on! We've gotta get going!"

"Coming, Grandfather!" She heads out the screen door, and it bangs behind her.

I stare at the beautiful lightning whelk. "For some reason this shell keeps coming back to me."

Holly pats my shoulder. "God created that shell. Maybe it's a reminder of what's important in life."

"Right. A financially secure future is not important. This magic shell will rid me of my dreams of wealth and ease." I slide the shell onto the table, bend, and pick up the chest. "If I only knew what was in here."

Holly smiles and pats my back. "You'll find out sooner or later."

"I think I already know."

"Oh yeah. And what would that be?"

"The stuff that dreams are made of."

I lug the chest over to my bunk. It's just the right size to slide under the bed. I get on my knees, push it to the middle, and find some dirty clothes to place around it just in case someone would peek under there for some odd reason.

"Do you have anything good to drink in these coolers?" Holly asks.

"Should be some sweet tea in a gallon jug."

"That sounds heavenly. All that digging dehydrated me."

"I'll get some cups." I walk over to the cupboard above the counter, open it, and take down a package of foam cups. After withdrawing the top two from the stack, I walk to the kitchen table and fill them to the brim with the tea. "Should be nice and cold."

Holly takes a long drink. "Oh, that's so good."

I plop down on the chair next to her. "What a week, huh?"

She takes another swig and nods. "I'll never forget this vacation."

I can't help studying her face. What a beautiful girl. I'll definitely never forget this vacation.

Her phone dings. She stretches her leg to extract it from her pants pocket. She's wearing tight white shorts and a yellow WVU t-shirt. It takes her a few seconds to jiggle the phone from that constricted location. Crimenetly, she's got great legs.

"It's a text from my mom."

"She must be missing you."

"That's odd. Listen to this: 'Have you seen the latest news story? I'm really worried.' Wonder what that's about?"

"I'll check CNN." I pull my phone out and quickly tap in the website. I read the first headline: "U.S. captures North Korean ship." Wow. I quickly skim down through the article. "Looks like our navy has captured a North Korean ship in international waters and has taken the crew hostage."

Holly shakes her head. "That's a pretty bold move. President Stamp wants a bargaining chip to trade for the U.S. hostages."

"I don't think it'll be that easy. Listen to this: 'North Korean leader, Kim Jung Ill, calls the U.S. maneuver an act of war. He has announced that he will hold a press conference this afternoon. Many international political experts believe he will officially declare war on the United States at this time. Both countries are scrambling in preparation for possible airstrikes. Rumors are spreading from undisclosed sources at the Whitehouse that President Stamp is considering a preemptive nuclear strike."

"No wonder Mom's upset." Holly takes a deep breath and blows it out. "Two crazy world leaders with their fingers hovering over the red buttons on their desks."

"Right. The question is who will fire first? Elsa may not get the chance to initiate her peace plan."

Holly stands and sniffles. Her eyes are watering. A tear trickles down her cheek.

"Are you okay?"

She shakes her head and cries.

I stand and draw her into my arms. Her tears are warm and wet against my neck. As she tries to settle herself, her body convulses against mine. I gently rub up and down her back. Her sobs slow to a few involuntary spasms. Now we are breathing together, slowly and in rhythm. I've never felt this close to a girl before, even with the few with whom I've awkwardly made out. We slowly separate and look in each other's eyes. We kiss, a long, soft, warm, moist kiss. An incredible rapture possesses me. I can feel it from my core to the very surface of my skin. We separate again, and she steps away and takes my hand. She leads me to my bunk.

Through the open window I can hear gulls crying in the distance and the gentle rhythm of waves against the shore. It feels like a dream. She releases my hand, sits on the bed, and stretches out on the mattress. "Lie with me."

I climb on the bed beside her and caress her cheek. We kiss again, a long, deep, intimate kiss.

Our lips break apart, and she says, "Make love to me."

Now I know I'm dreaming. Should I pinch myself? I want to say something romantic, but my practical side interferes. Instead I say, "Are you sure we should do this?"

"This could be our last chance. Tomorrow may never come." She reaches for the bottom of my t-shirt, tugs it up my torso, and manages to liberate it from my shoulders and head. She tosses my shirt to the floor and places her hand on my chest.

I reach for the bottom of her t-shirt and begin to pull upwards. There's a commotion at the door. We both sit straight up and spring off the bed. Holly straightens her shirt, and I scour the floor to see where mine landed.

Lisa and Don charge into the kitchen. They look like they just escaped a horde of zombies.

Don takes a double look at me as if he's never seen me shirtless before.

"You're not going to believe this," Lisa spouts, "We've got bad news."

"We've heard." My face feels like it's on fire. "We're at war with North Korea."

"Yeah but that's not all," Don says.

Lisa says. "Stephanie and Johnny went to talk to Reverend Swagger."

"What?" Holly gasps.

"I'm not kidding. We rode back down to the village on the ATVs and stopped near the church. Both Johnny and Stephanie started talking about their conservative Christian upbringing. They said they've heard the same sermon that Swagger preached at the campfire a hundred times: The world is about to end and you need to get right with God, that sort of thing."

"Then Johnny checked his phone," Don says, "and saw that World War III was about to begin. They started wondering about all those things Swagger said about surviving a nuclear apocalypse and building a new kingdom for God."

Lisa says, "Then Stephanie kept saying how she had gone astray from her Christian roots—too much partying and sleeping around. She needed to get right with God."

"I'm all for that," Don says, "but Swagger creeps me out. I guess Johnny and Stephanie didn't get that same vibe, or maybe they did the wild thing and felt they needed to repent. Anyway, Johnny said God had sent Swagger to this island to give us all a wakeup call. Right then and there he decided to go talk to him."

"That's when Stephanie said she'd go with him," Lisa says. "Off they went on their ATV to go talk to Swagger."

"What're we gonna do?" Holly says. "This morning we saw Swagger's true colors. He tried to steal something that didn't belong to him—some chests that Elsa and her grandfather had dug up. One of his so-called disciples punched Jonah Newland right in the face. Can you believe that? He's just an old man. When they tried to take the chests, Mr. Porter and Mr. Graham showed up in the nick of time and stopped them."

I glance from face to face, sensing the same panic that I see in their eyes. Keep calm. Think clearly. "Johnny and Stephanie are in trouble. Swagger's not an evangelical pastor. He's a cult leader. We need to tell them what happened."

"Let's go," Holly says. "They'll come to their senses when they know the truth."

Holly marches out the door, and we follow.

It's less than a two hundred yard walk to the two church cabins. All ten cabins sit back about fifty yards from the shore. We decide to walk along the beach and then cut through the short sections of sand fencing between the shoreline and the cabins. I can see the tall, thin figure of Disciple Clint leaning against the porch post. His shorter and wider sidekick, Disciple Tanner, is standing next to him. They're both dressed in old jeans and western-style shirts. I feel like we're about to face a couple gunslingers.

Disciple Clint pushes off the post, stands straight, and puts his hands on his hips. "What do you want?"

"We need to talk to Johnny and Stephanie," Holly says.

Disciple Clint's eyes narrow. "They're meeting with Reverend Swagger. You can't talk to them now."

An odd surge of courage rushes through me. "You either allow us to talk to them, or we'll get Sheriff Walton to come down here and arrest you for kidnapping and attempted brainwashing."

Both of the disciples laugh.

"What the hell are you talking about?" Disciple Tanner says. "Those two kids came to us. We didn't go after them. They showed up and wanted to talk to Reverend Swagger. We haven't done anything wrong. Go ahead and get the sheriff. He don't scare us."

I glance at Don, and he shrugs. Lisa stands there with her fists clenched. Does she want to fight these guys?

"Please," Holly says, "we just need to see them for a couple of minutes."

Disciple Clint juts his chin. "Go to hell."

I take Holly's hand. "Come on. Let's go talk to Sheriff Walton."

We whirl and march along the edge of the sand fences. The Walton cabin isn't far away, maybe a couple hundred feet. We climb the few steps to the porch and I rap on the screen door.

Sheriff Walton's wife Marla pushes open the door. She's a striking woman with long, dark brown hair, but the muscles around her eyes tense up when she sees us. "Is everything okay? You kids look like you just saw the devil himself."

She got that right. "We need to talk to Sheriff Walton."

She extends the door wider. "Come on in."

As my eyes adjust to the dimmer light inside the cabin, I immediately notice the four chests lined up on the floor next to the closest bunk where Sheriff Walton is standing. Russell Goodwin, his hands clasped behind his head, sits at the kitchen table next to Mee Mee Roberts. The older boy, Gabriel, sits on the floor reading a book to his younger sister Azy.

Sheriff Walton approaches us. "What's up?"

"We just came from Swagger's cabin," Holly says. "Johnny and Stephanie are in there, and they won't let us talk to them."

Sheriff Walton's brow furrows. "They kidnapped them?"

"No," Lisa says. "They went there willingly. That's the problem." She explains the circumstances and stresses our concern about the possibility of Swagger using religion and fear to control their minds.

Russell Goodwin slides out his chair and stands. "That's possible, but there's a fine line between respecting someone's free choice and rescuing them from a foolish decision."

Mee Mee presses her hands to the table and rises. "But they don't know what happened at the digging site. How can they make good decisions without all the facts?"

Sheriff Walton scratches his head, his thick, red hair springing up between his fingers. "Well . . . We can't force them to come out and talk to us, but I know a way to apply some pressure to Swagger that may just work."

I feel like someone just lifted a heavy rock off my chest. "Thanks. We appreciate any help you can give us."

"Besides that," Sheriff Walton says, "I wanted to talk to Swagger anyway. He needs to know that I'm guarding the gold for Jonah Newland. I don't want him getting any ideas of raiding Jonah's campsite. We can't force your friends to come with us. That'll be up to them."

"We understand that," Holly says. "But there's a much better chance of at least talking to them with you there."

"I'm coming, too." Russell Goodwin glances at Sheriff Walton. "I'm taking Annie with me just in case there's a problem."

Who's Annie? I haven't met her yet.

"Good idea." Sheriff Walton strides to the cupboard, opens it, reaches to the top shelf, and pulls down a holster with a handgun. "Gladys is coming with me."

After the two men strap on their weapons, we head out the door toward the church cabins. As we shuffle through the sand, Holly reaches for my hand. Feeling it tremble, I squeeze it tightly. For a few seconds my mind flashes back to my bunk, lying beside her, kissing her. Does she love me? Or does she just need me in these desperate hours?

As we approach the cabin, Tanner and Clint rise from their sitting positions on the steps and cross their arms. Their tanned faces, rigid with disdain, appear to be carved from walnut. We gather a few feet from the steps, Sheriff Walton and Russell Goodwin in front.

"We want to talk to Johnny and Stephanie," Sheriff Walton says.

Disciple Clint raises his chin. "They're busy."

"Tell Swagger I need to talk to him too. It's important. It's about the gold."

The two disciples eye at each other. Disciple Clint enters the cabin. Tanner shifts his gaze from us, to the steps, and then out to sea, as if he were pretending we weren't there. An uncomfortable minute or two of silence passes.

Finally, Clint steps back out onto the porch, followed by Swagger.

Swagger slips between the two thugs and stands at the top of the steps. "What did you want to talk to me about?"

"I wanted to make sure you knew about those four chests of gold coins."

"What about them?"

"First let us talk to the two college kids."

Swagger rubs his chin', stares at the ground, and then slowly nods. "Okay." He motions toward the door and Disciple Clint opens the screen.

"Send out our two new disciples," Swagger orders.

A few seconds later Johnny and Stephanie step out onto the porch. After making eye contact with us, they avert their gaze to the ground. Johnny has dark rings around his eyes, and Stephanie's normal smiling face looks haggard, the corners of her mouth turned down.

Swagger clears his throat. "These two young people came to us. They understand what's about to happen to this world. They know the prophetic scriptures. They grew up in a church like ours. We're not holding them captive. They're free to go with you right now if they want. But they also know the door will soon close just like the door on the ark."

"Is that true?" Walton asks.

Johnny and Stephanie look up and nod.

Swagger clasps his hands in front of him. "The old man claims ownership of the gold. He doesn't understand that all things belong to God. We are only stewards of our possessions. The old man had an opportunity to give to the work of the New Kingdom and he rejected it because of his greed. We're praying he has a change of heart. We believe God will provide the finances we need to pay off our underground shelter and purchase supplies whether it's through the gold or by some other means. Tomorrow we're leaving this island with or without the gold and heading to our shelter. With World War III about to begin, I would advise you to join us."

"I'll take my chances," Sheriff Walton says. "I wanted to make it clear, though, that Jonah Newland entrusted me with guarding the treasure chests until he leaves the island. If you planned on raiding his campsite and taking the chests, you're out of luck." He pats the handgun secured in his shoulder holster and nods toward Russell Goodwin. "We are armed. If you or your goons come to my cabin with those intensions, we will not hesitate to put a bullet between your eyes."

Disciple Clint and Disciple Tanner eye each other and then gaze at Swagger.

"Anything else?" Swagger asks.

"I just wanted to let these two kids know what kind of men you are." Sheriff Walton points at Swagger and then at Clint and Tanner. "Reverend Swagger and his two disciples have criminal records—fraud and extortion. These guys are conmen. Don't be their next victims."

"We're all sinners," Swagger says. "The difference between us and you is that we have repented, and you haven't." He turns to Johnny and Stephanie. "You're not our prisoners. If you want to go back with your friends, go ahead. If you do, though, don't come knocking when the world collapses. The door will be closed."

"I'm staying," Johnny says.

Stephanie gazes skyward. "Me too."

"Don't be stupid," Holly says. "These guys tried to steal those chests." Holly points to Disciple Clint. "That one even hit a defenseless old man right in the face."

"She's exaggerating to try to sway you." Swagger says. "But you believe who you want to believe. Make a decision. Either stay or go."

They look at each other as if trying to read each other's minds.

Finally, Stephanie grasps Johnny's hand and faces us. "We want to be a part of the New Kingdom. We're staying. You should join us."

"Please," Holly pleads. "Don't be so naïve."

Johnny says, "The world is about to end, and you call us naïve. I don't think so."

Swagger strides to the door and opens it. "We need to get back to our Bible study."

Johnny and Stephanie slink into the cabin.

Swagger turns and faces us. "We're studying Luke 17 where Jesus says, 'Just as it was in the days of Noah, so also will it be in the days of the Son of Man. People were eating, drinking, marrying, and being given in marriage up to the day Noah entered the ark. Then the flood came and destroyed them all.'" He steps inside and slams the door behind him.

Chapter 19

After leaving the church cabins, feeling disgusted and hungry, we decide to pool our resources and come up with a half decent lunch. With only a few days to go, our food supplies are dwindling. At noon Holly and Lisa come to our side of the cabin with a jar of peanut butter and a half loaf of bread. Don and I dig up a jar of strawberry jam and some apples. We sit at the table, slap together our sandwiches, and pour out the last of the sweet tea into four cups.

"We need to order more food," Lisa says. "There's a ferry that shows up a couple times a day. We can place an order at the camp office."

"That might not be necessary." Don holds up his cell phone.

I focus on the screen and see a weather radar map displaying nasty swirling clouds maybe a hundred miles east of Cape Hatteras. "Is that a hurricane?"

Don shakes his head. "More like a tropical storm, but those things can pack a punch—30 to 50 mile-an-hour winds and buckets of rain. If it comes our way, we could ride it out, but it might be wiser to leave tomorrow morning."

"What about Stephanie and Johnny?" Holly asks.

Don shrugs. "What can we do?"

"Hopefully, they'll come to their senses," Lisa says. "Our other option is to raid the church cabin and kidnap them."

"Yeah, right." I can picture the fiasco of trying to execute a surprise rescue. Disciple Clint and Disciple Tanner would counterattack by pounding the crap out of us. Then the other disciples would pile on like a scene from *The Night of the Living Dead*. No Thanks.

"Should we call their parents?" Holly asks.

"That might be interesting." Don thrums his fingers on the table. "Johnny's parents are Pentecostal. Don't know if they would disapprove or applaud this new development in Johnny's life."

"Still," Lisa says, "I'm going to text Stephanie's mom and let her know what's happening. Mrs. Ryder is religious but not crazy. I'm sure she'll call and try and talk some sense into her."

Lisa's reasoning makes sense to me. "I'll try to get a hold of Johnny's mom too. She needs to know what's going on."

"This all seems so surreal," Holly says. "We're worried about our friends who are headed to a fallout shelter. We're the ones who may not survive if a nuclear war erupts."

"Yeah," Don says. "What're we supposed to do? Go home, dig a big hole, and crawl into it in hopes of surviving a nuclear winter?"

"That would be a desperate move," Lisa says. "In all likelihood, you'd be digging your own grave."

"Well then . . .," Don temples his hands in front of him, "we might as well join Swagger's church. At least we'd survive the Apocalypse."

"Or . . ." Lisa raises her eyebrows. ". . . We can do what the Germans did before the Allies invaded Berlin."

"What's that?" Don asks.

Lisa raises her foam cup. "Eat, drink, and be merry."

Don raises his cup and tips Lisa's. "Amen."

"Or . . ." Holly says, "we could pray for peace."

Everybody mumbles in agreement.

To keep our minds off our unpleasant circumstances, we play euchre for about an hour, guys against the girls. The ladies seem to have all the luck, beating us every game. Could be they're smarter than we are, but Don swears they're getting the better cards. I can't seem to concentrate. My mind is a little unfocused.

A knock on the screen door interrupts the game. It's Mee Mee Roberts.

"Come on in," Holly says.

Mee Mee steps into the cabin. "I'm just delivering an invitation." She points at the cards on the table. "Looks like you're in the middle of a big game."

"Not much of one," Lisa says. "The boys can't keep up."

Mee Mee laughs. "Don't underestimate girl power when it comes to cunning and cards."

Don screws up his face. "What's that mean?"

"Never mind," Lisa says. "Not knowing has its own reward."

"Ahhh." Don waves his hand. "Joel and I are just tired and hungry."

"Well then," Mee Mee says, "I've got good news. We're having a potluck dinner tonight at the Walton cabin. You're all invited. There'll be plenty of hotdogs and hamburgers."

Don rubs his stomach. "That's the best news I've heard all day."

"We don't have much food left," Holly says. "Not sure what we could bring. Maybe a bowl of macaroni and cheese."

"That's fine."

I stand, shuffle to the counter next to the sink, and open the cupboard door. "We've got a big bag of potato chips left."

"That'll do. There'll be plenty of food to go around. We've made some good friendships this week with some of the campers. Tonight's dinner will be a chance to get together one last time before people start heading home in the next few days."

"That's a great idea," Holly says. "I wish we could let Johnny and Stephanie know about it."

Mee Mee steps closer to the table and puts her hand on Holly's shoulder. "I think your friends will come around sooner or later. They'll realize they don't fit in with Swagger's crew of lost souls."

Holly gazes up at Mee Mee. "I hope you're right."

***

That evening we head over to the Walton cabin with our bag of potato chips and dish of macaroni and cheese. The sunset over the Core Sound is beautiful, wisps of orange clouds against a pale blue background, but to the east cumulus clouds pile up over the ocean like mashed potatoes on a Thanksgiving dinner plate.

As we stroll along the beach the wind picks up, winnowing Holly's long blonde hair. Crimenetly, she's incredible. I wonder if I'm falling in love. I've never felt this way before. I want to be close to her all the time. Get a hold of yourself, Romeo. I need to lower my expectations, or else I could fall hard—flat on my face. Then again, I keep remembering how we almost Adam and Eve-ed it back at the cabin. She must feel something for me.

Mee Mee swings open the screen door as we mount the steps to the porch. "Come right in. Dinner will be ready in a few minutes."

Don takes a deep whiff. "That's a heavenly aroma. Nothing like the smell of sizzling ground beef."

"Yeah," Lisa says. "Garbanzo beans make you smart, but hamburgers keep you sane."

Don raises a finger. "I'll opt for sanity."

Quentin Porter and Jack Graham wave from across the room. They're standing next to Mary, the ex-disciple. The two kids sit at the table, Azy coloring and Gabriel playing a game on his phone. Elsa helps Marla near the stove, stirring a pot. I glance to the other side of the cabin where the bunks are located. Sheriff Walton, Russell Goodwin, and Jonah Newland stand next to the four chests aligned in front of the first bunk. Jonah is pointing at one of the chests and muttering something, but I can't understand him. I draw closer, curious about what he is saying.

"I truly believe God meant for me to find these chests." Jonah nods and grins. "That was my mission. God sent me to this island to find this treasure. I've been a believer all my life, and finally, I get rewarded. That's what the Bible says anyway. *Adversity pursues sinners, but the righteous will be rewarded with prosperity.* That's a proverb straight from God's word."

"You are a lucky man," Russell Goodwin says.

Jonah slaps his hip. "Don't I know it, but I'd call it blessed."

"Don't be so sure of yourself, Grandfather." Elsa thuds a big bowl of green beans onto the kitchen table. "I don't think one of God's priorities is to make you rich."

Jonah spreads his hands. "Now, Elsa, I'm not making these things up. I'm quoting scripture. You can't stand in the way of God's word: *The righteous will be rewarded with prosperity.* That's what it says, plain and simple."

"But didn't Jesus say, 'Blessed are you who are poor, for yours is the kingdom of God?'"

Jonah tilts his head and squints. "I don't think that's what he meant. You don't have to be dirt poor to be a child of God. He's talking about being poor in spirit. You know what I mean—humble."

"I agree." Elsa leans on the table and stares at her grandfather. "Jesus said, 'Blessed are the peacemakers for they shall be called the children of God.' God's children humbly seek peace not wealth."

"A man with wealth can do more for the cause of peace than a poor man." Jonah turns toward Sheriff Walton and Russell Goodwin. "Am I right, gentlemen?"

They shrug and wobble their heads.

"I'm no expert when it comes to scripture," Goodwin says.

Sheriff Walton pats Goodwin's back. "But he is an expert with a .44 Magnum revolver. You don't have to worry about your treasure. Russ is a former special agent. He was a body guard for several presidents. Believe me, he has all the right skills."

Jonah raises his wiry eyebrows. "Do you think Swagger's thugs will try anything?"

Sheriff Walton shakes his head. "I doubt it. But if Swagger has some kind of caper cooked up for tonight, we'll be ready for him."

"That's good," Jonah says. "Earlier today I made all the arrangements. A Brinks truck will arrive about noon tomorrow by ferry. It's costing me a pretty penny, but I don't want to take any chances. The chests will be delivered to my bank in Raleigh. I talked to the bank president himself."

"What did you tell him?" Goodwin asks.

"To be prepared to receive and store a large sum of valuables in his most secure vault late tomorrow afternoon. He said they'd be ready. He asked a lot of questions, but I was quite spare with my answers. Gave him just enough information to keep him enticed."

"Sounds like you've made the right moves," Goodwin says. "Tomorrow we'll make sure the four chests get from here to the ferry. Brinks will take it from there."

Sheriff Walton says, "After we deliver your treasure, we'll probably pack up and head home on one of the late afternoon ferries. There's a big storm brewing out at sea that may turn in our direction."

Goodwin nods. "We definitely need to keep track of it."

Jonah motions toward Quentin Porter and Jack Graham. "Fellas, come over here a second."

Porter and Graham stride to the bunk side of the cabin, Porter wearing his usual cut-off denim shirt and Graham decked out in a Hawaiian shirt and ragged jean shorts.

"Listen," Jonah says. "You four men have gone beyond the call of duty to help me. I plan on giving each of you a generous reward. How's a couple thousand dollars each sound?"

Graham raises both hands. "Like I told you before, that's not necessary."

Porter says, "That's up to you, but I'm not worried about getting paid."

Sheriff Walton and Goodwin follow suit.

What about me and Holly? Somehow I manage to bite my tongue, but my thoughts keep swirling. Didn't we help dig up that treasure? Didn't I stand up for you under the threat of Swagger's henchmen? When Porter and Graham showed up, I made it clear that Swagger tried to move in where he didn't belong. Crimenetly. How quickly good deeds are forgotten. It's hard to keep my mouth shut. I can feel my heartbeat accelerate. Maybe Jonah has temporary amnesia. Maybe I need to remind him.

"Believe me," Jonah says, "I'll be good to you. I don't forget my friends. God has blessed me, and I plan on sharing those blessings."

Someone coughs, and Porter and Graham separate. Mary steps between them, her forehead creased and eyes tense with deep crows' feet. "I hate to rain on anyone's windfall celebration, but Swagger won't give up this easily. I've heard him discuss plans and possibilities many times. He can see things other people don't see. Don't underestimate him. He's a smart man. I'll be surprised if he doesn't try to make some kind of move between now and noon tomorrow."

Sheriff Walton brushes his knuckles against the slight growth of whiskers on his jaw. "If he does, we'll be prepared."

Goodwin nods. "And Annie and Gladys will be loaded and ready to dance."

Jonah slaps his hip and laughs. "That's music to my ears!"

"Hey everyone!" Marla Walton raps a large wooden spoon on the counter. "Dinner is served."

Don slaps his hip. "Now that's music to my ears!"

***

The meal is delicious. Hotdogs, hamburgers, green beans, apple sauce, macaroni and cheese, and potato chips never tasted so good. Funny how food tastes better when you're really hungry. The conversation remains fairly light as we eat. Jonah does most of the talking. He can't shut up about his newfound riches and what he plans on doing with the money—new truck, new house, new fishing boat, new camping equipment, and of course, don't worry, he'll give plenty to charity. What about a couple of poor college kids? I catch Elsa looking my way from across the table several times. Is she sending me silent warnings to keep my mouth shut about the fifth chest? Don't worry, kid. I don't plan on blowing the cover off your world peace box. I keep refilling my plate and feeding my face. If I can't be rich, at least I'll be full.

After dinner the conversation turns more serious. What will happen with this conflict between the United States and North Korea? Will other countries take sides? If one nuclear bomb falls, will others follow? Lisa seems to have the best solution to the conflict: Put Stamp and Ill on some grade school playground and let them slug it out. Yeah, right. That'll work.

I clear my throat. "What do you think, Mr. Goodwin? You've been in the Oval Office. You must have an insider's view."

Goodwin rubs his chin. "Well, I've served under three presidents. I don't believe any of those three would have struck first with a nuke. That would have tainted their presidential legacy with a historical black eye. Remember how Japan was viewed after bombing Pearl Harbor. There's a reason no nation has resorted to nuclear warfare since we dropped the A-bombs on Hiroshima and Nagasaki. Nowadays too many countries have the technology. If we fire, then in all likelihood we will be fired upon. We could see a domino effect. It would end up being a nuclear battle of attrition. In that case, the whole world would be vulnerable to the destruction and nuclear winter that would follow."

"What about President Stamp?" Holly asks. "Do you think he's worried about his legacy?"

Goodwin shakes his head. "I'm not so sure about our current president. He seems impulsive. He doesn't have a good background in diplomacy. Often billionaires get to be billionaires by ruthless means. If he applies the same tactics to this situation, he may make a preemptive strike to gain an upper hand. Tactically, that may give us an advantage, but then again it may topple that first domino."

"Maybe Swagger has the right idea," Don says. "At least Johnny and Stephanie have a chance of surviving with him. Maybe we should find an underground shelter and live like mole people for a year."

Goodwin nods. "That's not a bad survival option. Many of our government leaders have that kind of plan in place. Hard to say what the world would be like once you came to the surface."

Gabriel peers up from the game he's playing on his iPhone. "I don't want to live underground for a year. Can't we just move to Alaska or someplace safe?"

Marla shakes her head. "We shouldn't be talking about this in front of the kids."

"I'm not a baby, Mom," Gabriel says. "We've talked about surviving a nuclear war in school."

"Jeesh," Marla says. "Reading, writing, arithmetic, and Armageddon. Times have changed."

"It's just not fair." Holly takes in a deep breath and lets out a long sigh. "These two children are just starting out in life. My friends and I will launch our careers in a couple of years. We want to have families and pursue our dreams. Why do these world leaders feel like they have to flex their muscles?"

Mee Mee swivels her head. "They don't consider the toll of human suffering that follows in the wake of their decisions. What took more than a lifetime to create can be destroyed in one afternoon. It's sad, but it's a reality we've got to face. These leaders have stockpiles of nuclear bombs and chemical weapons at their disposal. Living in America doesn't exempt us from war's death and destruction. 9/11 proved that."

Lisa says, "The United States could become another Portsmouth Island."

"That's true," Mee Mee says. "This was once a thriving community with schools, neighborhoods, churches, and plenty of activity. This island endured horrendous storms, the Civil War, and even an earthquake. What took years to turn this place into a ghost island could happen overnight to our country."

Jack Graham cups his hands behind his head. "I've lived my entire life under the dark cloud of nuclear annihilation. I've come to the conclusion that what will be will be. I can't complain. There's been ups and downs. I lost my wife a few years ago to cancer, but I've got lots of good memories. If I die tomorrow, I'll have no regrets. I feel bad for you young people, though. You haven't had the opportunity to live out your lives—marriage, family, career, kids—all that sort of thing. If Rocketman does send a nuke our way, I only have one request." He spreads his hands and looks up. "Let it fall right on top of me. That way I won't feel a thing."

Quentin Porter chuckles. "I'm with you, Jack. That wouldn't be a bad way to go. For me, the only better way to die would be wrestling a shark. Most people would say I'm a violent man. I've been in my share of fists fights. When my two best friends were killed in that shark attack, I got mad at God. I took it out on people for a while. My wife had me arrested for domestic violence. Eventually, we got divorced. Then I started taking it out on sharks. I've lost count of the number of sharks I've whacked to death with my machete. That would be poetic justice—dying in a battle with a shark."

"I'm not ready to die yet," Mary says. "My life hasn't been so good. I've made mistakes. Hurt people. I've got a six-year-old son that I haven't seen for more than a year." She holds out her hand, and it trembles. "Right now I need a smoke. I've struggled with addiction. When I joined the New Kingdom Church, things changed. I felt like I was given a new start. Their doctrine is similar to most evangelical churches. As time passed, though, I noticed Swagger didn't like to be questioned on anything. His word was law. He became obsessed with raising money to pay for the shelter and supplies. That's when I started getting cold feet."

Mary glances in my direction. "When Joel showed me the gold coin the other day, I knew Swagger would ask him to donate it. Obsession and addiction are similar. They skew your values. They make you do things and say things you normally wouldn't do or say. I guess I recognized that flaw in Swagger because I see it in myself. That's when I knew I had to get out. No, I'm not ready to die. I want another chance at life. I want to see my kid again. Maybe I could get my life straightened out and become a good mother to my boy one day."

Mee Mee reaches and cups Mary's hand. "You still have hope despite what's happening in the world. There's always hope. Our lives change with every decision we make. All of us are where we are in life right now because of our decisions—good or bad. A year from now, God willing, we will be in a different place because of our decisions. With time things could get much better for you."

"I believe you," Mary says. "If this world survives, I plan on making the right decisions. A year from now I want to be in a better place. I want to have my own home and a good job. I want to drop my kid off at school every day and be a member of the P.T.A."

"But that's the question." Don thrums his fingers on the table. "Will we be here a year from now? We may be gone tomorrow."

Jonah Newland laughs. "Wouldn't that be ironic? Wouldn't that be some dandy twist of fate—time runs out with my pockets full of gold. I was a laborer in the mill for almost forty years. Struggled from pay to pay to keep my family clothed and fed. My wife got sick, and everything we saved for retirement went to medical bills. Then my daughter died in a car accident, and Elsa came to live with us."

Jonah's eyes water and he blinks several times. "After my wife passed away, I was at my lowest. The one light in my life was Elsa. I knew she had the gift. She saw things differently. She had visions and dreams. One night she had this amazing vision of a treasure chest on some remote island. She loves the ocean and combing the shore for shells. She convinced me to come to Portsmouth Island for a camping vacation. I thought what the heck. I enjoy camping. When she loaded a couple shovels onto the truck, I knew something was up. Then I remembered her dream about the treasure. Like I said, she has the gift. We found the treasure." His smile fades, and the skin around his jowls sag. "But we might be out of time."

Elsa bangs her fist on the table. "Time is not going to run out if I can help it. What Mee Mee said is true. Tomorrow's outcome depends on what we decide today. These world leaders need to put their egos aside. I pray that God will give me the chance to help them see that peace is the right choice."

Lisa straightens and raises her eyebrows. "I don't mean to trample across your flower garden, but how is a twelve-year-old girl going to step onto the world stage and influence that kind of decision?"

Elsa smiles, her eyes seeming to focus on some far off scene. "God often uses the least expected to do the most."

Elsa's words trigger a long silence. I can feel the breath of the sea breeze through the screen door and hear the distant rumble of waves against the shore. Azy crawls up into her mother's lap and plants the side of her face against her chest. As Marla caresses her daughter's cheek, she hums a familiar lullaby. Slowly the conversation begins again, drifting away from war and destruction. We talk for another hour or so about hopes and dreams in a world with a more optimistic future.

Why did everyone's mood shift? It was as if Elsa's words of hope held some credibility. Tomorrow didn't seem so ominous. People began making plans for their last day or two on the island. Quentin Porter mentions that he wants to get up early the next morning and go fishing. Jack Graham says he has a date with his metal detector at sunrise. Mary and Mee Mee plan on taking a long walk along the beach. I don't say anything, but I want to spend as much time as I can with Holly. Porter and Graham scoot their chairs out from the table, say their goodbyes, and head out the door,

Holly says, "We better get going, too."

I agree.

Jonah stands and stretches. "Thanks for everything. You people are heaven sent. We're heading back to our campsite. It's been a long day."

After more thank-yous and hugs, we head out the door.

The first thing I notice is how dark it is. "It's kinda spooky out here."

Holly clasps her arms to her chest. "I'm cold."

Is that my cue? l put my arm around her and draw her close. She slips her arm around my waist.

Don peers into the sky. "No stars. No moon."

"Must be clouds moving in from that storm out at sea," Lisa says.

Elsa strides up to me, grasps my free arm, and tugs me toward the ocean.

I release Holly. "Whoa! Where're we going?"

"I need to talk to you alone."

Crimenetly, kid, can't you see I'm busy. "Okay. Okay. This better be important." We come to a halt about twenty yards away from everybody.

She draws close and whispers, "Remember. I'll be there early tomorrow morning to pick up the chest."

"That's fine. I'm not going anywhere. I'll be looking for you."

She puts her hand on my cheek. "You've been a tremendous help."

I shrug. "I do what I can."

"Thanks for being my friend."

"Elsa!" Jonah Newland hollers from a good ways down the beach.

She leans and kisses my cheek. "See you tomorrow." She turns and scurries into the darkness. "Coming, Grandfather!"

Chapter 20

The gray light of dawn creeps into my half-sleep. I blink and glance at my watch—6:05 a.m. That's odd. I figure Elsa should have been here by now. Maybe she got a late start.

Don is sleeping soundly. I rise, stretch, and peer out the window. It's overcast and misty outside but not raining . . . yet. I head to the bathroom and take care of business. After washing my hands and splashing my face, I stare at myself in the mirror. You're not the best looking guy in town, but there's hope for you yet. Rubbing my jaws, I notice my beard is coming in thicker. I expand my chest with a deep breath. Am I finally becoming a man? Maybe I ought to try growing the beard again. I hear the screen door rattle. Elsa? I lean my head out of the bathroom and take a peek. It was only the wind.

Now I'm starting to feel a little concerned. She should have been here by now. I slip on some shorts and decide to walk along the beach toward Elsa's campsite. In all probability I'll run into her along the way. Descending the porch steps, I notice visibility is limited because of the mist, maybe two hundred yards, if that. The wind is up, and the waves are cresting higher than usual, six or seven feet at their peak. With the ocean spray peppering me, I keep blinking my eyes to clear my vision. I see a dark, blurry hulk on the slope of sand up ahead. As I near I can make out the form of an ATV. Could it be Elsa's? Why would she stop there?

As I draw nearer, I notice the shark jawbone mounted on the front of the vehicle. Quentin Porter must be fishing nearby. I inspect the beach directly in front of the vehicle and notice two pole tubes embedded in the sand, one holding an ocean rod and reel and the other empty. A line stretches out to sea from the tip of the one pole. A large open tackle box and a bucket of bait sits nearby.

I turn and peer at the nearest cabin about sixty yards away just beyond the sand fences. Maybe he had to go to the bathroom. No lights are on. Something doesn't feel right. Turning slowly, I scan the shoreline to the south. The mist limits my vision, but I see no one within a hundred and fifty yards. I turn and look in the opposite direction. Thunderous waves pound the deserted shore.

Remembering Porter's shark-retrieving method from our first meeting, I gaze out to sea. Maybe he's wrestling a shark. The waves are huge, but I see something bobbing about forty yards out.

"Quentin!"

A dark shape tumbles and disappears under the water. A wave rolls the form forward, and an arm flops through the surface. My heart jumps into my throat. I catch sight of the body again, maybe thirty yards out, and charge into the sea. A wave smacks me and knocks me down. I struggle to my feet and manage to stand against the back-rushing water. Scanning the surface, I don't see anything. Another wave rises up, and I dive into the curl and swim a few yards before surfacing.

There! Twenty feet ahead of me. The backwash is tugging the body back out. The water is up to my waist, but I manage to thrust forward a few more yards. Another wave comes at me, and I duck under it just in time. When I break through to air, I gasp but manage to focus with an intensity fueled by adrenalin. I see a dark shape just ahead below the surface. Is that Porter's body? No matter. I plunge toward the form and latch on. Another wave crashes over me when I try to stand. I keep my right arm locked around the body as I tumble. It feels like I'm trapped in a washing machine.

Finally, I get my balance and rise to my feet, armed locked onto the body. It's Quentin Porter. He's heavy and lifeless. I begin backing my way toward shore, wary of the next wave. When it hits, I turn my back to it but can't handle its force. Down we go again, this time in shallower water where the broken shells gnaw at my exposed skin. I can't hold on. The body rolls ahead of me for a second or two, but then the back-charging water sweeps it ocean-ward. Crimenetly. I'm in a tug of war with the sea. I dive and latch on to Porter's arm. The water is only knee-deep now. It's easier to get to my feet and gain some leverage. I clamp my other hand onto Porter's other arm and drag him face up through the rushing shallows. His denin shirt is half torn off, and his prosthetic leg-blade cuts through the surface like a shark fin. Another wave hits, but I'm almost there. This time I stumble but manage to hold on. With all my strength I heave the body as far as I can up the slope of sand next to the ATV.

Porter's eyes stare blankly into the gloomy sky. His skin, once tawny and taunt, is pale gray. A fishing line wraps around his face and body as if he were a human spindle. Scratches and bruises mar his forehead, cheeks, arms, and legs. I drop to my knees and reach for his wrist. No pulse. I place my hands on his chest and begin pumping the way they taught us to do CPR in health class back in high school. His body just flops limply with each thrust. After a couple of minutes, I stop and catch my breath. No use. He's dead.

I've never been this close to death. It's cold and ugly and ghastly. As my breathing slows, I can feel my heart pounding. I'm not afraid, just shocked by it all. Standing,

I shake myself all over to regain some clarity. Did he go out after a shark and get thumped by a wave or a shark's tail? I don't see any bite marks on him, just scratches and bruises.

What should I do? The fishing line trails from his prosthetic leg out into the ocean. I reach, snag the line, and begin pulling it hand over hand back into shore. There's something heavy on the other end. The line is thick, strong enough to reel in a big fish. Could there be a shark on the other end? Whatever it is doesn't seem to be putting up a fight. It just has some weight to it. Now I see it—the rod and reel. I charge forward into the up-rushing water, grab the end of the rod, and drag it toward the body. What should I do with it? I lay the rod down next to Quentin Porter's corpse and shake my head. He said he wanted to die wrestling a shark. Maybe he got his wish.

Now I'm shivering. I need to get help. Does 911 work here? Oh no! Where's my phone? I press my hands against the pockets of my wet shorts. Not there. Thank God I left it back at the cabin. It wouldn't have survived the ocean. First I'll go back to Sheriff Walton's cabin and tell him. Then I'll get my phone and try to call 911.

"Hey you over there!" an anxious voice hollers.

I shift my focus in direction of the cry.

Chapter 21

Through the mist along the shore I see a thin, bearded figure carrying a long walking stick. His loose, white shirt flutters in the wind. Jonah Newland?

"Joel! Is that you?"

"Yeah, it's me!"

"Have you seen Elsa?"

"No." I glance at Porter's body and then back up at Jonah. He's still forty yards away. "I haven't seen her. There's been a terrible . . . a terrible . . ." I don't know what to call it. Accident? Drowning?

When Jonah draws to within a few yards, he stops and stiffens. "What happened? Is he dead?"

"Yes. I-I-I saw his body out in the waves and went out and lugged him back to shore. I tried to give him CPR. No use. He's d-d-dead." I can't stop shivering.

Jonah's face turns as pale as Porter's as he stares at the corpse. "I can't believe it. He was as fit as a pro athlete. How could he have drowned?"

"I don't know. Maybe he hooked a big shark and went out after it. The fishing line broke." I point to the rod and reel.

Jonah wobbles his head slowly. "That's strong line. Doesn't make sense to me."

"I need to go tell Sheriff Walton. Are you looking for Elsa?"

"Yeah. She left early this morning before I woke up. She's on foot. She knew she'd wake me if she started her ATV. That girl is going to be the death of me. I didn't want her to stray from camp today, but she's hardheaded. Probably wanted to go beach combing one last time before we left at noon."

My mind sloshes with a jumble of thoughts—Elsa, the chest, Quentin Porter's drowning, the strangeness of it all. Think straight. Should I tell Jonah about the chest and Elsa's plans to pick it up? Maybe she did walk up the beach to look for shells before stopping back at my cabin. First things first. Report Porter's death to Sheriff Walton.

I point in the direction of the cabins. "I need to tell Sheriff Walton about what happened to Quentin Porter. Maybe someone at his cabin saw Elsa."

"I'm coming with you."

I glance at the body one last time. There's plenty of clearance between the corpse and the water. We'll be back in a few minutes with Sheriff Walton. Not much chance the body will be disturbed. "Let's go."

The Walton cabin isn't far away, less than a two minute fast walk. We mount the steps to the porch, and I knock on the door.

About thirty seconds later Sheriff Walton pushes the screen open. He's unshaven, his red hair tousled. "Good morning." He blinks and rubs his eyes. "Is everything alright?"

"No." I thumb over my shoulder. "There's a dead body on shore—Quentin Porter's body."

Walton steps onto the porch and shuts the door. "Are you serious?"

"Unfortunately, yes."

"And my granddaughter is missing," Jonah says.

"What do you mean, missing? Have you seen her at all today?"

"No. When I woke up she was gone. Did anybody see her pass by your cabin?"

"No one mentioned it." He stares over my shoulder at the seashore. "Show me where the body is."

I pivot and ramble down the steps. "This way."

As we hurry toward Porter's body, Sheriff Walton asks, "Why did Elsa take off without telling you?"

"Who knows? I told her I didn't want her leaving camp today. She's a strong-willed child. She didn't take the ATV. It makes me nervous that she's on foot."

Walton nods. "Yeah. After yesterday's confrontation with Swagger's flock, you don't know what could happen."

"She . . . she . . ." I bite my tongue, remembering my promise not to say anything about the chest. "She said she would stop by our cabin to say goodbye sometime this morning, but I haven't seen her."

We arrive at the body, and Sheriff Walton falls to his knees. He checks for a pulse and examines the head, face and arms. "He's scratched up, but I don't see any signs of blunt force trauma. No lumps. No gashes. Apparently, he drowned, but that doesn't make sense. How can a man fishing from shore drown?"

I crouch and reach for the end of the fishing line. "When he catches a big shark, he goes out into the water after it. I've seen him do it. When I passed here earlier, I noticed his body tumbling out in the waves and managed to drag him to shore."

Sheriff Walton reaches and takes the end of the line. "Looks like the shark got away."

"This doesn't look right to me," Jonah says. "Porter was a well-trained jock. I can't believe he walked out into the ocean and drowned." He swivels his head, scanning the shoreline. "I've got to find Elsa. She couldn't have made it too far along the shore. She must have passed here when Porter was fishing."

Sheriff Walton rubs the short growth of beard on his jaws. "Hard to say. She could have walked by while he was out in the water. Maybe she saw something."

Jonah's thick, white eyebrows knot together. "Maybe she saw something she wasn't supposed to see."

I get to my feet. "Do you need me for anything else, Sheriff? I want to help hunt for Elsa."

"No. I'll get a statement from you later. Let me know if you can't find her."

Jonah and I decide to head north along the shoreline.

I glance to my left at the last few cabins. "I wonder if One-Eyed Jack saw her. He gets up early to go out metal detecting."

"He mentioned that last night at the dinner," Jonah says.

I stop and point to the third cabin from the end. "He's staying in that one."

"Let's go ask him."

We cut across the beach and angle between two of the sand fences. I'm guessing he already left, but it doesn't hurt to check. We climb the steps, and I cross the porch and pound on the screen door. No answer. I rap hard again and listen. I can't hear anyone moving around inside.

"I doubt if he's here. No lights are on." I motion toward the beach. "He's either farther north along the shore or up on the dunes."

Jonah steps to the side and peers through the window. He jerks backward, eyes wide. "Check the door! See if it's open!"

"Okay." Crimenetly. What in the world did he see in there? I reach for the handle and turn. The catch releases, and I swing the door open and enter the darkened cabin. "Mr. Graham? Are you here?"

The silhouette of a body slowly turns. I glance down and see a kitchen chair lying on the floor nearby. Jonah flips on the light. A rope from the rafters suspends Jack Graham by the neck. His good eye bulges, and his mouth is wide open, tongue hanging out. His black patch covers his other eye.

Jonah puts his hand to his mouth. "What in the hell is going on here?"

Jack Graham's body reverses direction, his feet only inches from the floor.

My knees go weak, so I slide a chair out from the table and sit down. My stomach feels like I just stepped off the Scrambler at a two-bit carnival. The only time I ever saw a dead person before today was at a funeral home. Two in the last ten minutes. Sheesh. I glance across the table and notice a piece of paper. I reach for it.

"What's this? Jack left a note."

"Read it," Jonah says. "I don't have my glasses."

"It says, 'I know this world won't last much longer. I don't want to burn to death in the flames of a nuclear blast. I'd rather go out on my own terms. See you on the other side, Jack Graham.'"

Jonah shakes his head. "He must have changed his tune. Last night he wanted the nuke to land right on top of him."

"No. I don't think he changed his tune."

"What do you mean?"

I pinch the corner of the note between my thumb and finger and lift it. "I don't think he wrote this. It's printed like a kindergarten kid's writing. Wouldn't you use your own handwriting for a suicide note?"

Jonah nods and steps closer to the body. He bends and examines Graham's wrists. "There's something else that doesn't sit right."

"What's that?"

"There's cut marks on his wrists. Someone strapped his hands together before they hung him."

Chapter 22

We step back out onto the porch. Dark gray clouds churn above the ocean. The wind picks up, making me shake uncontrollably. I feel like a scared teenager in a slasher flick. Who's next? I glance at Jonah. He's staring down the beach into the mist.

"Now I'm really worried," he says.

"We better go tell Sheriff Walton what happened to Mr. Graham."

"Go ahead." He turns and gazes down the beach in the other direction. "I'm heading back to camp to get my truck. If Elsa saw Swagger's two thugs trying to drown Porter, she may have ran. She's got good legs on her. They'd never catch her on foot." He pivots and points northward up the beach. "I'll head up that way for a couple of miles. Maybe she's hiding in the marshes on the other side of the dunes."

"That makes sense. She's a smart girl. I'll head in that direction as soon as I talk to Sheriff Walton."

Jonah reaches and grips my shoulder. "Thanks."

I decide to run back to the scene of the drowning. Maybe the physical exertion will warm me up. Through the mist I see two people standing near Porter's ATV. Judging by the second figure's tall stature, I'm guessing he's Russell Goodwin. They glance up as I near. It is Goodwin.

"Did you find Elsa?" Sheriff Walton asks.

"No." I come to a stop, catching my breath. "I've got more bad news. We were just up at Jack Graham's cabin. He's dead, too. "

"Damn." Goodwin straightens, eyes alarmed. "I guess we shouldn't be surprised. Could you tell how he died?"

"By hanging. We didn't disturb anything. His body is still strung up on a rope tied to the rafters."

"Did it appear to be a suicide?" Sheriff Walton asks.

"It appeared that way. A chair lay on the floor nearby, and we found a suicide note on the table. But I have my doubts."

"Why?" Goodwin asks.

"The message is printed, even the signature. Besides that, we noticed cut marks on his wrists. Jonah figured they strapped his hands before they hung him and then cut the strap off to make it look like a suicide."

Sheriff Walton rubs his chin. "That's a good observation, Joel. Sorry you had to see that scene, but we appreciate your help."

Goodwin paces around Porter's body. "We've got a couple possible murders on our hands."

Sheriff Walton nods. "I'll make a call to the Hyde County Sheriff's Department. We need to secure both crime scenes."

"What about the treasure?" I ask. "Do you think Swagger's gang will try to make a move while you're busy dealing with the bodies?"

"I'm not worried about that," Sheriff Walton says. "My wife can handle guarding the treasure. She's a deputy sheriff. Our cabin is in view. I don't think Swagger will make any moves in broad daylight."

I'm not so sure. After a double murder, why not a robbery? But I keep my mouth shut.

"Could you do us a big favor?" Sheriff Walton asks.

"Sure."

"The Hyde County Emergency Services will arrive shortly by ferry. Russell and I need to head up to Graham's cabin. Could you hang out until they get here? Just keep an eye on the body and don't let anybody disturb anything."

"I was going to help hunt for Elsa, but that can wait . . . I guess."

Sheriff Walton pats my back. "Thanks. It won't take long for the Hyde County people to get here, maybe twenty minutes."

The two men turn and stride in the direction of Graham's cabin. I glance at Porter's body. Death is so ugly. He lies there tangled up in that fishing line like the carcass of a dolphin that washed up on shore. It's not that I'm afraid of standing next to a lifeless body. Maybe it's the cold reality that death is no respecter of persons. It could happen to anyone, even me. The memory of meeting Porter on this very spot two days ago doesn't help. He was so alive and vigorous. A 250 pound bull shark didn't have a chance against him. Guess he wasn't invincible, though.

Then there's the possibility that both Porter and Graham were murdered. They opposed Swagger, and Swagger promised that the wrath of God would fall upon them. I stood up for Jonah and Elsa, too. Am I on his hit list? It's possible, but I doubt it. I didn't swing any machetes or threaten legal action. Maybe there weren't any malicious acts committed at all. Porter might have met his match out in the waves. Graham might have hung himself. Seems unlikely, though.

I glance southward down the beach. No one coming in my direction. I take a deep breath and try to stop shivering. The strong breeze has helped to dry out my clothes. Now it's nerves more than the cold. I better look the other way to make sure no one is sneaking up on me. I turn northward.

Someone is coming this way. Clint or Tanner? No. It looks more like a girl. Could it be Elsa? It's hard to tell through the mist. I hope it's Elsa. That would be a big relief. "Elsa! Is that you!"

"Joel, it's me! What's going on?"

It sounds like Holly. I hold up both of my hands. "There's a dead body over here. You probably don't want to look at this."

She stops about twenty yards away. "Who is it?"

"Quentin Porter."

"I'm not afraid. I've seen dead bodies."

She walks up to me and reaches for my hand. Her face drains of color as she stares at the corpse. "Poor Mr. Porter. What happened?"

"This morning I decided to walk toward Elsa's camp. Figured I'd run into her along the way. I noticed the fishing equipment and then saw a body out in the waves. I went out and towed him back to shore. He was already dead."

Her head slowly swivels back and forth. "He must have went out to cast his line. Maybe a big wave hit him unexpectedly."

I shrug. "I don't know. I've seen him charge into the shallows to haul in a shark that he's hooked."

"That's how he said he wanted to die—wrestling a shark."

"That's true, but Mr. Goodwin thinks someone murdered him. He and Sheriff Walton went up to Jack Graham's cabin. He's dead too."

"What?" Her eyes widen. "No way! How did he die?"

Remembering the scene, I try to swallow a lump in my throat. "Jonah Newland and I found him hanging by the neck from a rope in his cabin. There was a suicide note on the table, but I have my doubts. I don't think he killed himself."

"Do you think both men were murdered?"

I nod.

"Where's Elsa?"

"We don't know. When Jonah woke up, she was gone."

Holly gasps. "She told us she was coming to your cabin this morning to pick up the small chest."

"I'm worried that something happened along the way."

"You think . . . you think she may have been abducted?"

"Or worse."

"Why would they kill Elsa?"

"Sometimes members of cults go crazy. There's the Jonestown massacre, the Manson murders, the Hale-Bopp Comet deaths. People who are committed to cults have extreme beliefs and go to extreme measures."

Holly grips my hand tighter and scans the shoreline. "In other words, this could be the beginning of a killing spree."

Chapter 23

Holly and I spend the next fifteen minutes glancing up and down the shoreline, holding hands, feeling apprehensive, but not saying much. Our little isle of paradise has turned into a terror zone. I keep telling myself the two deaths could be an odd coincidence, but my heart's not buying it.

From the direction of the docks on the sound side of the island, I hear a siren. A white Chevy van with an orange stripe navigates its way between the dunes and onto the beach. I wave both hands. The flashing red and blue lights create an eerie luminosity through the mist.

"Thank God they're here," Holly says.

The van slows to a stop about ten feet from Porter's ATV. Two attendants exit the passenger side, a tall, dark-haired guy and a chunky short-haired blond. A bald, older man steps out from the driver's side. They're all wearing blue-green polo shirts and black pants.

"Good morning," the dark-haired guy says. He looks to be in his mid-thirties, about six-feet-two-inches tall. "I'm Albert Swingle." He points to the other young guy. "This is George Stenson, the county coroner." Stenson nods.

I let go of Holly's hand. "I'm Joel Thomas. This is my friend, Holly."

The older man walks directly to the body, stares at it, and shakes his head.

The dark haired guy motions toward the older man. "That's Bob Branson.".

The old guy glances up at us. "Where's Sheriff Walton?"

I point to Graham's cabin. "There's been another death."

All three attendants straighten up as if a cold breeze hit them in the face.

"What happened?" the old guy asks.

"That's what Sheriff Walton is trying to figure out," I say. "It appears to be a drowning and a suicide, but the Sheriff and his friend Mr. Goodwin believe both deaths are suspicious."

"Suspicious?" the old guy meets my gaze. "Are we talking a crime scene here?"

I nod.

He leans his head sideways as if he had a kink in his neck. "Well, that's good to know."

The blond coroner drops to his knees beside Porter's body. "Do you know anything about this man's death?"

"Yes. I . . . I pulled him out of the water."

They ask several questions, and I provide as much detail as I can remember. They seem to be satisfied with my account.

"Doesn't look like a murder to me. He got tangled up in his own fishing line," the coroner says as he checks over the body. "Just a typical drowning."

Holly clears her throat. "There are unusual circumstances."

"What do you mean?" The dark-haired guy asks.

"Well . . . you better ask Sheriff Walton about that. I don't know all the facts."

The dark-haired guy points over my shoulder. "Here he comes now."

Sheriff Walton cuts through the mist, striding at a brisk pace. "You Hyde County boys are always on the ball. Faster than a toupee in a windstorm."

The blond points out to sea. "We're trying to get ahead of that windstorm."

"Let's hope we can."

"What's going on here, Sheriff?" the old guy asks.

"We want to be careful. We may have a couple crime scenes on our hands." He points to Porter's body. "This one was found out in the waves by young Joel there. The autopsy will give us some clues. Other than that, I want to look for footprints along the beach so be careful where you walk. Sheriff Benson will take over when he gets here. Portsmouth Island is under his jurisdiction. I'd wait for his okay to move the body and ATV. "

"He better get here soon," the old guy says.

Sheriff Walton turns and points to Graham's cabin. "The other body is hanging from a rope in that eighth cabin. Don't know if it's suicide or murder. I'm sure the CSI team will want to comb that place for evidence. Sheriff Benson should be getting here in the next thirty minutes, so be patient." He spreads his hands. "Gentlemen, this may simply be a drowning and a suicide. But until we know for sure, I want to leave no stone unturned."

"Not too many stones on this island," the tall guy says. "Lots of grains of sand, though."

"Hopefully, I'll find some footprints in the sand," Sheriff Walton says.

"We'll be careful not to gum things up too much, Sheriff," the old man says.

"I'd like one of you boys to stay here with this body. The other two can head up to Graham's cabin. My buddy Russell Goodwin is keeping his eye on things there for now. You can relieve him. Please be careful. Don't touch anything."

"We know the protocol." The old man pats the tall guy on the back. "Come with me, Swingle. Stenson, you stay here with the drowning victim."

The blond gives a half-hearted salute. "Whatever you say, boss."

"I appreciate your help," Sheriff Walton says.

As the old guy and Stingle walk away, the blond mutters, "The old fart thinks he's in charge."

Sheriff Walton turns to me and says, "Can you come with me while I talk to Swagger and his followers? I want a witness there just in case anything happens. Try to observe how Disciple Clint and Disciple Tanner react to what I have to say."

"Sure."

"I'll come too," Holly says. "I'm a good observer. I'll watch one of them."

"You take Tanner, and I'll take Clint."

Holly takes a deep breath and nods.

Sheriff Walton wags his head toward the cabins. "Let's go."

Swagger's cabin is the first one on the far left, right next to the other church cabin. Both are octagonal in shape. There's a fifty-yard gap between those two and the next two octagonal cabins. After another fifty yard gap, the six rectangular cabins follow, spaced fairly evenly, maybe twenty to thirty yards apart. Sheriff Walton wants to walk along the shore to look for footprints in the wet sand. I immediately notice one set along the top of the slope. We stop and stare at the prints.

"Those look like Jonah's to me," I say. "He came up the beach earlier this morning looking for Elsa."

Sheriff Walton pulls his cell phone out of a lower pocket of his cargo shorts. "I'll take a photo for comparison purposes."

"There're lots of footstep indentions in the dry sand." Holly points to the stretch of sand between the shore and the cabins.

Sheriff Walton glances up to where she's pointing. "Those could have been made three or four days ago. None of them are clearly defined. I was hoping to find a couple of fresh sets in the wet sand heading in the direction of Porter's body." He turns and stares at the first church cabin. "Let's go pay a visit."

When we reach the cabin steps, we hear singing, some old hymn about the roll being called up in heaven. Sheriff Walton points to footprints that go around to the back of the cabin. "Those prints aren't very clear, but it looks like two people cut up over the dunes. Maybe they approached Graham's cabin from the rear."

I nod, picturing Tanner and Clint on their murder mission.

We climb the steps, and Walton raps hard on the door. The singing stops.

Swagger opens the door. "What do you want? We've just begun our morning worship service."

"I would like to talk to you and all of your followers. This is very important. There have been a couple of deaths on the island. The authorities will be arriving soon to determine the cause of death and if there needs to be an investigation."

"I see. Well . . ." Swagger peeks inside. "We have nothing to hide." He leans inside the door. "Everybody come out onto the porch. Sheriff Walton wants to speak to us." He steps out and holds open the screen door.

To make room, we back away, descend the steps, turn, and face the gathering disciples. There must be at least twelve or thirteen of them. I notice Johnny and Stephanie in the back, Johnny a head taller than most of them. His eyes look strained and face pale, as if he stayed up all night. When we make eye contact, he offers a grim smile but quickly averts his gaze. Stephanie doesn't look happy either. Her eyes are red-rimmed with dark circles like she aged ten years overnight. They look like they're turning into zombies.

Sheriff Walton puts his hands on his hips. "I want you all to listen to me carefully. Last night two men died on the island. As of now, we're not sure if the cause was accidental, self-inflicted, or criminal."

"Self-inflicted?" Swagger says. "That's sounds like suicide."

"One of the deaths may be classified as a suicide, but both are suspicious."

Swagger spreads his hands. "Why are you bothering us? We had nothing to do with these deaths."

"For two reasons. One—you and your people may be in danger if there's a killer on the island. Two—you are not above suspicion. I'm not sure what your plans are, but no one is to leave this island until the authorities have a chance to question all of you."

"I've got two things for you to consider." Swagger raises his index finger. "One—we're not afraid of anyone on this island because God's protection is over us. The scriptures tell us that the Lord will keep us from all harm and watch over our lives."

Several amens break out behind him.

He raises a second finger. "Two—our departure boat is scheduled to arrive at five this afternoon. We intend to get off this island before the storm hits later this evening."

"That shouldn't be a problem," Sheriff Walton says. "The authorities will be here soon. They should be done with their questioning by noon. I do have one question that I would like to ask all of you. Did anyone here leave the cabin this morning?"

They all shake their heads. Many of them say, "No."

"Then whose footprints are these?" Sheriff Walton points to the ground in front of him. "They go around the back of the cabin to the dunes."

"It hasn't rained all week," Swagger says. "We always go on prayer walks. Those could have been made yesterday or three days ago."

"Or maybe early this morning or the middle of last night," Sheriff Walton says.

"I don't think so," Swagger says. "I'm curious, though, Sheriff. Who died last night?"

Sheriff Walton glances at Holly and me, his eyes alerting us to pay attention. He refocuses on Swagger. "Quentin Porter and Jack Graham."

I observe Disciple Clint and notice that his eyes shift downward. Clearly, he doesn't want to make eye contact with us.

"That doesn't surprise me," Swagger says.

"Why's that, Swagger?" Walton asks.

"Both men opposed God's will yesterday. Porter threatened us with violence and Graham with deceptive legal mumbo-jumbo. The treasure we found and dug up was meant to help build the New Kingdom. It was an answer to our prayers. Those men met their deaths because of God's hand of judgment upon them."

I can't keep my mouth shut. "But you didn't find that treasure. I was there. Elsa Newland found the treasure. She and her grandfather were digging it up when your gang showed up and tried to take over."

Swagger holds both hands up as if ready to give a benediction. "Listen to what I'm saying. Elsa was God's means of bringing the treasure to us. Those chests of gold were not meant to be mammon wasted selfishly on the few. God provided the treasure to help us prepare for Armageddon. Believe me, the end is coming soon. By opposing us, Porter and Graham opposed God." He lowers his hands and points at Sheriff Walton. "You and

Jonah Newland need to come to your senses before the hand of God's judgment falls upon you."

"I'm not worried." Walton opens his jacket to reveal a holstered handgun. "If one of your goons comes after me, he's a dead man."

"You're mistaken. We don't resort to violent means." Swagger points skyward. "But remember this: The hand of God is bulletproof."

I hear the sound of an engine, turn, and stare down the beach. Jonah Newland's pickup truck emerges through the mist. The old Ford skids to a stop just on the other side of the sand fences.

Jonah throws open the door and jumps out. "I've been all the way to the end of the island and back. No sign of her."

"Who?" Swagger asks.

The old man's voice crackles in desperation: "Elsa! My granddaughter!"

Swagger closes his eyes and holds his hands palms up. "I've seen her."

Chapter 24

"When did you see her?" Sheriff Walton asks.

Swagger opens his eyes and lowers his hands. "It was early this morning just before sunrise."

"Where?" Jonah shouts.

"Some distance away from here."

"What're you talking about?" Sheriff Walton says. "A few minutes ago you told me nobody left this cabin."

"I saw her in a vision just before I woke up. I saw the surroundings very clearly. I could describe the exact location."

"You're full of crap." Sheriff Walton turns toward us and shakes his head. "What a load of phony horse shit."

Swagger's bushy eyebrows lower, darkening his eyes. "Say what you want to say about me. Your opinion matters nothing. I tell the truth whether you want to hear it or not."

Jonah steps closer. "I want to hear about your vision. What did you see?"

Swagger shakes his head. "I don't share my visions with those who oppose me. You and Sheriff Walton have set your prideful hearts against God's plans. We were led to this island by God for a purpose. We welcomed you with open arms to join us. We offered you a place in the New Kingdom. Because of your greed you have made a stand against the very One who offers you deliverance and salvation."

Jonah frowns, his face wrinkling. As he takes a deep breath, his body trembles. "Please, if you know anything, tell me."

"I will tell you this. In my vision she was in great danger." Swagger spreads his hands as if receiving an offering. "If you have a change of heart, I will tell you more." He turns and pulls open the screen door. One by one the disciples file back into the cabin.

"Stephanie! Johnny!" Holly shouts. "Don't go back in there. Come with us."

They stop and face us. Their eyes meet our gaze for a few moments but then cast downward.

With his free hand, Swagger grasps Johnny's shoulder. "You're free to leave, my son, but like I told you, once the door closes, it stays closed."

They glance up at us again, hesitating, almost stepping in our direction. Swagger's grip tightens on Johnny's shoulder as if trying to steady him.

Stephanie wipes a tear from her cheek. "It's too late."

"It's never too late. Come with us," Holly pleads.

I feel like charging onto the porch and pulling Johnny away from Swagger's grip. "Let go of his shoulder!"

Swagger lifts his hand from Johnny's shoulder and lowers his arm to his side. "Like I said, they are free to go if they want to return to this fallen world."

Both Johnny and Stephanie shake their heads, turn, and walk into the cabin. Swagger smiles and nods like a spook house ticket-taker. He enters the cabin and slams the door behind him.

Chapter 25

Sheriff Walton places his hand on Jonah's shoulder. "Don't put too much stock in a lunatic preacher's visions, especially one who has been convicted of fraud."

Jonah blinks as if he just glimpsed a ghoul. "What're we gonna do?"

Walton scratches his chin. "Let's go up to my cabin and formulate a plan. We definitely need to organize a search party."

I grasp Holly's hand as we walk the short distance to the Walton cabin. We squeeze each other's hands tightly like a couple of kids passing through a graveyard. I wonder if Don and Lisa are up yet. It's still fairly early in the morning.

When we reach the Walton cabin, I say, "We'll go recruit Don and Lisa. Be back in a few minutes."

"Good idea," Sheriff Walton says. "The more volunteers out looking the better."

My legs feel wobbly as we trudge through the sand to the last cabin. "This seems like a nightmare, doesn't it?"

"Worse. It's really happening. I'm scared, Joel."

"Me too."

"I can't believe Stephanie and Johnny chose to stay with Swagger."

"They looked like they were brainwashed."

Holly stops and turns toward me. "You're right. They weren't in their right minds. I pray to God they snap out of it. And poor Elsa, I pray to God we can find her." She closes her eyes. "Joel, could you say a prayer."

The request throws me off guard. The last prayer I said out loud with someone listening was 'Now I lay me down to sleep.' When I was a kid I prayed a lot, but I've drifted from my spiritual roots since heading off to college. Oh well. If I ever I needed some help from above, now's the time. I face Holly, take her other hand, and bow my head. "Lord, you haven't heard from me in a while, but we're in trouble here. Our friends have gone off the deep end joining that crazy cult. Shake them up so they come to their senses. Please get them away from Reverend Swagger and out of there."

"Yes, Lord," Holly says. "Rescue them from that weird bunch of wackos." After a few moments of silence, she says, "Go on, Joel, you're doing good."

"And Lord, we're really worried about Elsa. With all that's happened, we fear for her life. Help us to find her. Give us a clue or a sign or something. May we find her safe and sound. Amen."

"Amen. " Holly draws closer and gives me a quick kiss on the lips. "Thanks for praying."

"You're welcome." It felt more like a holy kiss than a passionate kiss. That's okay. It felt right. This girl is definitely different. We've gone from parallel-body parking to prayer partners in less than twenty-four hours.

She grasps my hand and leads me toward the cabin. "Let's go. Mom always says that God answers our prayers when we get off our butts and get to it."

As we near the cabin, I can hear Don and Lisa's voices coming from our side of the duplex. Lisa must have dropped over to join Don for breakfast. I think we had half a box of cereal left. We enter the door. Sitting at the kitchen table, they both look up at us, mouths chomping away like a couple of goats.

"Breakfast of champions," Don garbles through a mouthful of Wheaties.

Lisa swallows and wipes her mouth with the back of her hand. "Where have you two been?"

"You're not going to believe what happened," Holly says.

Lisa closes her eyes and hangs her head. "Please tell me it's not more abominable news."

Abominable? Crimenetly. "It's worse than bad news," I say.

Don sits straight up. "How could it get worse? Two of our friends joined a cult, and a tropical storm is closing in on us."

"Believe me, it's much worse." I quickly cover the basic details of this morning's happenings—the murders, Elsa's disappearance, Swagger's hold over Johnny and Stephanie.

Lisa places her hands flat on the table and rises from her chair. "We've got to get off of this island."

"You've got that right," Don says. "A ferry should get here about three this afternoon. I say we set sail for home even if Johnny and Stephanie refuse to come with us."

"What about Elsa?" Holly says.

"We can help hunt until the ferry gets here," Lisa says.

"For sure," Don says. "Who knows? We might find her in the next hour or two."

"Let's hope so." I'm disappointed that they seem more concerned about themselves than Elsa, but I keep my mouth shut.

Holly thumbs over her shoulder toward the door. "Sheriff Walton is organizing a search party right now. Let's head over there. We've got lots of ground to cover."

***

We head back to the Walton cabin. As soon as we get there, Sheriff Walton takes a headcount.

"We've got eleven people counting my two kids. We're definitely shorthanded. Somehow we've got to cover a thirteen mile island as thoroughly as possible. Sheriff Benson and his crew will get here soon, but they'll be busy with the investigation. Maybe we can recruit some of the fishermen in the third cabin, the one next to the church cabins. However, those good ol' boys may have plans to get off the island sooner than later. I've been keeping track of the storm. The worst of it is predicted to hit here by sunset. We're on the fringe now. Expect the winds to pick up and some drizzle. Hopefully, the hard rain will hold off until this evening."

"We can help for a few hours," Don says, "but our ferry is supposed to arrive about three this afternoon."

"I understand." Sheriff Walton says. "We appreciate any help you can give us. Hopefully, we'll find Elsa in the next couple of hours."

Jonah Newland places his hand on his heart. "May the good Lord be with us."

I pat his back. "I don't plan on leaving until we find her."

"Me too," Holly says.

"I appreciate that."

"Listen." Sheriff Walton glances around the circle of faces. "Swagger is a real snake. He made up a story about having a vision of Elsa in danger somewhere on the island. Of course, he's not willing to share the vision unless Jonah hands over the treasure. It's a ploy. The guy is a convicted conman. He knows how to manipulate people. If Jonah would give him the gold, he'd give some nebulous description of his so-called vision, and then he'd take the treasure and run with it. The law wouldn't be able to do anything about it. I've advised Jonah not to go in that direction."

"Wait a minute," Mee Mee says. "There is another angle to consider. Let's say Swagger sent a couple of his disciples out to murder Porter and Graham. After they do the dirty deeds, they see Elsa walking along the beach. They don't want any witnesses, so they decide to grab her. Now Swagger has a plan B to get his hands on the gold."

Russell Goodwin tilts his head. "That is a possibility."

Marla Walton steps forward. "If that's the case, then Swagger may know where she is. Maybe they took her back to one of the church cabins."

"That'll be my first stop." Sheriff Walton pats the handgun holstered at his side. "Good ol' Gladys can open doors that are hard to open. I'll check both cabins thoroughly."

Mary shakes her head. "I doubt they took her back to the church cabins. Most of the church members are sincere believers. They may be naive when it comes to trusting Swagger but sincere about their faith. They wouldn't go along with an obvious kidnapping."

Sheriff Walton nods. "You're probably right. Elsa is either lost on the island or tucked away somewhere— Swagger's ace up his sleeve."

"Then maybe I should give him the gold," Jonah says. "If he knows, that may be our only hope."

"That's up to you," Sheriff Walton says. "But there's another possibility no one has mentioned. I didn't want to bring it up."

"Well, tell me!" Jonah's eyes widen.

"These men are murderers. They may have killed your granddaughter and buried her body out in the marsh somewhere. She may never be found."

Jonah's whole body trembles. "Why'd you have to say that?"

"I didn't want to say it, but it's a possibility. I recommend you don't hand over the chests until it's absolutely necessary."

Jonah swallows and steadies himself. "That makes sense." He glances from face to face. "Well, we're wasting time standing around talking about it. Let's go find Elsa."

Chapter 26

Heading up the beach, we rumble along on our ATVs through the misty half-drizzle toward the north end of the island. What a difference a couple of days make. The first time we drove up here everything was new and exciting. Johnny and Stephanie were with us. The sun shone down from a brilliant blue sky, and Elsa was safe. Come to think of it, Jonah was hunting for her that day. She was hanging out at the abandoned village in the Methodist church. I remember walking into that church and seeing her kneeling at the altar. Wouldn't that be incredible if we walked in there today and found her?

Sheriff Walton divided the island into four sections and assigned us the northern end. That's fine. Chances are she didn't make it this far, ten miles from her camp, but you never know. We'll do our best to look through every building and search the marshes, trails, and shoreline.

This dreary day doesn't help to raise my hopes. Holly keeps telling me that God's hand of protection is on Elsa, and we need to have faith. Crimenetly. I wish I had an ounce of Holly's faith. She's hanging on to me tightly as we ride along. Her nearness makes me feel like a different person, more than just a stressed-out college kid. I feel manlier, I guess. More complete. I don't know if it's love, the warmth of her body, or hormones, but I don't want this feeling to end. Sheesh, I need to snap out of it. Come on, Romeo. Focus on the task at hand.

Up ahead to the left I see the trail that leads to the abandoned village. I turn the ATV off the firm wet surface and cross over the softer, bumpier sand toward the path. Glancing over my shoulder, I check on Don and Lisa. They're not far behind. Good. I'll slow down as we travel along the trail to the village just in case we get lucky and spot Elsa. When we get to the old lifesaving station, we can stop and formulate a search plan.

I keep my head on a swivel, panning just above the sea grasses and live oaks but see no signs of Elsa. The wind has picked up to maybe twenty miles an hour, making the grass and trees ripple and undulate like a turbulent green and yellow sea. After five minutes of plodding along, we arrive at the lifesaving station. The building appears much more sinister today with roiling gray clouds above its dark-gray-shingled gables and blood-red trim. We slide to a stop on the side of the building in front of the garage doors. I cut the engine on the ATV, and Don follows suit.

"I doubt if she walked all the way up to this end of the island," Don says. "That's a good ten miles."

"We don't know exactly what happened," I say. "If Swagger's men chased her, she may have gotten away. Who knows? She could be hiding out up here somewhere."

Lisa steps off the back of the ATV. "There's another possibility to consider. If they did catch her, what would they do with her? We know she's not at the church cabins. Sheriff Walton made sure of that before we left. My guess is they would tie her up, gag her, and stash her away in one of these abandoned buildings. There's got to be thirty or forty of them. Are we going to check every nook and cranny of every house and edifice on this end of the island?"

Holly nods. "We have to."

Don throws up his hands. "That'll take forever!"

"Listen to me," Lisa says. "With that big storm hitting this evening, all of us need to be on that three o'clock ferry. These storms are incredibly dangerous. I'm not kidding."

I throw my leg over the front of the ATV and step off. "I'm not leaving if we don't find Elsa."

Holly climbs off the vehicle and stands next to me. "Me either."

"Hell's bells," Lisa says. "You two are crazy. Absolutely insane."

Don says, "Well, we're leaving no matter what you two do."

"That's fine," I say. "Just help us hunt for the next couple of hours until you have to leave."

Holly holds out her hands pleadingly. "We're wasting time arguing about it. Let's get going."

We decide to split up. Holly and I head up to the lookout room of the lifesaving station. Don and Lisa start checking the lower rooms. The hallways and staircases seem long and foreboding.

On the way up the final staircase, Holly shouts, "Elsa! Can you hear me?"

No response, only the whine of the wind through cracks in the old building.

It's obvious no one is in the small upper room. We gaze out windows on the side facing the village. If ever the place looked like a ghost island, it's now. Mist shrouds the ten or so structures scattered across the expanse below us. A few hundred yards away the church steeple rises from the mist like a strange obelisk out of a cloud.

I glance at Holly. "Man, it looks spooky out there."

"Like a weird dream."

"Yeah."

She takes my hand, and we head back down the stairs. We spend about fifteen minutes helping Don and Lisa check through all the rooms and closets. Nothing. We exit the building through the garage doors and cross over to the stable where the rescue horses were once kept. The place is empty, just like the hollow feeling growing inside me. As we head out the doors, I try to have faith. *God, I don't pray that often anymore, but we need your help. Somehow show us the way. Give us some kind of sign.*

Staring across the field at the village, Lisa says, "Don and I will take the buildings on the right, you two take the ones on the left. We'll meet at the church on the other side."

"That's as good a plan as any," I say.

I climb onto the ATV, and I start the engine. Holly jumps on and wraps her arms around me. I feel better already. Is my faith growing, or has Cupid thumped me with a sledge hammer? Clearly, I'm turning into a love-sick fool.

One by one we go through the buildings. Some of them are locked, so we look through the windows and check for signs of forced entry. Nothing suspicious. Most of them are old residences, the bygone houses of fishermen, storeowners, school teachers, and post masters. The houses that are open to the public are nothing fancy, a few rooms with small closets. The Portsmouth Island people definitely lived a simple life.

On the far left side of the village we see a sign designating a building as the schoolhouse. It's definitely of the one-room variety with white wooden siding, black shutters, and a hipped roof. A white water-storage tank, like a mini silo, sits close to the right side of the structure. We scramble up the three steps and take a quick look inside. I feel like I just walked into a scene from Little House on the Prairie. A dozen or so old fashioned desks take up most of the room with the teacher's big wooden desk up front. Old slate chalkboards cover the walls with alphabet cards tacked to the wall above.

Holly glances around the room and takes a deep breath. "Do you feel what I feel?"

Uh oh. Are we talking a confession of love here? I doubt it. My eyes drift around the room from the pint-sized desks and chairs to the bookshelves filled with dusty old dictionaries, encyclopedias and readers. "Feels like we've gone back in time."

She nods. "But it's more than that. I sense the spirits of children gathered here for the school day."

I didn't quite feel that. "Most of the kids who sat in these desks are long gone."

"Yes. That's what I mean. They all grew up and left or passed away here on this island, but the ghosts of their childhood remains—the laughter, the learning, the innocence. I feel it. Elsa is still a kid. I wonder if they know where she is."

I'm not sure what to say. I don't see any ghosts.

Holly eyes the desks and nods slowly. A weird chill runs down my back. She shifts her gaze to me. "We need to get over to the church."

Whoa. Did she just hear from the spirit realm? "Alright. Lisa and Don are probably waiting for us there."

We head out the door and mount the ATV. The wind is gusting harder, maybe 25 or 30 miles an hour, and the half-drizzle has turned into a full drizzle. It's definitely not cold out, but the wind blowing against our wet clothes and skin makes it hard not to shiver. It doesn't take long to get to the church. As we approach, I can see a blue ATV near the entrance. Don and Lisa must have gone inside to get out of the weather.

We slide to a stop in the wet grass near the corner of the church, and I cut the engine. It's a small white church with the bell tower front and center that also serves as the entrance and foyer. Three arched windows are spaced evenly on the side. The structure sits on brick supports about two feet off the ground. As we climb the steps, I notice an old wooden maintenance ladder half-slid under the building, almost hidden in the grass. We open the large front door and go inside. Don and Lisa are standing in the middle of the sanctuary. They stride up the aisle and join us in the entryway.

"We've looked through this building," Don says. "No one's here."

"Any signs at all at the other buildings?" I ask.

Lisa shakes her head. "Nothing."

"You guys have any luck?" Don asks.

"Nope." I wipe droplets of water from my face and glance around the small empty foyer.

Holly stamps her foot. "She's got to be here somewhere. Elsa! Can you hear me!"

We stand and listen. The wind blowing through the open door creates an eerie, low moan.

"I'm sorry," Lisa says, "but I don't think she walked all the way to this end of the island. Let's hope the others had better luck."

Don peers out the door "It's getting darker out there. What time is it?"

Lisa checks her watch. "It's almost one-thirty."

"We've got to head back," Don says. "Our ferry is supposed to get here at three. I haven't packed yet. That storm may move in quicker than expected."

"You might be right," I say, "but like I said before, I'm not leaving until we find Elsa."

Holly grips my arm. "I'm staying too."

Lisa leans her tall body toward us, eyes wide, the bill of her red ball cap shadowing her face. "Don't be foolish. Use your heads. You are putting yourselves at great risk by staying on this island. Those cabins aren't that sturdy."

My eyes focus on the floor. Maybe she's right. I take a deep breath. Should we go with them?

"Some risks are worth taking," Holly says. "We're not asking you two to stay. You don't understand. We are persuaded by circumstances you don't know about."

Okay. I guess that answers my question.

"What! What are you talking about?" Lisa says.

Holly holds up her hand. "Please. I can't say anything now, but I'll explain it when we get back home."

Lisa straightens and crosses her arms. She looks taller than ever. "That's assuming you make it back. This is preposterous! I give up. We're taking my Jeep and leaving on that ferry. Come on, Don. We tried. Let's get going."

Don holds his hand out toward me. "I hope I see you again someday, buddy."

I shake his hand. "Don't be ridiculous. We'll be fine." I hope. I've always heard that falling in love clouds one's good judgment.

They hurry out the door, mount their ATV, and zoom away. I reach for the door and pull it closed to stop the chill of the wind.

Holly turns and embraces me. "I'm so proud of you. You give me courage."

Sheesh. I almost took off with Don and Lisa with my tail between my legs. "Thanks." I rub her back, relishing her warmth against me. "Well, we better keep looking. We still got a lot of ground to cover." Obviously, she doesn't know how erratic my courage can be.

Holly releases me, walks into the sanctuary, and glances around the room. There's no place to hide. A red aisle runner separates two rows of eight wooden pews. An altar rail stretches across the front of the church. Behind the rail stands the pulpit in the middle covered by a red parament. To the left sits an old piano and to the right an old organ. One big room. No closets or cubbyholes.

Holly clasps her hands to her face. "I don't understand." She lowers her hands. "Back at the schoolhouse I felt such a strong sensation that she would be here."

"Maybe she was here." I put my hand on Holly's shoulder. "Maybe she's nearby."

"Do you hear that?" She turns quickly and faces me. "It's a high pitched sound."

I listen. The wind whistles through the crevices of the old structure. "I can't hear anything but the wind."

She nods and takes my hand. "You're right. Come on. We've got a lot more ground to cover."

We head toward the door, but in the foyer Holly stops and grips my arm. "There it is again."

I tilt my head and listen. Nothing but the moaning of the wind.

"Sounds like the church is crying," she says.

"It's probably lonely. It's been a long time since people worshiped here."

A tear trickles down her face. "It makes me cry, too."

I bend and kiss the tear track on her cheek. I want to tell I love her, but instead I say, "We got to keep the faith."

She nods. "Let's go."

Chapter 27

We spend the next couple of hours checking through the remaining buildings on the north end of the island. No luck. We head over to the sound side and ride along the trails through the marshes. A light rain falls, saturating the sandy paths and creating a multitude of muddy-brown puddles. We're both soaked to the bone. I bring the ATV to a stop atop a sand hill and check my watch—3:35. I can feel Holly shivering as she hangs on to me.

"What do you think?" I swivel my head, scanning the dreary scene—dark skies, the whipping wind rustling the trees and grasses, the choppy sound waters fading into a misty fog as they stretch toward the North Carolina mainland.

Holly releases her hold on me and straightens up. "I don't know. We've looked everywhere."

"I say we head back. Maybe someone found her. Maybe she showed up at her grandfather's camp."

"Maybe. I pray to God you're right." She re-clamps her arms around me and plants the side of her head against my back. "Let's head back."

The drive to the cabin along the seashore seems like a bad dream. The falling rain stings my face, and the wind blasts us like a high powered fan. The gray clouds turn almost black above the ocean. I can see lightning strikes maybe twenty miles out but can't hear the thunder because of the ATV motor. We don't say much. We're wet, cold, tired, and hungry. I hope the heart of the storm stays out at sea longer than anticipated. The outer bands are bad enough. Maybe it will turn and won't hit us as hard as expected. Yeah, right. Not the way our luck is going.

I bring the ATV to a stop in front of the Walton cabin. I'm guessing we're the last ones to arrive. Sheriff Walton assigned the job of guarding the gold to his wife. Hopefully, the cult didn't make a raid while we were hunting for Elsa. We climb the steps to the porch, and I knock. Mee Mee Roberts opens the door, and we step inside. It feels good to be out of the weather, but the relief doesn't last long. Everyone stares at us, waiting for a report. By their discouraged expressions I can tell they didn't have much luck either.

I shake my head. "We didn't find her. Not a sign. I'm sorry."

Mee Mee pats my shoulder. "We were worried about you two. You were out there a long time."

"We gave it our best." Holly sniffles and wipes her face with her sleeve.

"We all gave it our best," Sheriff Walton says. "We need to figure out what to do next."

Jonah, sitting on the bed next to the chests, hangs his head and rakes his fingers through his long gray hair. "I saw Swagger's people carrying their belongings over to the dock. Their boat will get here soon." He raises his head and gazes in our direction. "He knows where she is. I know his vision is a bunch of bullcrap. They kidnapped her and hid her away somewhere on the island. But what else can we do? We're out of time. There's no other choice. I have to hand the treasure over to Swagger."

Sheriff Walton shrugs. "It's your decision, Jonah. There's no guarantees with a man like Swagger. He cast his vision out to us like bait on a hook. If you want to hand over the gold, we'll stand with you. You never know. He may give us enough information to find her."

"It's not what I want to do; it's what I have to do. Whatever Swagger knows, whatever he is willing to tell us is my last hope."

Russell Goodwin rises from his seat at the kitchen table. "I could call the Coast Guard. I'll tell them there's a legal question concerning the ownership of the gold. When their boat lands on the North Carolina mainland, the authorities will detain Swagger and hold the treasure until the legalities are sorted out."

Jonah raises his eyebrows. "I'd be okay with that." He stands. "I'm going to go talk to Swagger. I'll be back in a few minutes. I want to thank all of you for your help. In hard times like these, you can count on your good friends." He stares at the treasure chests. "There may be gold in these old cedar boxes, but you people are truly golden." He heads out the door.

Marla Walton hands Holly and me each a towel. "You two need to dry off and get something to eat. I've got some chicken noodle soup heating up on the stove."

Holly rubs the towel briskly over her head, scouring the moisture from her hair. "That sounds good to me. I need something to warm me up."

I wipe off my arms and face. "It was frustrating out there. We looked everywhere but didn't find a clue—no footprints, no pieces of clothing, nothing."

"The weather didn't help," Sheriff Walton says. "The rain deteriorated any footprints."

Mee Mee wrings her hands. "It's impossible to cover every inch of this island in a few hours with a limited number of people. Let's hope Swagger tells us something to narrow our search."

"Don't count on it," Sheriff Walton says. "Two men are dead, possibly murdered. If Elsa is still alive, she may know something. Why would he risk handing over a witness? He may do just the opposite and try to misdirect us."

Mary, standing in the shadows against the wall by the farthest bunk, steps forward into the light. "One thing to consider is that Swagger did have a religious conversion. It was a warped one for sure, but he truly believes God called him to begin a New Kingdom. He reminds me of the T.V. evangelists who send out prayer cloths to get donations. He'll justify anything to bankroll his mission. He may have authorized the hits on Quentin and Jack because he believed they opposed God's will, but I doubt if he ordered the murder of an innocent girl."

Holly drops her towel over the back of a chair. "At the digging site Swagger called her a prophet. He said God sent the vision of the gold through her. I believe that's true. She is a prophet."

"That makes a sticky situation for him," Mee Mee says. "Through this young prophet he can secure the funds he needs to accomplish his mission, but then she becomes a big problem. What do you do with a prophet of God who may testify against you?"

"Perhaps you put her in God's hands," Mary says.

"What do you mean by that?" Sheriff Walton asks.

"You put her some place only God knows. If she is found, then God willed it. If she dies, then again, God willed it."

"That's how Jesus died." Holly glances from face to face. "The religious leaders demanded his death, and God willed it. He didn't deserve it, but it was God's will."

Wow. That girl is deep, but it makes sense. I'm no Bible expert, but I made it through a Presbyterian communicant's class. That's exactly what happened. God worked through the schemes of corrupted men to accomplish a higher purpose.

"If that's the case," Mee Mee says, "let's hope for a resurrection."

Chapter 28

Jonah pushes open the door and tramps into the Walton cabin. His hooded sweatshirt, soaked and heavy, hangs on his thin frame like a monk's robe. He takes a deep breath, blows it out, and frowns. "Their boat has arrived. In ten minutes, Swagger wants us to carry the chests over to the dock." The stark kitchen light above him rakes deep shadows across his wrinkled face. "What a wily bastard that sonovabitch is. He wants me to make a public declaration that I'm donating the treasure to the New Kingdom Church. Then, to make sure there's no doubt about my intensions, he insists we carry the chests onto the boat."

"Doesn't surprise me," Sheriff Walton says. "I'm guessing he'll have one of his disciples record the video on a cell phone. He's preparing a legal case."

Jonah shrugs. "If we don't do exactly what he says, he won't reveal his so-called vision. We're cornered."

Russell Goodwin clears his throat. "That'll make it tougher to sort things out in court, but don't give up hope. I called the Coast Guard while you were gone. They'll be waiting for him on the other side."

Mary glances out the back window toward the Core Sound. "It's a chess game to Swagger, and he always thinks two steps ahead."

The dock is only about a hundred yards from the cabin. We take a few minutes to figure out how to get the treasure from here to there. Each chest weighs nearly a hundred pounds. Sheriff Walton thinks loading up the truck and driving over won't be necessary. He and Russell Goodwin can each carry one. Holly and I volunteer to team up and haul the third one over. Jonah and Mee Mee agree to handle the fourth one. Marla Walton, of course, needs to stay at the cabin with her kids, but the boy, Gabriel, insists on coming.

Sheriff Walton tousles his son's dark brown hair. "You stay here with your mom and help keep your sister safe."

"Ahhh, Dad."

"I'm serious, Gabe. It's important there's a man here at the cabin. You never know what might happen."

Gabe nods slowly. "Okay, Dad. I'll help guard the cabin."

We pick up the chests, and Gabe holds the door open. A harsh wind greets us as we step out onto the porch. We carefully descend the steps into a steady rain. I glance out to sea where dark clouds blend into choppy waters. It doesn't look good. Russell Goodwin and Sheriff Walton lead the way around to the back of the cabin. The Long Point Cabin Camp Office is directly behind the Walton cabin. To my left I see Jack Graham's cabin, and the memory of finding his suspended corpse sends a sickening feeling into my gut. I glimpse an emergency vehicle and a sheriff's car on the sea-side of the cabin. They must be finishing up their investigation.

We climb a small sand hill and follow a trail toward the sound. From the top of the hill I can see the dock and a white boat, maybe forty-five feet long, hitched to it. Usually ferries moor up here, but this looks like a fishing vessel. A lot of people are standing on the dock and on the deck of the boat. It's one of those two-story jobbers with the helm on top and a passenger compartment below. I squint through the rain to read the name on the bow. Stenciled in black are the words: THE SEA WEASEL. As we draw closer, I spot Johnny and Stephanie standing on the dock next to Swagger. Disciple Clint and Disciple Tanner hand baggage up to the people standing on the boat's deck. The ranger who works in the camp office observes the bustling scene from near the ferry ramp.

We get to within a few yards of where Swagger is standing and lower the chests to the ground. I notice the ranger is watching us carefully. Did Swagger ask him to witness the exchange? Probably. A large bearded man dressed in a green rain jacket and pants stands front and center on the deck of the boat. He peers down at us, frowning, with his arms crossed. Captain Ahab I presume. The strong wind pelts the steady rain against us. It feels like a shower of pellets.

Swagger says, "Jonah Newland, a few minutes ago you told me you wanted to give a donation to the New Kingdom Church."

Jonah stands silently for what seems like an eternity. Finally, he says, "That's right. I'm giving the New Kingdom Church these four treasure chests that my daughter Elsa and I found on the island. Each chest is filled to the top with gold coins."

Swagger strokes his chin and nods. "That's quite a generous donation. In today's gold market that would be worth well over six million dollars."

Jonah crosses his arms. "Men with dollar signs for eyes sure know the price of gold."

Swagger knots his brow. "Are you sure you want to give this amount of money to our ministry?"

"I'm sure," Jonah says.

Swagger's facial muscles relax. "We thank you for your

generosity. May God bless you and pour out his abundance upon you. Could you please carry the chests and place them on the boat?" Swagger smiles like a poker player who just bluffed his way to a winning hand.

Sheriff Walton and Russell Goodwin pick up their chests and haul them across the dock over to the boat. They have to lift the cedar boxes chest high in order to place them onto the deck. The vessel rocks unsteadily in the choppy sound waters as several of the disciples reach down and slide the chests farther from the edge.

Mee Mee and Jonah go next. Jonah struggles to lift his end high enough to set the chest on the deck. The disciples quickly pull the chest away from him, but his hand locks onto the top corner until they yank hard enough to break it free.

As Holly and I carry our chest across the dock, I feel totally humiliated. Not only did Swagger get the gold but also the satisfaction of watching his opposition do the labor. Crimenetly. What a reversal he pulled on us. We lift the chest and heave it onto the boat with a thud. I rub my hands against my wet sweatshirt as we stride back to where the others are standing.

Swagger clears his throat.

We turn and face him. I'm guessing it's vision revelation time.

Swagger raises his hands like a prophet from the Old Testament. He's wearing a long gray hooded poncho and dark blue jeans. The rain splashes off the plastic surface of the poncho like mini eruptions. "My prayers are with you, Jonah Newland, because I know your granddaughter is still missing, lost somewhere on this island. Early this morning before the sun came up, I had a dream, a vision of your granddaughter Elsa. She was walking along the beach, but then she turned and headed over the dunes to a marshy region nearer the sound. I sensed danger. She was looking for the fifth treasure chest—the smaller one she spoke about the night of the bonfire. I saw her feet sinking slightly into this soggy terrain, but she kept going, driven by her obsession to find that chest."

My heart thumps like bongos against my ribcage. What a lie! I picture the fifth chest under my bunk back at the cabin. Should I interrupt and call him out? I promised Elsa not to say anything. What good would it do anyway?

Swagger lowers his hands. "She decided to cross what looked to be a shallow pond to get to a sandy area on the other side. She thought the chest was buried there. Halfway across the pond she began to sink in the mud. She screamed. That's when I woke from my dream."

"That's it?" Jonah says.

"That was my vision."

Jonah's hands form fists. "That gives us almost nothing to go on. There's thirteen miles of marshes out there."

Swagger spreads his arms. "I told you I'd share my vision of your granddaughter with you. I saw her sinking in the mud. Your time left to find her may be running out. There's nothing more I can do." He turns and points to the boat. "Disciples, hurry! Climb the ladder onto the boat. The eye of the storm is approaching. We need to cross over before it hits. The end is near, and the New Kingdom is about to begin."

"Stephanie! Johnny!" Holly yells. "Don't go with them!"

The remaining disciples on the dock stop in their tracks, turn, and stare in our direction.

I holler, "Can't you see he's a liar and a fraud! I know that for a fact. We already found that smaller chest. Elsa gave it to me to hide. He's a false prophet!"

"He lying!" Swagger yells. "They'll say anything to get you to turn back like a dog returning to its vomit."

"It's true!" Holly hollers. "I was there!"

Stephanie grabs Johnny's arm. "Come on. Let's go back with Holly and Joel." They turn to cross the dock toward us.

Swagger steps in front of them. "Get on the boat!"

A gunshot explodes in my ears.

Chapter 29

Sheriff Walton points his gun into the sky, the barrel smoking. "Get out of the way, Swagger, and let those two college kids go!"

Swagger turns and faces the sheriff. "You don't understand. God has granted them the privilege of rising again with us after the Apocalypse. They can't return to this doomed world. They will bear children for the New Kingdom."

Sheriff Walton lowers the gun and aims at Swagger's chest. "Step out of the way, or you'll see the kingdom come sooner than expected."

Swagger frowns. "You and your violence. This is why the world as we know it will end soon."

"You've got three seconds."

Swagger glances at Disciple Clint and then at Disciple Tanner, hesitates, but then steps aside. Stephanie and Johnny, carrying their baggage, hurry across the dock and up the slope to where we are standing. Stephanie, bawling like a lost kid, drops her suitcase and embraces Holly.

Swagger motions toward the boat's ladder. "Get on board!"

Disciple Tanner climbs the few rungs to the deck followed by Disciple Clint. The boat's motor rumbles and roars to life. Swagger reaches for the top rung on the ladder.

Russell Goodwin yells, "Don't think you're going to get too far with that gold! There're legal questions that need to be answered!"

Swagger lets go of the ladder, wheels around and faces us. He looks like he wants to say something but can't come up with the right words. Instead, he turns and gazes across the Core Sound to the North Carolina shoreline.

Disciple Clint extends his hand to him. "Reverend Swagger, we need to get going. Let me help you up."

Swagger stares across the sound for a few more seconds, pivots, grasps Clint's hand, and climbs onto the boat. He edges across the gunwale, climbs the ladder, and enters the upper compartment where the captain sits at the helm. Bending, Swagger says something to the bearded man. They seem to be having an intense discussion. After several minutes, the boat slowly backs away from the dock into the choppy sound waters.

"Look at that," Sheriff Walton says. "They're backing away to the right. That's not the shortest route to the mainland. What are they doing?"

Russell Goodwin grunts. "They're heading south toward the inlet. The storm's approaching from the south."

"Maybe you scared him," Sheriff Walton says.

Goodwin grimaces. "I should have kept my mouth shut."

Sheriff Walton stares at the boat. "He might be heading down to Cedar Island or across the Core Sound to Whortonsville."

"I'll notify the Coast Guard about those possibilities. He'd be crazy to head out to sea into the teeth of the storm."

"Gold makes you do crazy things," Jonah Newland says.

"What are we going to do about Elsa?" Holly asks.

Jonah points northward in the direction of our cabin. "I'm heading up the island to look in the marshes. I know Swagger's vision is bullcrap, but I've got to try to find her."

"We'll help," Mee Mee says. "Even with this storm bearing down, we've got a couple hours of daylight left."

"There's a lot of marshy areas and ponds on this island," Sheriff Walton says. "We better divide it up like we did this morning."

Holly steps forward. "We'll take the north end again." She turns to me and speaks lowly, "I can't shake that feeling I had at the church. We've got to go back there and look again."

"We're coming with you," Stephanie says.

Johnny nods. "Yeah, we wanna help."

"Well, time's a wasting." I start to jog toward our cabin. "Let's go get the ATVs!"

Chapter 30

I feel reenergized and run at a good pace to our cabin. When I get there, I stop and catch my breath, trying to clear my mind. I have my doubts that Elsa sunk into some pond out in the marshes. They must have hid her somewhere or did something worse. I hate to think about that possibility. Looking in the church again may be a waste of time. There're only two rooms—the entry way and the sanctuary. Obviously, she wasn't there when we looked the first time.

Johnny pulls up beside me, breathing hard, lugging a big gym bag. "Hey, what happened to the other ATV?"

"Don took it back on the three o'clock ferry. He and Lisa wanted to get out of here before the storm hit."

Holly and Stephanie stride up to us.

"What're we gonna do if we find her?" Johnny says.

"What do you mean?" Holly asks.

Johnny points to the ATVs. "There're only two ATVs. It'll be hard to fit three people on one of them."

We stand in silence for a few seconds. Johnny's got a point. The northern end of the island is ten miles away. That'd be a long walk back in a storm.

Johnny taps Stephanie on the shoulder. "Steph, can you drive one of these?"

"Sure. My younger brother has one at home. I ride it all the time."

"Well," Johnny says, "Stephanie could go with you two. If you find Elsa, she can ride back with her. I'll help Jonah hunt wherever he decides to look."

"That'll work." I motion toward the cabin. "Better put your stuff away so we can get going."

They haul their gear up the steps and peel off in two directions, Stephanie toward the girl's side and Johnny toward the guy's.

Holly gazes at me. "I'm surprised Johnny wants to split up. Maybe their romance has cooled off."

I nod. "They've been through a lot these last couple of days. Who knows what went on in those church cabins?"

The sound of an engine catches my attention, and I shift my gaze down the beach where Jonah Newland's old pickup cuts through the slashing rain. I wave my hands and trot toward the shore to get him to stop. He hits the brakes and skids in the wet sand.

I approach the driver's side window. "Can you take Johnny with you? He wants to help hunt for Elsa, but we need room on the ATV in case we find her on the north end of the island."

"Sure thing. Where is he?"

I glance over my shoulder and glimpse Johnny coming out the cabin door. "Here he comes now."

Jonah pounds the steering wheel. "Damn that Reverend Swagger and his crew of creepy fanatics. If they did something to my granddaughter, I hope they all burn in hell."

"We can't give up hope, Jonah. Maybe Johnny knows something. He spent the last couple of days in the church cabin."

"I'll try to jiggle his memory. He might have overheard Tanner or Clint talking to Swagger. Maybe he didn't understand what they were talking about, but it could be a clue."

"I'm coming!" Johnny hollers. He runs across the beach to the other side of the truck, opens the door, hops in, slams the door and slaps the dashboard. "Let's get rolling!"

"God help us." Jonah hits the gas, and the pickup speeds away spewing sand.

I head back over to the cabin, and we get on the ATVs. The gas gauge reads low, so we make a quick trip over to the ranger's cabin and pull up next to the gas pump. The ranger steps out the door and gives me the thumbs up to fill the tanks.

After uncapping the tank, I insert the nozzle and glance up. "Can I ask you a question?"

He ambles in our direction. "Sure." The man looks like an old sailor with a white beard and yellow rain coat and rain hat.

"Did Reverend Swagger ask you to come over and witness the donation?"

"Yeah. He didn't' tell me what was going down, but he wanted me to be there. I thought that was strange. I just got off the phone with the National Park Service people. They claim that finders aren't keepers in this circumstance. They intend to contest the rightful ownership of the treasure."

"I hope they do." I hand the nozzle to Stephanie so she can fill her tank. "We think Swagger kidnapped Jonah's granddaughter to force his hand."

"Hmmmh. That's serious. Do you have any proof?"

I shake my head. "No, but we're going to keep looking for the girl."

"I'll take a walk around here and keep my eye out."

"We appreciate that," Holly says. "Come on, Joel, let's get going."

I open the small storage box on the back of the ATV where I put my wallet and cell phone to keep them dry. "It came to twenty even." I hand him the money.

"Thanks. You kids be careful out there. I hope you find her."

I glance up at the angry sky. "We'll give it our best. The weather's definitely not cooperating."

We speed northward along the shore, Holly and I leading the way. I glance over my shoulder and see Stephanie not far behind. She's not having any problem keeping up with us. The wind, probably thirty-five or forty mph, pelts the rain against us. The way Holly is hanging on to me, I feel like we've become one person.

She hollers in my ear, "Let's go directly to the village! I want to check out the church first thing!"

I know she's got this odd inkling, but that doesn't make sense to me. The lifesaving station has more rooms, closets, and cubbyholes. Maybe we missed something the first time we looked through it.

The storm has crept over us, flashes of lightning crackle like hell's fireworks above the ocean. It's not even six o'clock but it feels more like eight. I keep the throttle cranked and try to stay on the smoother part of the beach, but the ride is definitely bumpy.

We make it to the north end of the island in less than twenty minutes. I veer to the left across the beach to the trail that leads to the village. Huge puddles and small ponds have formed on the path. I throttle down the ATV but can't help making tremendous splashes as we plow through the water and ramble up slick sand hills.

I spot the lifesaving station just ahead. "I think we ought to stop and look here again."

"I don't know. I just have this strong feeling about the church."

I slow to a stop in front of the lifesaving station, and Stephanie pulls up beside us. We cut the engines, and I hear my ringtone. "My phone's in the storage box behind you."

Holly reaches back, unclasps the box, pulls out the phone and hands it to me.

I can see by the caller I.D. it's Johnny. "What's up?"

"Jonah wanted me to call you. I remembered something."

"Okay."

"I overheard Clint telling Swagger something about a white church this morning. I didn't think much about it. Church is a common word when you're in a religious group, but I'm almost sure he said 'white church.'"

"That could be important. Thanks for letting us know." I end the call. "That's odd."

"What did he say?" Stephanie asks.

"Johnny said Clint mentioned the white church to Swagger this morning."

Holly slaps me on the back. "Let's not waste time here. Drive to the church!"

I start the engine and peel out toward the other side of the village. The wind and slicing rain has dispelled the mist, but the darkening clouds make the setting look like a scene from an old Dracula movie. The few scattered houses and stores cower in the gloom, their murky shapes blurred by the downpour. At the end of the village, the church steeple towers into a malicious, swirling sky. We skid to a stop in front of the church steps.

Just as Stephanie pulls up beside us, lightning strikes over the Pamlico Sound. "It's not safe out here."

Holly climbs off the back. "It's only going to get worse. The storm is just cranking up. Let's get inside the church."

Stephanie and I climb off the ATVs and trail Holly up the steps and into the foyer. We stand there for a few seconds. Rivulets of water run down our clothing and puddle on the wooden floor. I reach for the knob and close the door. The sound of the wind quiets to an eerie moan that climbs the scale and lowers again like a ghost playing an old pipe organ.

Holly marches into of the sanctuary and stands in the middle of the aisle. Slowly she pans the entire room.

I wipe droplets from my face. "I hate to say it, Holly, but there's no place to hide in here."

Holly cups her hands to her mouth. "Elsa! Elsa!"

"Maybe there's a secret hatch somewhere on the floor." Stephanie points to the pulpit. "There's a stage up front raised up a foot or so. Let's look up there."

I follow Stephanie to the front of the church. A brown wooden railing stretches across the stage with two entry gaps, one on the right and one on the left. Stephanie cuts to the left, and I veer to the right and take the two steps onto the stage. An old organ sits to my right, and a bookshelf stands against the back wall in the corner. I don't see any hatches on the floor. Another little stage, maybe six inches high and about ten feet wide rises directly behind the pulpit. In the middle of the back wall hangs a picture of Jesus, the one you always see in protestant churches—long brown hair and beard with a slight olive glow on his face. I stare at the picture and send up a quick prayer for help.

Stephanie says, "I don't see anything on this side. Any cut-outs on the floor over there?"

I glance down. I'm standing on a red rug, maybe six feet long. I step to the side and pick it up. Nothing but a wooden floor underneath. "Nope."

"Shhhhhhhhhh!" Holly tilts her head. "I hear something."

I listen, but it's the same sound I heard before. "That's the wind, Holly. It's a louder than before because the storm is on top of us."

Holly shakes her head. "It's not the wind. It's an odd, high-pitched sound. Elsa! Elsa!"

Man, she's got good ears. I don't hear it.

Stephanie cups her ear and listens. "Are you sure?"

Holly nods, turns, and points toward the door. "It's out there."

I make an about-face. "Outside?"

Holly leads the way out of the sanctuary through the arched entryway and into the foyer.

"What's up there?" Holly points to the corner of the ceiling.

A rope snakes through a small hole and then loops back up to a hook.

"That's how they ring the bell," Stephanie says. "We have something rigged up like that back at our church in Harmony Grove."

"That's gotta be the access hatch to the bell tower," Holly says. "We've gotta look up in there."

I focus and see the thin line of the hatch cutout.

"How're we gonna reach it?" Stephanie glances around the foyer. "That's got to be twelve feet high. I don't see a ladder."

Something clicks in my memory. "Wait a minute. I saw a ladder somewhere this morning."

Holly stiffens. "The sound is definitely coming from up there."

"Now I remember!" I walk to the door, grab the knob, and turn it. The wind blasts the door open, knocking me backwards. I manage to regain my balance and thrust forward, the wind blowing debris into the church. "I think there's a ladder in the churchyard!"

I ramble down the few steps and spot the old wooden ladder half-slid under the church. I tug it out and get a grip on the middle rungs. It's not heavy, maybe fifteen feet long. Perfect!

"You need some help?" Holly rushes out of the church and takes one end of the ladder.

I maneuver down to the other end, and we carry it into the foyer. Stephanie manages to push the door shut against the wind.

I wag my head toward the right corner. "Set your end down."

Holly lowers the ladder, and I raise my end up and prop it against the wall just below the hatch.

Stephanie points upward. "Use the end of the ladder to push open the hatch."

"Good idea. Get that end, Holly."

Holly lifts her end slightly and moves a couple steps backwards. I angle my end so it butts against the ceiling. We push upwards, and the hatch pops open. She moves her end forward, and the top of the ladder edges a foot or so into the opening. The movement makes the rope swing slightly from the hole in the hatch to where it hooks to the ceiling. The bell makes a gentle bong sound.

"There. Did you hear that?" Holly says.

"The bell?" I ask.

"No. The crying."

All I hear is the same moaning of the wind. "Hold the bottom of the ladder. I'll climb up."

At the top of the ladder the hatch is leaning, half slid off the opening. I push it up and off to the side on the floor above. Now I hear the sound—a high-pitched whine as if someone was struggling to cry but couldn't. I climb up into the darkness but can't see a thing.

"Do you need a flashlight?" Holly says. "I got my phone here."

"Yeah." I climb back down a few rungs, reach down, and take her phone. She already activated the flashlight app.

Back up the ladder I climb into bell tower. I thrust the phone into the darkness. The high-pitched whining gets louder. Not two feet away is what looks like a big brown and silver sack of potatoes. I reach and touch it. There's something solid but soft underneath. It moves slightly. "Elsa!"

The high pitched whining intensifies.

"Stay calm! We're gonna to get you out of here." I grab the end of the sack and tug it toward me. The first thing I notice is that the burlap bag is wrapped in silver duct tape making its contents look like a redneck mummy.

"Is she up there?" Holly yells.

"Yeah! It's gotta be her." I get a better grip, my hands grasping what seems to be her knees. Are her legs bent backwards? I pull her toward me.

"Be careful!" Holly says. "I can climb halfway up the ladder and help."

"That'll work." I glance down at Holly and Stephanie. "Steph, hold the ladder. Holly can help me bring her down."

Holly climbs a few rungs. Slowly, I slide the body through the opening down toward Holly. She grips the bottom. I can hear wheezing coming from my end of the taped-up sack. Elsa is tall but skinny. Knowing she doesn't weigh much more than a hundred pounds, I feel confident we can get her down without dropping her. Weird thing, though, the bag definitely doesn't match Elsa's height. Carefully, we descend the ladder one rung at a time. At the bottom, Stephanie helps us to lower the sack onto the floor.

"Quick," Holly says, "we gotta get her out of this thing."

The top of the sack has been cinched shut with duct tape. I find the end of the silver strip and peel it away, unwinding it several times until it breaks free.

Holly grabs the edge of the burlap and pulls down. It's Elsa, but she's taped up like a silver mummy. Black hair juts through the gaps in the tape on the back of her head. How could she breathe? Somehow she forced a little gap open just above her lips. I reach and gently tug the tape away a fraction of an inch more from her mouth to give her more room to breathe. She sucks in air like someone surfacing after crossing the pool underwater.

"Let's get this tape off of her," Stephanie says.

Holly drops to her knees. "Be careful. We don't want to tear her skin."

We work on the outside of the bag first, loosening all the tape so we can pull the sack completely off of her. Once we peel down the bag, I can see why the sack is much shorter than Elsa's height: Her legs are bent back at the knees and her arms taped behind her to her feet. Man, how could she stand that position for all these hours? She has to be in incredible pain.

I work feverishly on removing the tape around her hands and feet to give her some relief. Holly and Stephanie carefully peel off the tape from around her head. Once I get the hands and feet separated, I gently stretch her legs out.

Holly frees the tape from her mouth, and Elsa whimpers, haltingly catching her breath.

Stephanie pats her head. "You're gonna be okay. You're safe now."

Holly works on removing the tape across her eyes.

Elsa takes a deep breath and says, "I kept praying you'd find me. I didn't give up. Somehow I knew you would."

Holly peels away a strip across her forehead. "We're sorry we didn't find you sooner."

"I don't think I could have lasted another five minutes. I just couldn't breathe anymore."

A jolt goes through me. Johnny's phone call saved her. I wanted to search through the old lifesaving station again. That could have been a fatal mistake.

We take our time peeling away the rest of the tape. Elsa doesn't complain even though our efforts had to feel like a thousand Band-Aids being ripped away. Once we get most of the tape off, I help her sit up and stretch out her arms and legs.

"Where's my grandfather?" Elsa asks.

I slap the side of his head. "I forgot to call everybody to let them know we found you. They're all out in the middle of the marshes looking for you."

Elsa grabs my arm. "Hurry. Call them and tell them to meet us at your cabin."

A flash of lightning blazes the window next to us, and thunder instantly erupts like a bomb, causing the old church to vibrate.

"Jeesh!" Stephanie gasps.

The thunder continues to rumble and slowly fades away.

Holly crisscrosses her arms, grasps her shoulders, and shivers. "That gave me the oddest feeling."

Elsa peers up into the darkness of the bell tower. "That was the voice of God."

Chapter 31

Stephanie leads the way with Elsa riding on the back. As we turn off the trail and rumble southward along the beach, rain pours down in buckets, and waves crash violently against the shore. The wind howls like a hundred wolves, making it challenging to hang on at the speed were going. Crimenetly, I hope Elsa doesn't fall off the back. Lightning flashes all around us like cannon fire, followed immediately by explosions of thunder. It feels like we're in a war zone.

Holly holds on to me tightly with her head pressed against my back. Man, is it dark out here. Hopefully, everybody made it back to our cabin safely. For some reason Elsa wanted to meet there. When I called Johnny, he handed the phone to Jonah, and I told him we found his granddaughter. He cried like a baby. Now we need to get her back safely. I blink through the rain and gaze down the shoreline. We're still several miles away, but I keep looking for the cabin lights. Finding Elsa brought incredible relief, but I won't feel like the job is complete until were snug inside that cabin.

I keep thinking of that song, *Riders on the Storm*. That's us. Nothing is guaranteed. We're out here— exposed, vulnerable, at risk. The storm is oblivious, heartless, and merciless. It's coming through whether we like it or not. It doesn't care one way or another if we survive. But we keep riding, pushing through, doing our best to escape its mindless fury. Dear God, I hope we make it back in one piece.

Hallelujah! I see lights, maybe a mile ahead. We're only two minutes away. "We're almost there!"

Holly hugs me extra tight. "Thank God! I'm soaked to the bone and worn out like an old pair of Adidas."

I try to capture the essence of her arms around me. It feels so good. Reality will hit soon. Another day and we'll go our separate ways. Have we made a strong enough connection to pursue a long distance relationship? I guess time will tell.

Finally, we make it back. Stephanie steers the ATV toward the gap in the sand fences, and I follow. We park near the steps and cut the engines. Holly jumps off and rushes over to help Elsa climb off the back. I collect my phone and wallet from the back compartment. Elsa's legs and arms have got to be sore and stiff from being bound for all those hours. What a horrendous day! But Elsa's alive and well, and I'm incredibly thankful for that. I follow the girls up the steps and into the cabin. I squint as my eyes adjust to the stark light. As we enter, everyone cheers and smiles.

Jonah rises from a kitchen chair, and Elsa rushes into his arms. They embrace for what seems like minutes. Elsa sobs, and Jonah blinks several times causing tears to run down his cheeks. Mee Mee hands us each a towel. It feels so good to be inside. No rain soaking our clothes. No wind battering our bodies. No lightning flashing in our faces. I want to get out of these wet clothes and sit down. I'm sure the girls do too.

Mee Mee rushes over to my bunk and snatches up a beige cover. Holding it up, she walks over and wraps it around Elsa as the girl steps away from her grandfather. With the blanket covering her head like a hood, Elsa looks like a saint from the middle ages, a modern day Joan of

Arc. Mee Mee rubs Elsa's back and shoulders to generate some heat.

Holly and Stephanie stand there shivering.

I place my arm around Holly's shoulders. "I've got some extra t-shirts and sweatpants, if you gals want to change."

"That'd be great." Stephanie says. "Our stuff is right next door, but I'd rather stay here until the storm passes."

I head over to my bunk to where I keep my baggage against the wall. As I bend down to pick up my red nylon suitcase, I remember the fifth chest. Is it still under my bed? I drop to my knees, dip my head, and look. It's dark and hard to see. I reach under and move clothes out of the way. It's still there. I can feel the rough wood and metal. I move my hand over and grab the lock. Whew! Still intact. I straighten up and plop my suitcase on the bed, pull out some t-shirts and sweat pants, and hurry back to Holly and Stephanie.

"Here you go."

"Thanks, Joel." Stephanie grabs a long-sleeve t-shirt and sweat bottoms.

Holly points to the bathroom. "You can change first, Steph." Holly leans and kisses my cheek as she takes the clothes. "You're the best, Joel."

Mee Mee reaches and grips Elsa's shoulders. "Finding you in this storm was nothing short of a miracle. Are you feeling okay?"

She nods. "I'm wet, tired, and sore, but I think I'm okay."

Sheriff Walton pulls out a chair. "Let the girl sit down."

Elsa sits, wrapping the blanket tightly around her.

"Are you feeling well enough to answer some questions?" Russell Goodwin asks.

"Sure, but I just need something to eat."

I scour my mind and remember I stashed a candy bar in my suitcase. "Do you like Snickers?"

"Love 'em."

I rush over to my bunk and dig through the suitcase until I find the candy bar. My stomach rumbles. Man, I'm hungry too. There's got to be some corn chips or crackers up in the cupboard. I hurry back to Elsa and hand her the Snickers. She swipes it from my hand like an osprey snatching a fish, rips off the top half of the wrapper, and takes a big bite.

"Do you remember what happened this morning?" Goodwin asks.

Elsa munches the candy bar and swallows. "I got up very early before sunrise to go to Joel's cabin. He has something that belongs to me, and I wanted to pick it up and pack it away before we left."

"We heard about the other chest," Sheriff Walton says. "Joel mentioned it when we were at the dock talking to Swagger."

Elsa's mouth drops open, and she glares at me.

I spread my hands, palms up. "I had to tell them about it."

"You promised you wouldn't tell anyone!"

"I had no choice. Swagger said he had a vision that you went looking for that small chest this morning and had become stuck in a marsh. I had to prove he was lying so that Johnny and Stephanie would come to their senses and leave the cult."

"I'm glad he did," Johnny said.

Stephanie bobbles her head. "Me too."

Jonah pans the cabin. "Where is the small chest?"

"It's under my bed. I'll get it." I cross over to my bunk and bend down. After clearing away the clothing, I grasp the corners and carefully slide it out. It's not heavy, maybe twenty or twenty-five pounds. I carry it over to the circle of people and place it on the floor.

Mee Mee asks, "Didn't you say the contents of this chest could save the world?"

Elsa nods slowly, examining the cedar box. "Yes."

Jonah's eyes grow wide. "Let's open it."

"No!" Elsa shouts.

Everyone straightens, our eyes shifting around the circle of faces.

"This is not yours, Grandfather. And it's only mine to give away."

"Okay." Sheriff Walton raises his hands and then lowers them gently. "I'm sure your grandfather will respect your wishes. Let's get back to what happened this morning. Did you make it to Joel's cabin?"

Elsa wobbles her head. "I was walking along the shore. It was very misty and still dark except for a glimmer of light above the sea. Suddenly, I came upon two people standing near an ATV. They wore hooded sweatshirts making it hard to see their faces. I assumed they were Mr. Porter and Mr. Graham. We weren't far from Mr. Porter's cabin, and that's where he always sets up his fishing gear. Then I looked down and saw this dark shape at their feet—a body. When I noticed the prosthetic leg, I knew it was Mr. Porter. I asked what happened, and one of them said that they were taking their morning walk when they found him lying there."

"Did you recognize the man's voice?" Sheriff Walton asks.

"It sounded familiar, but I was too worked up to worry about who they were."

"What happened next?" Goodwin asks.

"I dropped to my knees to see if he was still alive. His hat was lying next to him, and his shirt was slightly wet but not soaked. I didn't think he drowned. I put my hand on his cheek. He still felt warm. I yelled his name and shook him, but he didn't respond. I thought maybe he had a heart attack. I tried to remember the steps to do CPR. We had a speaker in health class that taught us what to do. I knew I had to turn him over on his back.

"When I reached for his shoulder, everything went black. From behind, one of those men covered my face with a cloth and held it there. My head started to spin. That's the last thing I remember. When I came to, I couldn't move, or see, or hardly even breathe. Then I realized someone had wrapped my whole body up with something. I couldn't feel my arms or legs. I thought I was paralyzed. But I could still hear."

Goodwin clears his throat. "Sounds like Swagger's men used chloroform to knock you out. They probably did the same thing to Porter and Graham. Hopefully, the autopsy results will confirm traces of the drug."

Elsa's eyes narrow. "Mr. Graham too?"

Sheriff Walton nods. "We believe both men were murdered."

That made a lot of sense to me. "I spotted Porter's body tumbling in the waves this morning when I went for a walk. After they knocked Elsa out, they must have dragged Porter's body into the ocean to make it look like a drowning."

Sheriff Walton thumbs over his shoulder. "Then they carried Elsa back to the church cabin to see what Swagger wanted to do with her."

Goodwin says, "I noticed they have a side by side ROV they must have rented. That's how they transported her up to the village."

"Why'd they put Elsa in the bell tower?" Stephanie asks.

"Swagger's an odd man," Mee Mee says. "In my opinion he's delusional. He really believed God's will required the possibility of a sacrifice. He admitted that Elsa was God's prophet. In the Bible the lives of the prophets were often placed in jeopardy. Sometimes God rescued them. Sometimes they paid the ultimate price—death. The church bell tower seemed like the logical place to allow God's will to unfold."

Jonah scratches his beard. "I think I know what you mean. It's like the Abraham and Isaac story. Swagger believed God demanded that Elsa be sacrificed to benefit his church. Hiding her in that bell tower was the raising of the knife. If she died there, it was God's will—the knife plunged. If we found her, then God intervened. Either way, he felt justified."

Elsa wipes a tear from her cheek. "God did intervene. Poor Mr. Graham and Mr. Porter didn't have a chance. I feel terrible about what happened to them. They stood up for us."

Jonah grips Elsa's shoulder. "They were courageous men. I'll never forget what they did."

Elsa takes a deep breath. "I thought for sure I was going to die, too. When I woke up in that dark place, I heard voices below me. I tried to scream, but my mouth was taped over, and I could hardly get air into my lungs. All I could do was make a whistling noise through a small gap in the tape. It wasn't very loud."

"I heard that sound," Holly says. "That's when we came to the church the first time. We thought it was the wind, but it stuck with me. I couldn't get that sound out of my mind."

"I'm glad of that," Elsa says. "As the hours went by, it became harder and harder to breathe. But I kept praying and praying. I prayed that God would send somebody to find me. In the darkness, I kept seeing the church in my mind. I wondered why. Then it came to me—that's where they hid me, somewhere in that church. For hours I kept sending out this mental message: I'm at the church. I'm at the church. Finally, when I could barely take another breath, I heard someone yell my name: 'Elsa! Elsa!'"

Holly smiles. "That was me, too. I knew you there. I felt it deep inside."

"You were my angel sent from God."

Holly pans the circle of faces. "Instead of going to hunt for Elsa in the marshes, we went back to the church. I just knew we had to go back there. I heard the high-pitched sound again. This time, though, I knew it was coming from the bell tower. Joel found a ladder, and we managed to use it to move the panel on the ceiling. That's when Joel climbed up and found Elsa stuffed in a burlap sack and wrapped like a mummy with duct tape."

"We need to call the Coast Guard," Sheriff Walton says. "They'll want to know about the kidnapping. Hopefully, with kidnapping and murder charges we'll have enough evidence to retrieve Jonah's gold."

Russell Goodwin rubs his chin. "If they went back to the Carolina coast, the Coast Guard will be waiting."

"What if they went out to sea?" Jonah asks.

Russell Goodwin grunts. "In that fishing boat?" He thumbs toward the cabin door. "With that kind of storm at sea they better have one helluva skipper."

A loud clap of thunder vibrates the cabin. The lights flash off and on.

Jonah hunches his shoulders, glancing around the room. When the rumbles fade out, he drops to his knees and places his hands on the small chest. "At least Swagger didn't get his hands on this one."

"No, Grandfather!" Elsa shouts. "Don't touch it."

"I was just going to brush off some of the dirt."

"Please don't." Her eyes shift around the circle of faces. I know this sounds crazy, but I want to make a video right now."

Jonah's forehead furrows. "A video?"

"Yes. My cellphone is back at camp. Joel, can I borrow yours?"

I pull my phone out of my back pocket and hand it to her.

Elsa takes the phone and activates the video camera. "Let's hope this goes viral."

Chapter 32

Bright sunshine through the window assaults my eyes as I struggle to break out of a deep sleep. What time is it? I blink and squint, adjusting to the light, and check my watch—8:00 a.m. Crimenetly. I haven't slept in this late all week. The storm finally passed about midnight, and everyone went back to their cabins except for Holly and Stephanie. We stayed up until about two in the morning, talking about all that happened during the week. Then we conked out on the beds in our cabin. No funny business, though. Stephanie and Johnny's romance had cooled off in their time at the church cabins. Holly and I were too tired for any fooling around.

Johnny confessed that Swagger convinced them the world was about to end, and sinners were in big trouble. That poured a bucket of cold water on their raging hormones. As time passed, doubt spread like an afternoon shadow in both of their minds. My revelation of Swagger's faulty vision convinced them to break away. They didn't want to follow a false prophet but still worried about the possibility of an apocalypse. I can't blame them with all the news outlets reporting the maneuvers of President Stamp and Kim Jung Ill. We all fear we're on the brink of nuclear war.

I glance over my shoulder and see Holly, Stephanie, and Johnny sleeping in the other bunks. Stephanie starts to stir. Holly looks like an angel, facing me with her eyes closed, strands of blonde hair draped gently on her cheek and crossing her full lips. I hate to admit it, but I'm in love. Man, this is such a helpless feeling. Is it possible for a girl like Holly to be in love with me? I have my doubts. Maybe it's just my low self-esteem. Should I go all goofy and tell her I love her? I'd be taking a chance. I hope I don't end up blurting it out in a moment of weakness.

We need to get up and start packing. Hopefully, we can catch a ferry back to Ocracoke by ten o'clock. Don and Lisa took the Jeep Wrangler back to the mainland on the ferry yesterday. The car belonged to Lisa. By now they're probably back home in West Virginia. I'm guessing Don dropped her off in Morgantown and then headed north to Wheeling. They must have figured that Holly could ride with me. They'll be glad to know that Johnny and Stephanie are with us. My car is parked on Ocracoke Island. We'll take a ferry from Ocracoke back to Hatteras Island. From there we can drive north along the Outer Banks and cross the Wright Memorial Bridge at Kitty Hawk back to the mainland.

"Good morning," Stephanie says.

I smile. It feels good to smile. "It's a bright and beautiful morning."

Holly opens her eyes and stretches her arms above her head. "What a week. I'm ready to head home."

I agree on both counts. "It's a week I'll never forget."

Holly sits up on the bunk and stretches again, arching her back. "I wonder if Elsa and her grandfather left yet."

"They wanted to get out of here as soon as possible," I say. "Jonah mentioned scheduling a pre-dawn ferry. I'm guessing they're gone by now."

Holly's brow tenses. "Let's check to see if Elsa's video is getting any hits."

I stagger to my feet, shuffle over to the kitchen table, and pick up my cell phone. With a couple of taps, I browse to the YouTube homepage. There it is! "I can't believe this. Elsa's video is on the most popular list. It has more than two hundred thousand hits already. It's only been published for about twelve hours."

"I want to watch it again." Holly springs out of bed and darts to my side.

I click on the video title—*The Treasure of Portsmouth Island*. Elsa appears filming herself. "My name is Elsa Newland, and my grandfather and I recently found the *Treasure of Portsmouth* Island, more famously known as the *Lost Treasure of El Salvador*. The treasure consisted of four chests of gold weighing about a hundred pounds each and one smaller chest containing a mysterious object that some say has special powers."

Elsa zooms in on the smaller chest and then back to herself. "We haven't opened the small chest yet. I am hoping and praying that it will be opened in the presence of President Ronald Stamp and North Korean Leader Kim Jung Ill. You may be wondering what happened to the other four chests of gold. I am going to ask Sheriff Walton of Dare County, North Carolina, to explain what happened." She redirects the phone's camera to Sheriff Walton.

Walton blinks and smiles. "I didn't prepare for this speech, but I can at least tell you what I know. As Elsa said, she and her grandfather dug up the treasure. While they were digging, Noah Swagger, the pastor of the New Kingdom Church, and his followers arrived. They claimed that God led them to Portsmouth Island to find this treasure, and by divine providence it belonged to them. Two brave men, Quentin Porter and Jack Graham, stepped in and prevented Swagger and his followers from taking the treasure. The four chests of gold were then brought to my cabin and entrusted to my care until the Newlands were ready to leave the island. At that point, Elsa made a video confirming that she and her grandfather discovered the legendary treasure.

"The next morning we found the dead bodies of Quentin Porter and Jack Graham. We suspect they were murdered. But that's not all. We then discovered that Elsa was missing. Pastor Swagger claimed he had a vision of where Elsa could be found. However, he would not reveal his vision unless Jonah Newland donated the treasure to the New Kingdom Church. Because of the deaths, we figured Swagger kidnapped Elsa but couldn't prove anything. Noah turned over the four chests to Swagger. His vision, though, proved false. We did not find her where he said she would be found. Fortunately, we did find her last night. She had been kidnapped, taped up with duct tape, placed into a burlap sack, and hid in one of the abandoned buildings on the north end of the island."

Elsa turns the camera back on her. "I want to personally thank Joel, Holly, and Stephanie for finding me last evening. They saved my life." She points the camera at Holly, Stephanie, and me. We wave and smile at the camera.

She points the phone back at herself. "I am now going to ask Russell Goodwin, former special agent for the secret service, to verify all that's been said here, and, hopefully, make an appeal to our president to schedule a meeting with me and the North Korean Chairman." She focuses the camera on Goodwin.

"Well," he says, "my name is Russell Goodwin. As Elsa mentioned, I served as a body guard to three presidents during my time as a special agent for the Secret Service. Like Sheriff Walton said, this video is a spur of the moment thing, so I didn't prepare to make a speech. But I can confirm everything that's been said. The treasure is real. One of my hobbies is history, especially the history of the Outer Banks. Historically, these islands have been infamous for shipwrecks and pirates. For centuries, rumors have spread about great treasures buried on these islands. I was familiar with the legend of the *Lost Treasure of El Salvador*. Now I know it is no longer just a legend. I've seen it firsthand. Where it is right now, I do not know. Like Sheriff Walton explained, Reverend Swagger and his cult absconded with it.

"However, the smaller treasure chest is right here in front of me."

Elsa quickly flashes back to the small chest and then refocuses on Goodwin.

"Who knows what this smaller chest may contain. Some say it has healing powers. Elsa believes it could become an offering of peace to the world, perhaps a covenant of peace between the United States and North Korea. Therefore, I would urge President Stamp to consider arranging a meeting where this chest would be opened and negotiations begun. As John Lennon said, 'Let's give peace a chance.'"

Elsa turns the camera on herself again. "President Ronald Stamp, please listen to me. My grandfather and I will be leaving Portsmouth Island early tomorrow morning with the chest. We're heading directly for Washington D.C. We plan to arrive there by four in the afternoon. Through Mr. Goodwin's connections, I'm hoping my cell phone number will be forwarded to you. Call me, and we will work out the details of a peace negotiation between the United States and North Korea."

The video ends, and I refresh the page to see if the count has increased.

"That video is so powerful," Holly says.

"Look," I point to the screen on my phone. It has over three hundred thousand hits! That's another hundred thousand in the last ten minutes."

Chapter 33

Standing beside the two ATVs and our luggage, we wait at the dock, watching the ferry slowly edge toward the ramp. The sun blazes down from a cloudless azure sky, and the waters of the Core Sound ripple gently. It's just after ten o'clock, but the temperature has climbed into the eighties already. A half dozen or so seagulls flitter about on the bow of the ferry. They'd rather ride than fly, I guess. The ferries that drop off people and vehicles at Portsmouth Island are much smaller than the ones that cross back and forth between Ocracoke and Hatteras Island. The ferries from Ocracoke only haul ATVs for campers and daily tours of the island. This one's from Ocracoke, loaded with a bunch of ATVs and a tour group. It doesn't take long for them to unload. The tourists, dressed in shorts and colorful t-shirts, smile and chatter. They have no idea what happened here over the last few days.

Johnny and I drive the two ATVs across the ramp onto the ferry. Then we go back and help the girls lug the baggage. Sheriff Walton and his gang decided to stay another day to help with the investigation. With all they learned last night after questioning Elsa, they wanted to share notes with the Hyde County Sheriff's Department. Five more ATVs are driven onto the ferry. All of them will be returned to the rental place on Ocracoke. As the ferry backs away from the dock, we lean on the rear rail, gazing across the Core Sound at the North Carolina mainland.

"It seems like a dream, doesn't it?" Holly says.

"More like a nightmare," Johnny says.

Stephanie rubs Johnny's back. "It wasn't all bad."

He smiles and nods. "No, we had some good times too."

I glance up at Holly. "It was the best of vacations. It was the worst of vacations."

She cups her hand over mine. "Okay, Mr. Dickens, let's do our best to hold on to the good memories."

That won't be hard for me. Just feeling her hand touching mine brings back a slew of wonderful flashbacks: seeing her skinny dipping in the ocean, walking with her on the beach, sitting next to her around the campfire, driving the ATV with her arms wrapped around me, lying close to her on my bunk. No, holding on to those memories won't be hard for me.

"Yeah," Stephanie says. "We won't forget what happened this week even when we're old and gray."

Holly laughs. "I've got an idea. Fifty years from now when we're in our seventies, let's come back here and rent a cabin."

I chuckle. "That's a good idea. I'll put it on my calendar."

Johnny shakes his head. "I don't think this world will last another fifty years. We'll be lucky to make it to next week."

"We're not even guaranteed tomorrow," Stephanie says.

Holly arches her neck and gazes into the wide blue sky. "Enough of the doom and gloom. We've been given this day. Let's make the most of it."

Johnny straightens and crosses his arms. "I'm just being realistic. World War III is about to begin."

"You're both right," Stephanie says. "We need to be realistic but positive. That's the lesson I learned from those two days in the church cabin. Swagger and his disciples were realistic about the state of this world, but they went off the deep end."

Johnny nods. "We almost went with them."

"That's true." Stephanie raises her head and stares into the sky. "I'd rather die in the sunshine than live in a hole with a bunch of gloom-and-doom fanatics."

Her words trigger a thought. "That reminds me." I pull my cell phone out of my back pocket and open the link to Elsa's YouTube post. "Unbelievable! Look at this. Elsa's video has over three million hits!"

"The world is taking notice," Holly says. "Let's hope the world leaders do."

***

Crossing over to Ocracoke Island only takes about twenty minutes. Once we arrive, Johnny and I load the ATVs up with our luggage and haul it over to the parking lot near the Ocracoke Visitor Center where I parked my Chevy Cruze. The girls follow us on foot. After we unload and pack the car, we decide to take the ATVs back to the rental place on Loop Road. Johnny and Stephanie volunteer to drive the ATVs, and Holly rides with me. It feels good driving my car again. I guess after a week of exploring the exotic, something familiar feels comforting.

Holly says, "Did you notice that Stephanie and Johnny are warming up to each other again?"

"Yeah. I thought Swagger's preaching put out the flame, but there must be some embers left."

"No doubt about that. Maybe the whole experience with the cult was a test of their love."

Hmmmm. That's interesting. Does she really think they are in love? "I heard someone once say there's a fine line between lust and love."

"That may be true. It's like that old song, *Will You Still Love Me Tomorrow*. You don't know until tomorrow comes."

I swallow a knot that just formed in my throat. Is she testing the waters here? Does she want me to say the words? Should I blurt it out? But what if she doesn't feel the same way? I'd feel like a damned fool. I take a deep breath and let it out. Go for it you coward. "Holly, . . . I . . . I . . ."

"Joel, do you believe there's one special person in this world meant for each of us?"

"I . . . I . . . uhhh . . . What?"

"Do you believe God has appointed a special someone for you to be with until death do you part?"

Good question. I'm not sure about that. "Do you mean that there's only one person in this entire world that would make me complete?"

"Yes."

"Even if that person is halfway around the world? How would you ever get together if that person is in China?"

"Somehow God would bring you together."

Uh oh. Now I'm back on unfamiliar ground. "Well . . . they say that anything is possible with God, but if that's true, why do most people end up marrying their high school or college sweethearts?"

"Maybe because most people don't wait for that special someone."

"I think you're special."

"Really?"

"Really." Did I just say *I love you* without saying it?

She reaches across the cup-holder compartment and places her hand on my knee. "I think you're special, too."

Hmmmm. Get real, Romeo. You didn't say it. I think you're special isn't I love you. If you're gonna say it, say it. I bite my lip. Not now. The right moment has passed.

Up ahead, Johnny and Stephanie pull into the Portsmouth Island ATV Tour center. They park their vehicles in front of the building, which looks like a small beach house raised up on posts like most of the other houses on the island. To the side there's several advertising signs and a couple big umbrellas shading a counter, but no one is at the counter. I pull up next to the ATVs and park. Stephanie hops off the ATV and climbs into the back seat. The girls wait in the car while Johnny and I go inside and wrap up paperwork with the rental company.

Within ten minutes we're heading up Route 12 to the north end of the Ocracoke where we can catch a ferry over to Hatteras Island. Ocracoke is long and narrow and incredibly rustic and beautiful. To the left the Pamlico Sound stretches to the North Carolina mainland, and the Atlantic Ocean spreads endlessly to the blue horizon on the right. No houses. No stores. No construction. Instead just dunes and sea grasses on one side, and scrubland and live oaks on the other. No one says much during the ride. We're all pretty tired. The amazing surroundings have a hypnotizing effect. As we pull into the line of cars waiting to board the ferry, I ask Holly to check Elsa's YouTube video again.

"Almost four million."

"Wow," Stephanie says. "Do you think President Stamp has heard about it yet?"

"No doubt," Johnny says. "Not much happens in this world that Big Brother doesn't take notice."

I chuckle. "Now you're starting to sound like Swagger."

"It's true. I guarantee you President Stamp and Kim Jung Ill know about that video."

"The question is," Holly says, "Are they going to do anything about it?"

Chapter 34

All of us nod off on the ferry ride from Ocracoke to Hatteras Island. A loud horn awakens me. I check my rearview mirror. The guy in the red SUV behind me raises both hands. Crimenetly. I'm holding up the line of cars waiting to drive off the ferry. I start my car and throw it into drive. The traffic guy standing by the exit ramp shakes his head.

"Sorry," I mumble through my open window.

Holly giggles. "I think you need a strong cup of coffee if we're gonna get home in one piece."

"Definitely." I focus on the ramp ahead. "I'm stopping at the first coffee joint we see." I drive across the ramp and along the designated lane to the red light. Turning left puts us on Route 12. From here it's a long drive up the Outer Banks to Kitty Hawk where we will cross Wright Memorial Bridge to the mainland.

Holly turns and glances into the back seat. "They're totally zonked."

I take a peek at the rearview mirror. Johnny's head is sunken into a pillow that's propped against the car door. Stephanie, slumped on his arm and chest, dozes away. Baggage is stuffed all around them. It was challenging getting everything packed into my little car.

Less than a half mile up Route 12, I spot the Dancing Turtle Coffee Shop on the right. Perfect. I need a large, strong, black cup of coffee and a cinnamon roll to go with it. I pull into an empty parking space.

"My treat," Holly says and pops open the door. "Be back in five minutes."

"Get me a cinnamon roll too, would ya?"

"Sure thing."

The shop is quaint with wood-shingled siding and an overhanging porch. Three dormers, spaced evenly across the steep roof, face the road. I could work at a place like this all summer. Maybe that's what I'll do next summer. Come down here and get a job at a coffee shop. That would be the life. Forget about the real world for three months and live at the beach.

The real world. Hmmmmm. I wonder what's happening with Elsa and Jonah. They must be nearing Washington D.C. by now. It's only about a five hour drive from here. I slide my phone out of my front pants pocket and check the YouTube link. 5,286,452 hits. Sheesh, that's incredible. To think I could have kept that small treasure chest for myself. Yeah, right—me, the guy that stood in the way of world peace. I guess I still have a chance of owning what's inside, maybe a good chance. Elsa said she'd give the treasure back to me if things didn't work out with President Stamp and Kim Jung Ill. We have a *covenant*. I'm not going to count on that. So much for the real world.

Holly manages to sidle through the doorway of the coffee shop with her hands loaded with two large cups of java and a bag of goodies. She looks more beautiful now than when I first saw her on the beach. I could spend the rest of my life with that girl. I've got tell her how I feel. What do I got to lose? Pride? Wouldn't be the first time I've been humiliated by life's realities. Besides, didn't some guru say that humility is the key to success? If that's the case, I should be independently wealthy by now. When the moment's right, I'm going to tell her.

The ride up Route 12 along the southern Outer Banks is picturesque: small, folksy towns separated by stretches of unspoiled natural habitat. In between towns, the sea breeze blows sand from the tall dunes across the road. Huge cranes, ospreys, and gulls flap and float above the scrubland and marshes. As we near Buxton, I spy the Cape Hatteras Lighthouse. The tall, black-and-white-spiraling tower offers a magical quality to the place—a beacon high above the land, guiding ships that sail near the dangerous shoals at night.

Holly points to my left. "Look! Buxton Village Books. Isn't that Mee Mee's bookstore?"

I glimpse a white-framed sign mounted on green posts in front of a white house with a small front porch. "I think you're right. She did mention owning the bookstore in Buxton."

"The sign says established in 1984. She's been selling books here for thirty-five years. Can you imagine living most of your life surrounded by this kind of beauty?"

I take a deep breath and picture my future living in paradise. With Holly by my side, we'd create our own Eden. "Yeah. I'd like that."

"Me too."

Is this the right time? No. Not yet.

As the miles pass we travel through the small towns of Avon, Salvo, Waves, and Rodanthe. Someone wrote a love story about Rodanthe. I can't remember the title, but I think they made a movie from the book. I guess I'm not the only fool who falls hard for a woman in these parts. It must have happened to at least one other love-struck sap.

"Have you ever read *Nights in Rodanthe*?" Holly asks.

Whoa! That's a weird coincidence. "I was just thinking about that. I couldn't remember the name of the book. Did you read it?"

"Yeah. It's one of my favorite books."

"What's it about?"

"A couple meets in Rodanthe and fall in love. When a storm hits, they work together to save an old beachfront inn. It's a beautiful story."

Get it together, Romeo. This could be the right moment. "That sounds a little bit like us. We worked together during a storm to save Elsa."

"Yeah." She reaches across the divider compartment and places her hand gently on top of my leg. "We made a good team."

"Did the couple in the book end up getting married?"

"No."

"What happened?"

"The guy died unexpectedly."

That's a bucket of cold water dumped on my flaming heart. "Oh. Too bad."

"Yeah. I wish they would have gotten married and lived happily ever after, but not all stories end that way. Sometimes lives cross passionately for a short while, and then go their separate ways." She lifts her hand from my leg and rests her arm on the divider.

"I guess so." Is she trying to tell me something? I better cool my romantic jets.

We don't say much for the next ten minutes. I need some quiet time to face reality. I've only known this girl for less than a week. One of my closest friends jumped off the cliff of love after meeting a girl on vacation two years ago. He went crazy. Lust, love, and hormones took over his life. He traveled hundreds of miles on the weekends just to see the girl for a few hours. Eventually, she let him know her life was going in a different direction than his. He got over it, but it took a while. That's a cautionary tale I should take to heart.

I take a deep breath and let it out slowly, like a tire going flat.

"Are you okay?" Holly asks.

"I'm fine. Just focusing on the road ahead." I was speaking figuratively, but literally, something strange is happening up ahead. This is a lonely stretch of highway, a part of the Pea Island National Wildlife Refuge, but a bunch of vehicles have pulled off along the right shoulder. What's going on?

"Joel, something happened up there. Look at all those people on top of the dune."

"Must be twenty cars or more parked on the berm. Wonder what happened?"

I hear stirring in the back seat.

"Hey!" Johnny says. "Where are we?"

"We're about fifteen miles from Manteo."

"Pull over, Joel," Holly says. "Let's see what's going on."

"Good idea," Stephanie yawns. "I need to stretch my legs. It's a sardine can back here."

Chapter 35

There's plenty of room on the shoulder. I park behind the last car, a black Cadillac Escalade. We all exit the car and stagger up the steep sand hill. There must be at least thirty people lining the top of the dune and staring out to sea. When I reach the top, I can see the object of their fascination: A medium sized fishing boat is hung up on the shoals about a hundred yards off shore. It must have lodged there during the storm. Along the shoreline another ten or so people stand watching.

A larger vessel floats about a half mile out to sea. Between the two, one of those orange motorized rafts speeds back toward the bigger boat. Standing a few yards away from me, a chubby guy wearing a fedora peers through binoculars. His long black hair and goatee gives him a scholarly look, like a young college professor. He lowers the binoculars and shakes his head.

I tap his shoulder. "Sir, do you mind if I take a look."

He turns and smiles, blinking to readjust his vision. "Not at all. We've got quite a mystery happening out there."

He hands me the binoculars, and I zero in on the fishing boat. "What happened?"

"About two hours ago some guy caught sight of the boat stranded on the sand bar." He motions toward the people standing along the shore. "There he is, the guy wearing the red ball cap. He waved down a couple cars to get help. He didn't know what to do. More and more people kept stopping. Someone was able to contact the Coast Guard. They showed up about a half hour ago and sent a raft to investigate the wreck."

Crimenetly, that boat looks familiar. I focus on the bow and check out the lettering: THE SEA WEASEL! "Did they unload the passengers?"

"That's the funny thing. There were no passengers. It's a ghost ship."

"What!"

"I'm not kidding."

"There had to be passengers. I saw that boat leave Portsmouth Island yesterday with at least twelve people on it."

The chubby guy shakes his head. "No sirrree bob, not a one."

"Did they unload any boxes that looked like old treasure chests?"

The man grins and raises his eyebrows. "Treasure chests? No. I've been here the whole time watching the entire proceedings. They didn't unload a thing from that boat. The people on shore are waiting for bodies to wash up."

I turn and face my friends. "That's the *Sea Weasel.*"

"No way," Johnny says. "Can I look through the binoculars?"

"Sure," the guy says.

I hand Johnny the binoculars, and he focuses on the boat.

"What happened to them?" Holly asks.

"They're gone. Disappeared." I wave in the direction of the Coast Guard vessel. "They didn't find a soul on board."

"That's freaky," Stephanie says. "Remember the story Lisa told at the campfire?"

Holly's eyes widen. "Yes! The story about the ghost ship, the Carroll A. Deering. The passengers and crew disappeared without a trace."

A weird chill prickles up my spine. "I wonder what happened."

"It's the *Sea Weasel* for sure." Johnny hands the binoculars back to the chubby guy. "Thanks." He turns toward us, his face drained of color. "I hope it wasn't the rapture."

"Yeah, right." I can't help smiling.

"I'm not kidding. If it was the rapture, then we missed the boat, and World War III is about to begin."

Holly's eyes narrow. "If crooks, cons, and murderers get raptured, then count me out. I don't want to spend eternity with people like Noah Swagger and his followers."

Stephanie reaches and grips Holly's arm. "Don't say that. If sinners don't get into heaven, then we're all out of luck. I won't complain to God if Reverend Swagger shows up at the Pearly Gates with his followers. Who are we to question God's grace?"

Holly stiffens and stares at Stephanie but then slowly relaxes. She shrugs. "I guess you're right. I'll let God be the judge."

"Let's get out of here," Johnny says. "Seeing that boat again creeps me out. I want to go home."

Chapter 36

As we cross over the Wright Memorial Bridge to the North Carolina mainland, I feel like a different person. Before leaving on vacation I longed to be free. At times on Portsmouth Island I felt that sense of freedom. Will life clamp the chains of responsibility back onto my wrists? Or is it a matter of growing up and facing the challenges of adulthood? I want to become a man. I don't want to have to escape the real world to feel free for a few fleeting days. What is freedom, anyway? Is it living on the beach with no responsibilities? Or is it becoming a person who is strong enough to handle whatever life throws at me and somehow manage to keep my balance in this crazy world?

I'm alone with my thoughts. Everyone else has nodded off. The bridge, two lanes heading east and two west, crosses the wide expanse of the Albermarle Sound, a little over two miles long. Glancing to the left or right, I see the choppy sound waters. In front of me the long bridge stretches out to the vanishing point on the opposite shore. The rhythmic rumble of the tires on expansion joints feels like a mother's heartbeat.

In a few short days I've enjoyed nature's incredible beauty, fallen in love, found treasure, faced death, and witnessed a resurrection. I doubt if I'll ever experience another week like that in my life. Beside me sits the most wonderful girl I've ever met. But I'm not sure what to do about it. I keep getting mixed signals from her. Does she love me or not? Are we a one-week affair, or is there hope for something lasting? I won't know until I risk rejection and tell her how I feel.

Perhaps something more important happened on Portsmouth Island than falling in love with an amazing girl. Perhaps finding Elsa surpasses my romantic encounter with Holly. I helped save a life. Meeting Elsa that morning along the shore must have been ordained. Somehow she knew we would meet. When I traded the shell for the golden coin, I thought she was crazy. Now I'm not so sure. That kid sees things most of us don't see. All I could see was that shiny gold coin. When I found the small chest, I wanted it for myself. I guess I was no better than Noah Swagger. There's something inside of me, inside all of us, that's not so noble. It's easy to give in to that ugly side. Elsa helped me to see that.

The bridge finally ends, and I turn north onto Route 158. The afternoon sun beams brightly, splashing the world with amazing color—blues, greens, yellows, reds. The little towns with their fast food joints, roadside fruit stands, and gas stations help to spur me out of the drowsiness that threatens to overtake me. Holly still sleeps soundly. Johnny and Stephanie are dead to the world. The last few days wore them out completely. I'm tired but feeling upbeat. I'll keep driving. My anxiety about the future is gone. No matter what happens, I'll be able to handle it. If Holly and I aren't meant to be, I'll be fine. I'll get through my senior year of college. I'll apply for teaching jobs. The adventure of life will unfold, and I'll be okay. I feel something completely new—a new kind of freedom.

***

By the time we reach Williamsburg, Virginia, I can barely keep my eyes open. Holly, Johnny, and Stephanie stirred back to life a few minutes ago. I keep slapping myself on the cheek and shaking my head to stay awake.

"Joel, take the next exit," Holly says. "You're weaving back and forth. I can drive. You need to get some sleep."

"There's got to be a rest stop up ahead. I'd rather get off at a rest stop than some random exit."

"That's fine," Johnny says. "You sound just like my dad. Just don't kill us all between here and there by drifting off into dreamland."

Stephanie groans. "Oh, my butt and legs are numb. I've got to get out of this car in the next ten minutes, or I'll never be able to walk again."

"Your legs?" Johnny says. "My legs are twice as long as yours. How do you think I feel? After we stop, I'm taking over the driving duties. I can't survive another ten minutes in this back seat."

"Whatever," Holly says. "If you want to drive, I'll sit in the back. I see a rest stop sign—the New Kent Safety Rest Area twenty miles ahead. I think we all can hang in there another twenty miles."

"Twenty miles?" Johnny says. "Are you kidding?"

Stephanie whines, "I'll pee my pants if we don't stop soon."

"Quit complaining, kids." I chuckle, remembering long trips with my family. "We'll be there in less than twenty minutes."

"Let's sing a song," Holly says. "It'll make the time go by faster."

"Okay," Stephanie says. "How about *I've Gotta Pee* sung to the tune of *Under the Sea*?"

"How does it go?" Johnny asks.

"I've gotta pee. I've gotta pee. It won't be better, if everything's wetter underneath me. We've been in this car all day. My bladder is 'bout to give way. And it won't get better, if everything's wetter underneath me."

Johnny laughs. "That's a good one."

They sing silly songs for the next twenty miles, and I join in just to stay awake. As I pull into the rest stop and park, everyone cheers. I cut the engine and toss the keys over my shoulder to Johnny. Heading to the restroom, I can't get the song out of my head: I've gotta pee. I've gotta pee. It won't be better, if everything's wetter underneath me. I start to laugh, and the guy standing next to me at the urinal glares at me like I'm crazy. Man, I am really tired.

I make it back to the car first and climb into the passenger side front seat. Holly's pillow is stuffed between the seat and the compartment divider. I puff it up and place it in the gap between the headrest and the window. Slowly, I ease my shoulder and head into the comfort of the pillow. I can smell the remnants of Holly's shampoo and skin cream on the pillowcase, a mixture of coconut and mint. It feels so good to close my eyes and sink into the softness. I can hear the car doors open and my friends' voices. The engine starts, but everything seems far, far away.

A huge wave breaks onto the shore, and the water rushes up the slope and swirls around my bare feet. It feels good, soothing. I shade my eyes from the morning sun and gaze along the shoreline. Squinting into the brightness, I see a figure casting a line into the ocean. He has a prosthetic leg, one of those blade legs. I know him. What's his name? Quentin. That's right. Quentin Porter. I'll go see how he's doing.

"Mr. Porter! It's good to see you!"

"Hi, Joel." He inserts the fishing pole handle into a white tube embedded into the sand, stands, and faces me. "It's good to see you."

"Catch anything today?"

"Not even a bite, but I don't mind. I'm enjoying the sea breeze and sunshine. It's beautiful here, isn't it?"

"Yeah. This is a special place."

I glance at his red ATV. Something is missing. "Hey, what happened to all those shark jaws you had mounted on your vehicle?"

He shakes his head and smiles. "I don't need them anymore. Got rid of the machete too."

I thumb toward the ocean. "The sharks will be happy to hear about that."

"Yeah. Things have changed." He turns and gazes toward the dunes. "Look who's coming."

I glance over my shoulder and see a man walking toward us wearing a red pirate do rag and an eye patch. He's carrying a metal detector. I know him. What's his name? Jack! One-Eyed-Jack Graham. "Mr. Graham, how's it going?"

He waves. "Argh, matey, good to see ya. It goes well."

"Have you been scouring the dunes again, Jack?" Mr. Porter asks.

"Aye, matey. Spent the morning in paradise with me friend here." He lifts the metal detector. "Found something special too."

"Let's see it," Mr. Porter says.

One-Eyed-Jack reaches into his pocket and extracts a golden ring. He raises it to our eye level, and the sun's rays make it sparkle.

I've never seen anything like it. "It's beautiful!"

"It's yours."

"What?"

"I'm giving it to you, young Joel."

"Why?"

"You'll need it some day."

He drops the ring into my hand, and I trace the circular edge with my finger. "Thanks!" I slip the ring into my pocket.

He smiles. "Believe me, I don't need it here."

Mr. Porter grunts and motions out to sea. "Look. Someone's coming."

I glance up and see a head break the surface of the water. What in the world? It's a man with dark hair and Elvis sideburns. His wide shoulders and torso rises from the depths as he makes his way toward shore. I know him. What's his name? Noah! He's the preacher, Noah Swagger.

We stand silently as he approaches. He stops a few feet away, the water dripping off of him.

Swagger smiles. "Surprised to see me here, aren't you?"

Mr. Porter shakes his head. "Life is full of surprises, but death isn't."

"That's right," Mr. Graham says. "Who are we to question who shows up on these shores?"

Swagger points at me. "What's Joel doing here?"

All three stare at me. What am I doing here?

"Joel."

From behind, someone grasps my shoulder.

"Joel, we're here."

Chapter 37

I blink my eyes and struggle into consciousness. "Where are we?"

Holly says, "We're at a Buffalo Wild Wings in Fredericksburg. Everyone's starved to death. Come on. Let's get something to eat."

Johnny opens the driver's door and steps out of the car. "Let's go, Joel. I'm hungry."

I stretch and reach for my seatbelt. "Man, you woke me up out of a crazy dream."

"What was it about?" Holly asks.

"I'll tell you in the restaurant. It was one of those vivid dreams that seem so real that I could touch and feel everything." I glance into the back seat. "Where's Stephanie?"

"She jumped out of the car as soon as we stopped. Said she had to pee again."

Holly and I walk toward the sports bar, and I can't help humming *Under the Sea*. It's a typical Buffalo Wild Wings with a brick exterior, big yellow letters, and black awnings with yellow squares repeating across the bottom edge. When I open the door for Holly, I see Johnny standing by the hostess counter, waving.

"They've got a table for us already," Johnny points in the direction of a ponytailed brunette. "Right over there by the big TV. I'm heading to the bathroom."

The waitress, wearing a black football jersey with the number 32 on it, raises her hand and motions us toward her. Holly and I head in that direction. The table is near the back wall with a large high-def television mounted a few feet above us. Some soccer match is playing. A blue team and a red team chase the ball down the field. It's midafternoon on a Friday. The place isn't crowded. We sit across from each other, and Holly smiles at me, those China blue eyes reigniting that fire within me.

The waitress plops down four menus. "I'll be back to take your drink orders when your friends get back."

"That's fine." I glance around and notice no one is sitting near us. Maybe now's the time.

Holly leans forward on her elbows. "So what was your dream about?"

"I'll tell you in a minute. First I want to give you something that One-Eyed Jack found on the Island. I want you to have it. Then I want to tell you something that's been on my mind."

Her smile widens. "Okay."

I funnel my hand into my pocket, slide it out, and then reach toward Holly. She cups her hand underneath mine, and I open my palm.

She stares at her empty hand. "Is the gift invisible?"

"You could say that."

"I get it." She leans closer to me. "The stuff that dreams are made of."

"That's right. In my dream Jack Graham gave me a golden ring. I could actually feel its weight, its circular shape. He said that I would need it someday. Today's the day."

She jiggles her hand. "What do you think this golden ring means?"

"It's a vision, a promise, a possibility."

"Something that could happen."

"Yes, if we want it to happen."

"Do you want it to happen?"

I bob my head slowly. "Holly, I love you."

Her eyes widen, and over the cheers of soccer fans, she mouths the words: I love you, too.

Goallll!!!!

"Hey you two!" Stephanie calls out. She rushes toward our table from the direction of the bathroom. "Did you order appetizers yet? I wanted some onion rings."

"No. We haven't even ordered drinks yet," Holly says.

"Good. Let's get some onion rings and chicken wings with some barbeque sauce for starters. My stomach's growling."

Holly shrugs and laughs. "Sure, whatever you want." She glances at me, her dark eyebrows rising slightly.

I can't believe it. She loves me. I'm in love. We're in love. I open the menu and try to focus on the food selections. She knew exactly what I was talking about—the stuff that dreams are made of. I raise my head and peer at the air-conditioning ducts crossing the ceiling. Thanks for the ring, Jack.

Johnny returns from the bathroom, and the brunette waitress struts over to take our drink orders. Johnny wants a beer, and both girls order sweet tea, but I'm craving coffee again.

"Jeesh," Johnny says. "When did you start drinking so much coffee?"

"I don't know. My tastes are changing."

Johnny laughs. "You're starting to turn into your old man."

"We want some appetizers," Stephanie says. "Onion rings and barbeque sauce wings."

The waitress nods and jots the order.

I hear a ding. Someone just got a text.

The waitress says, "I'll be back with your drinks and appetizers in a couple minutes."

"Wait a minute." Holly stares at her phone. "My mom just messaged me. There's a special report about a peace summit coming on the news right now." She points to the big TV on the wall. "Could you change the channel to CNN?"

"No problem." The waitress pivots and reaches for a button along the bottom edge of the television. The channels keep flipping through until the CNN logo appears.

"Thanks," Holly says.

The ponytailed brunette whirls and smiles. "Sounds like this could be important." She steps to the side and gazes at the television.

The guy with the white beard appears on the screen. What's his name? Wolfe Blister? He's shuffling papers and reading notes. Finally he stares into the camera. "This is a CNN Special Report. We have a most interesting development occurring this afternoon on the world stage. President Ronald Stamp has called a news conference for what he has termed, and I quote, 'The most significant opportunity for the establishment of world peace in the Twenty-First Century.'"

Holly gasps.

"Wow," Stephanie says. "Can you believe this?"

I put my hands flat on the table and lean forward. "Elsa's video must have gotten through to the White House."

The reporter continues: "Apparently, a viral video caught the attention of both President Stamp and North Korea's leader, Kim Jung Ill. In the video a young girl appeals to both world leaders to meet with her for peace talks. You may have seen the video by now. It has over twenty million views on YouTube. Do we have that video cued up?" He nods toward someone off screen. "Let's play it."

Elsa's video plays on the huge television. We watch in amazement. When the part comes where she turns the phone's camera at us and thanks us for saving her life, Holly and Stephanie shriek. My heart thumps like a base drum as I watch all three of our faces on the big screen, smiling and waving. People in the restaurant begin to murmur. Some stand and walk over to our table.

"That's them," one woman says. "They're on TV."

When the video concludes, the reporter appears on the screen again. "As you saw for yourself, this teenager, Elsa Newland, and her grandfather, Jonah Newland, found the *Lost Treasure of El Salvador*. According to the law officer, Sheriff Dugan Walton, two possible murders and a kidnapping occurred the next day. Shortly afterwards, some church group departed Portsmouth Island with the treasure. Our sources confirm that authorities are on the lookout for Reverend Noah Swagger and his followers. The boat on which they left the island, the *Sea Weasel*, was discovered stranded on the shoals just off Hatteras Island. However, the vessel was totally abandoned—no trace of the people on board or the treasure."

Someone off screen hands the bearded reporter a piece of paper, and he reads it. He straightens and gazes into the camera. "It has been confirmed that Elsa Newland has arrived at the White House with the smaller chest she mentioned in the video. According to former Special Agent Russell Goodwin, the chest is rumored to contain a relic that has healing properties. Young Miss Newland believes its contents may offer a path of peace for the world.

"We received another report earlier today that Chairman Kim Jung Ill recently made an unannounced trip to the Odette Cancer Center at Sunnybrook Hospital in Toronto Canada with his seven-year-old son, who is suffering from leukemia. A clinician-scientist at the center, Dr. David Spencer, has made great strides recently in the treatment of this childhood disease. When Kim Jung Ill was briefed by his Secretary of State about the Portsmouth Treasure Video, he expressed great interest in a possible summit with President Stamp. It is well known that Kim Jung Ill is a collector of ancient relics."

The reporter adjusts his wire-rimmed glasses, places his hand on his ear, and nods several times. "We are going to send you to the Oval Office where Press Secretary Sarah Huckleberry is now addressing the few media people who have been given permission to cover the event."

The scene shifts to the Oval Office where Sarah Huckleberry, wearing a bright red dress and a string of pearls, stands at a podium. "Good afternoon." She glances around the room. "As you well know, for the last several months the threat of nuclear war between the United States and North Korea has escalated. Less than a week ago, North Korea captured the U.S.S. Shawnee in international waters and took its crew hostage, claiming the ship was on a spy mission. The United States retaliated by capturing a North Korean Vessel. The world has been shaken by these military actions and the possibility of world war. Russia and China have sided with North Korea. South Korea, France, and England have pledged their support to the United States. President Stamp and Secretary of State Michael Pompadore have been working tirelessly to improve relations between the two countries but to no avail . . . until today."

She motions toward the other side of the room and the camera shifts to a doorway where several secret service agents, dressed in black suits, stand on each side. The President's ornate, oak desk sits to the left. A large leather chair sits behind the desk and two Federalist style chairs face the desk. "I would like to welcome North Korea's Chairman Kim Jung Ill and his Secretary of State Kim Chung Choe into the Oval Office in hopes of resolving our differences and establishing a lasting peace."

The chubby, bespectacled leader enters the room followed by a much older North Korean official. Chairman Ill is wearing a button-up black shirt and his assistant a black suit and blue tie. A secret service agent leads them to the two chairs facing the desk. They stand behind the chairs, glancing around the office.

The camera shifts back to Sarah Huckleberry. "Next, I would like to introduce a young lady by the name of Elsa Newland."

Elsa appears in the doorway holding the small treasure chest, her forearms bearing its weight. A Secret Service agent leads her to the side of the desk opposite the door. Wearing a long sleeve white t-shirt and faded jeans, she smiles and nods at the two Korean officials standing to her right. They bow slightly.

The camera returns to Sarah Huckleberry. "Elsa and her grandfather, Jonah Newland, discovered the chest she is holding on Portsmouth Island, North Carolina. She believes the contents of this chest could offer a pathway to peace between our two nations. Finally, I would like to introduce the President of the United States of America, Ronald J. Stamp."

Wearing a dark blue suit and red tie, the President steps into the doorway. He smiles broadly, his trademark blondish-gray hair swooping down and back across the top of his head. He strolls to the other side of the desk and stands behind the leather chair. Secretary of State Michael Pompadore enters and stands beside the President. They all bob their heads at one another.

The camera zooms in on President Stamp. "I would like to thank North Korea's Chairman Kim Jung Ill and his Secretary of State Kim Chung Choe for meeting us here on such short notice. As most of you know, this young lady . . .," he motions toward Elsa, ". . . has found a treasure chest—the legendary *Lost Treasure of El*

Salvador. She believes it contains something that could help ease the strained relations between our two countries, perhaps even bring about peace negotiations and the exchange of prisoners." He spreads his hands. "Please have a seat."

The two North Koreans settle into their chairs. President Stamp slides out his leather chair and sits. Pompadore remains standing next to the President. Elsa, her face straining and arms slightly shaking, still stands at the side of the desk.

The camera zooms in on President Stamp. "Both I and Chairman Kim Jung-Ill found Elsa's video very interesting. Chairman Ill has a direct line of communication to the White House. He immediately sent word to Secretary of State Michael Pompadore that he would like to meet with me and Elsa. I must say, for a twelve-year-old girl, Elsa is quite the ambassador for peace. She wants to say a few words before the proceedings begin."

Elsa takes a deep breath and lets it out. She bends and places the chest on the desk. She straightens, faces the North Koreans, and then bows slightly. "Greetings and peace to you."

They nod and smile.

She turns and repeats the words to President Stamp.

"Likewise, young lady," the President says.

Elsa clasps her hands. "This is the offer I would like to make. I am willing to give this chest to President Stamp if he is willing to present its contents to Chairman Kim Jung Ill as a peace offering. If accepted, the gift would seal a covenant between the two countries to exchange prisoners and hammer out a peace agreement that would rid the world of this dark cloud of nuclear war."

President Stamp temples his hands in front of his chest and then lowers them onto his desk. He glances at Elsa. "Let me make sure I understand you clearly. You want me to agree to give whatever is inside this chest to Chairman Ill as a peace offering. It would be my gift to him. Then it would be up to him whether to accept it or not."

"Correct," Elsa replies.

Secretary of State Pompadore bends and whispers something into President Stamp's ear, and he quietly answers back.

I reach and grasp Holly's shoulder. "Did you hear what he said?"

She nods. "Something about establishing President Stamp's legacy as a great peacemaker."

President Stamp places his hands flat on the desk. "Okay. I'm willing to give the contents of this chest to Chairman Kim Jung Ill in hopes of establishing peace between our nations."

Secretary of State Kim Chung Choe leans and speaks quietly to Kim Jung Ill. The Chairman bobs his head slowly and smiles.

"Okay then," the President says, "let's open the box."

A Secret Service agent strides toward the President and hands him red bolt cutters.

He rises, and then opens and closes the cutter handles several times. "I'll be happy to do the honors."

Elsa steps out of the way, and President Stamp moves to the side of the desk where he has a better approach to the padlock on the chest. He smiles at the camera, spreads the bolt cutter handles, and lowers the steel jaws onto the lock. With a quick jerk of his arms the lock snaps and falls off.

He tilts his head and smiles. "That wasn't too difficult." He hands the bolt cutters back to the Secret Service agent.

Kim Jung Ill and his Secretary of State scoot their chairs back and stand up. They both lean on the desk, hovering near the chest.

President Stamp lifts the clasp and slowly opens the lid. "What do you know? It's an old wooden cup." He extends his hand into the box, picks up the cup, and holds it above his head for all to see. "This is a tremendous ancient relic. I would say one of the best ever found. I would like to call it the Cup of Peace. I'm not an expert, but I'd say it's from the 1500s. Very, very valuable."

Kim Jung Ill's eyes grow wide. His hands shake as he speaks Korean to his Secretary of State.

"We will accept," Kim Chung Choe says in broken English.

President Stamp pulls the cup away from the two North Koreans. "Does that mean you are willing to exchange prisoners and work out a nuclear arms agreement?"

Kim Chung Choe nods. "Yes. Yes we will."

President Stamp extends the cup, and Kim Jung Ill quickly grasps it and cradles it against his chest.

Grinning like the cat that just gobbled up a fat mouse, President Stamp turns and winks at Sarah Huckleberry. She rushes from her podium over to his side.

"Is there something wrong?" He asks.

She stares at the cup clenched in Kim Jung Ill's hands. Her face grows pale. "Do you know what you just gave away?" she says in a hushed tone.

President Stamp shrugs, his eyes narrowing. "No. What?"

She shakes her head. "Never mind."

PEACE

Please turn the page to learn how to receive your free gift.

I wish you the gift of PEACE, but more than that I would like to send you something that I hope will complete your experience and enjoyment of *The Treasure of Portsmouth Island*.

I am interested in your opinions on certain questions the novel raises. To receive your gift, I ask that you answer one of the five questions below and complete a two-minute task.

The task is to like and share The Treasure of Portsmouth Island's Facebook page on your Facebook timeline. If you do not have a Facebook account, ask a friend to like and share it. You may also share the Facebook link on Instagram or Twitter. The Facebook address is:

https://www.facebook.com/JoeCEllisNovels/

Here are the five opinion questions. Choose one:
1. Do you believe Reverend Swagger's New Kingdom Church was a cult? Why or why not?
2. Do you believe Holly's philosophy about love—that there is one special person in the world meant for you? Why or why not?
3. Do you believe Joel Thomas discovered the true meaning of freedom? Why or why not?
4. What do you think happened to the passengers of the *Sea Weasel*?
5. Are you a bunker builder or a peacemaker?

Please send your answers to: **JoeCEllisNovels@comcast.net**

As soon as I receive your email and confirmation that you liked and shared The Treasure of Portsmouth Island Facebook page, I will send you your gift.

Thanks for reading my novel. Please check out my other books on the next page.

Books by Joe C. Ellis

Outer Banks Murder Series
The Healing Place (Prequel to Murder at Whalehead)
Book 1 – Murder at Whalehead
Book 2 – Murder at Hatteras
Book 3 – Murder on the Outer Banks
Book 4 – Murder at Ocracoke
Book 5 – The Treasure of Portstmouth Island

Other Books

The Old Man and the Marathon
A Running Novel

The First Shall Be Last
A World War II Novel

The Christmas Monkey
A Children's Book

About the Author

Joe C. Ellis, a big fan of the North Carolina's Outer Banks, grew up in the Ohio Valley. A native of Martins Ferry, Ohio, he attended West Liberty State College in West Virginia and went on to earn his Master's Degree in education from Muskingum College in New Concord, Ohio. After a thirty-six year career as an art teacher, he retired from the Martins Ferry City School District.

Currently, he is the pastor for the Scotch Ridge Presbyterian Church and the Colerain Presbyterian Church. His writing career began in 2001 with the publication of his first novel, *The Healing Place*. In 2007 he began the *Outer Banks Murder Series* with the publication of *Murder at Whalehead* (2010), *Murder at Hatteras* (2011), *Murder on the Outer Banks* (2012), *Murder at Ocracoke* (2017), and the latest installment, *The Treasure of Portsmouth Island* (2019).

Joe credits family vacations on the Outer Banks with the inspiration for his stories. Joe and his wife Judy have three children and eight grandchildren. Although the kids have flown the nest, they get together often and always make it a priority to vacation on the Outer Banks whenever possible. He comments, "It's a place on the edge of the world, a place of great beauty and sometimes danger—the ideal setting for murder mysteries.

CPSIA information can be obtained
at www.ICGtesting.com
Printed in the USA
LVHW050900051119
636383LV00002B/90